Timothy
and the
Dragon's
Gate

Adrienne Kress

■SCHOLASTIC

First published in the UK in 2009 by Scholastic Children's Books
An imprint of Scholastic Ltd
Euston House, 24 Eversholt Street
London, NW1 1DB, UK
Registered office: Westfield Road, Southam, Warwickshire, CV47 0RA
SCHOLASTIC and associated logos are trademarks and/or registered trademarks of
Scholastic Inc.

ISBN 978 1407 10290 0

A CIP catalogue record for this book
is available from the British Library.

Printed in the UK by CPI Bookmarque, Croydon, Surrey
Papers used by Scholastic Children's Books are made from
wood grown in sustainable forests.

1 3 5 7 9 10 8 6 4 2

www.scholastic.co.uk/zone

For Bubie

CONTENTS

THE NOT-QUITE-FIRST CHAPTER

In which we begin the story

Headmaster Doosy was having a bad day. He didn't usually have bad days. Usually he had days that made him feel special and important. But today was proving to be one of the worst days in recent memory.

It had started out with a visit from a large bearded man who claimed to be a doctor. This man had trashed his office and made violent threats to his person, explaining how he could switch around Headmaster Doosy's leg and arm if he so chose. Headmaster Doosy had been inclined to believe him.

Fortunately the man had left rather quickly, and Headmaster Doosy had felt a great sense of relief to be alone in his office once more.

Only to discover he wasn't actually alone at all.

"Headmaster Doosy, I believe?" asked a soft voice behind him.

Headmaster Doosy jumped in his seat and violently swivelled his SwivelChairPro chair (headmaster grade) to meet the voice.

"Who are you and what are you doing in my office and how long have you been standing in that darkened corner?!" he asked, trying to sound composed and failing utterly.

"My name is of no concern to you. I am here to ask you a few questions. And I've been in this office since before you arrived this morning," replied the young woman who was stepping out of the shadows. She walked calmly by Headmaster Doosy and took a seat on the edge of his desk.

"Well, that's . . . trespassing. . ." Headmaster Doosy was pretty sure the young woman didn't much care, but he said it anyway.

"Headmaster Doosy, I understand you were sent an employee by one Evans Bore, were you not?"

"What?"

"An employee. I believe he works in the sanitation department. A custodian?"

Headmaster Doosy thought for a moment, though thinking was proving difficult, as he was still suffering from a great deal of shock. Then he remembered.

"Mr Shen! Yes. Yes, he worked here, but that was several years ago. He's since left."

"Left?"

"Yes, he left. That Bore fellow came and took him back. I think he works for him now. In the city."

2

The young woman stared at Headmaster Doosy. Then she leaned in and brought her cheek to his. Whispering in his ear, she said, "Well, I do hope you are being honest with me, Headmaster. Because if you are not, I can assure you that the things I could do to your person would be so horrific, you would be begging for that large bearded gentleman to act on his threat instead. Have I made myself clear?"

"Perfectly," squeaked Headmaster Doosy.

The young woman stood up, smoothing her skirt as she did so.

"Good." She gave Headmaster Doosy a small wave and a smile, and opened the door to his office. "Thank you so much for your cooperation." And she passed through the door, closing it behind her.

Headmaster Doosy stood up like a shot and took a careful, though slightly manic, turn about his office. He even opened his closet door and called out, "Anyone in there?!"

When he was secure in the knowledge that no one else was hiding in his office, he took his seat once more. He reached for the school intercom and, in a barely audible voice, said, "I regret to announce that the school musical has been cancelled. That is all."

Headmaster Doosy leaned back in his chair with a satisfied sigh. At least now he wouldn't be the only one having a bad day.

THE FIRST CHAPTER

In which we meet Timothy Freshwater on the
day he is expelled from the last school in the city
at the tender age of eleven

T
imothy Freshwater was used to people telling him
he was too smart for his own good. No, not quite
used to it, more like tired of it. Every parent-teacher
conference it was the same thing:

"That lad is bored, that's the problem."

"Timothy knows too much, have you been reading to
him?"

He would stare past whichever teacher it was this
year and cross his eyes so his vision would get all blurry.
And whichever teacher it was – they too blurred all
together – would drone on and on about his potential.
That really he would be a lovely boy, if only he would . . .
you know . . . (and they would give him a hasty glance) . . .
apply himself.

Whatever.

Because Timothy knew the truth. What worried his

teachers wasn't that he was too smart for his own good. What did they care if he was bored in class? The same could be said of two-thirds of his peers. No, what worried them was that he was too smart, period. He was smarter than all of them, and this put them on edge. And what he was smartest about, although Timothy himself didn't know it, was figuring out what other people were thinking. Especially grown-ups. Especially authority figures. He could interpret every twitch of their eyebrows and every drop of sweat on their upper lips. He could just about watch their thoughts go by like pictures on the telly. He was that clever at reading the signs.

So his teachers drew back from him. They shrank into corners when he walked down the hall, and they punished him whenever they got the chance, and that's why they expelled him. Time after time. Sure, at Reeling Comprehensive they said it was because he stuffed Dirk Walker into his locker. And at The Fortunate School for Boys because he carefully placed steaming dog droppings in his year-five teacher's briefcase. It wasn't because he organized a student walkout protesting the removal of chips from the school lunch menu at Central Tech. Oh, and it most definitely was not because he plastered posters around Arlington Elementary showing the headmaster kissing the art teacher.

No.

It was because he could out-think them all and they knew it. And it terrified them. In year three, for example, he had tormented his teacher by answering all the maths problems on the chalkboard before Mr Inklemeyer had finished drawing the "equals" sign. It had become a bit of a race, and had resulted in Mr Inklemeyer spraining his index finger in his haste to beat Timothy to the punch. There was that year-four science class when he had drawn an anatomically correct picture of Mr Plink, complete with labels, and made a photocopy for everyone. And, of course, there had been his rather short-lived glory of winning the creative writing award in year two, until a supply teacher pointed out that Timothy's piece, "The Happy Chipmunk", was actually an allegory for something far more sinister.

Yes, they were all petrified of him, sitting there in the back row, scrutinizing them carefully. They never knew when he would strike next. He would rock back and forth in his chair, making sure it squeaked ominously. He always found a chair that squeaked ominously. He was so good at squeaking ominously that he managed to make year-six teacher number two burst into tears.

Well, bully for them. He wouldn't sit idly by and let them smugly tell him what was what, when they didn't really know themselves. They knew what was in their textbooks, but if you asked them questions, real questions, then they'd crumple on to the floor. Timothy used the Socratic method. He asked questions he knew the answers to, just to get a rise out of them.

So, of course, it was no surprise when he was finally expelled from Montgomery.

"Well, that's that then," said his father, squinting over his steering wheel and taking a left turn rather abruptly. "There are officially no more schools left. You must be really proud of yourself."

Timothy shrugged. "Whatever."

"What am I going to write to your mother?"

"Why're you asking me that?"

His father sighed.

Timothy's father sighed a lot. When he wasn't sighing because of his son, then he was sighing because of his job. And when he wasn't sighing about his job, then he was sighing because he missed his wife. His wife, and Timothy's mum, Kathryn Lapine, was a very glamorous theatre actress, or, rather, considered herself a very glamorous theatre actress, or, rather, wished she were a very glamorous theatre actress, and had never really understood why she had had such limited success. When she wasn't on tour she was at very chic parties. Or very fabulous gallery openings. Or very resplendent book launches.

Yes, Timothy's father sighed a lot. But no one ever noticed. And this made him sigh all the more. And of course no one ever noticed that either.

The car turned down a leafy street and pulled to a stop in front of a very tall terraced house.

"I'll find a spot, you go on in."

Timothy, who had already stepped out of the car, slammed the door fiercely.

"And no telly! You're grounded!" his father shouted, leaning his head out the window.

7

"Whatever." The standard reply.

The Freshwater house at 18 Wither Way was very narrow. It was also full of books, and the walls were lined with theatrical posters, many of which featured Timothy's mother in elegant poses. Timothy leaned against the front door and gazed at the dust floating in the coloured shards of light from the window. He hated his house. Especially in the day. During the day, the Freshwater house could be quite claustrophobic. The rooms were small and closed off from each other by French doors. The walls varied between mustard and burgundy, and the floors were a dark hardwood. And because the house was tall and there were lots of nooks and crannies, Timothy's father never quite managed to catch all the dust, so it floated around in clumps, like aimless schools of fish. Which was a pity, seeing as Timothy's father was rather allergic to dust.

Timothy ran up to his room on the fourth floor, stripped off the brown corduroy jacket that he wore everywhere, even when the weather turned cold, and flung himself on to his bed. He gave a quick glance over to the pile of unopened letters from his mother on his bedside table. Next to it was the picture of her with her arms around him backstage at some insignificant theatre in the middle of nowhere. It had been taken last year, but Timothy thought he looked ridiculously young. He reached over and slammed the photograph down on the table, grabbed the remote sitting next to it, and turned on the television.

He wasn't particularly fussed about what was on, just as he wasn't particularly fussed about having been expelled from every school in the city by the tender age of eleven. He didn't get fussed about anything. He ran his fingers through his hair. It fell purposefully over his eyes, just as he liked it. He did have to wonder, though, what would happen now. Maybe he could get a real job. He knew his parents wouldn't hire a tutor again. That experiment had ended in miserable failure.

Timothy laughed to himself. And then stopped. And then threw the remote across the room.

So there you go. You've now met Timothy Freshwater, the boy who knew too much for his own good. But perhaps this description isn't entirely accurate. In fact, I would say that Timothy Freshwater didn't truly know how much he actually knew. And how much good what he knew would turn out to be. At least not yet. See, he had never met a dragon. But he was about to. And that would make all the difference.

THE SECOND CHAPTER

In which Timothy visits the Tall and Imposing Tower of Doom

The headquarters of the Appliance, Furniture and Rubber Gloves Consortium was located deep in the heart of the city. A tall modern building of glass, it rose a full twenty storeys over the other office structures in its vicinity. From the top floor you had a completely uninterrupted 360-degree view of the downtown core. It was a really terrific view, and most of the employees assumed it must be something special. However, only one person ever got to experience it. That person was owner and CEO of the Appliance, Furniture and Rubber Gloves Consortium, Evans Bore (a short, round, absent-minded fellow, whose favourite joke was introducing himself to people as a "fridge magnate"). The rest of the employees, like Timothy's father, had to content themselves with offices somewhere in the middle region of the building, quietly sensing the weight of several hundred tons of steel bearing down on them from above.

From the outside, the building seemed to grow taller and less stable as you approached it. Possibly this was because in order to see the full building you had to tilt your head back so far that you often fell backwards. And because it had an unmistakably daunting presence, and because you would feel this slight sense of dread when you approached it, it had quickly acquired the nickname "the Tall and Imposing Tower of Doom".

Even Timothy, who had long ago decided not to let anything bother him, ever, was taken aback ever so slightly when he and his father came upon it the morning after he was expelled from the last school in the city.

"You work here?"

His father looked up, teetered dangerously for a moment, and sighed.

They passed through the revolving door into the large lobby area and made their way to the elevators.

Timothy's father worked on the thirty-ninth floor.

The thirty-ninth floor was considered "open plan". This meant that instead of individual offices, or even cubicles, which you could decorate with ferns, or possibly a cactus, everyone worked out in the open under the scrutiny of everyone else. This arrangement was meant to encourage productivity. Since no one had an office, or even a cubicle, or even their own desk to decorate with ferns or possibly a cactus, no one was superior to anyone else. Everyone was part of a team.

At least in theory.

In reality, the thirty-ninth floor was comparable to the cafeteria at school, with each clique occupying its own area. The men who liked to play squash before work had claimed the desks closest to the windows on the north side, decorating their desks with posters of famous squash players (although Louis LeBoeuff had managed to slip a football player into the mix). The ladies who lunch had taken the east and had carefully adorned every inch of their area with mirrors. The men and women who liked practical jokes were in the south and enjoyed constantly tormenting the ambitious workers at the west end.

The centre housed the strays. Here, dotted about in threes or twos or ones, the rest of the workers on the thirty-ninth floor had made little hovels for themselves. Some had done most impressive constructions, like Barney Winterwobble, who had created a palace with turrets out of cardboard boxes, complete with a moat of little polystyrene bits.

It was in the centre that Timothy's father worked, next to an incredibly tiny woman with wispy black hair and opposite the tallest man Timothy had ever seen, who had to rest his chin on his knees while typing on his computer. They both made a small grunt of hello as Timothy's father sat to join them. In moments his gaze, too, was fixed upon the computer monitor in front of him, his fingers spasming across the keyboard, his back hunched ever so slightly.

The first few hours passed pretty slowly. Timothy had tried at the start to watch his father work, but there was only so much to appreciate about data entry. Then he watched the other employees doing what they were doing, which wasn't much, though a very plain red-headed woman liked to go to the bathroom every five minutes. Then he watched the big clock on the far wall tick its way through the seconds. And then Timothy thought that maybe for a lark he would go jump off a bridge.

His salvation came in brown velour.

"It's time for the eleven-fifteen meeting," said a breathless small blonde woman approaching his father, the very tiny woman and the very tall man.

Timothy's father stood up and cracked his neck. Then he looked at Timothy. "Think you can stay out of trouble for forty-five minutes?"

"Whatever."

Timothy's father sighed and looked sadly off into the distance.

"I can keep an eye on him if you'd like," said the blonde woman in velour, following Timothy's father's gaze and looking back at him bemusedly.

"Are you sure?"

"Of course! He can come make the rounds with me now, get the blood circulating again!"

The possibility that spending time with this blonde cheery woman in a brown velour jacket and matching skirt could be even more unpleasant than sitting at his father's desk did occur to Timothy as he followed her towards the elevators. But at this point, Timothy was willing to risk it. Plus he didn't plan on staying with her for very long.

The woman in brown was known to everyone on the thirty-ninth floor simply as Sarah. And it was her task to inform all personnel, on each floor, of their respective meetings beginning at eleven fifteen (by the time she reached the top it was the eleven-thirty meeting). Eventually it would be her job to inform each floor of the three-forty-five meeting. What she did between those two times was up to her.

It was a strange job to have. Sarah, having graduated with honours from Oxford, might have felt it beneath her, had she felt such things. Sarah did not like to judge the class and rank of various people and their work, and believed that every job, however small, was vitally important in a free-market economy. She might have felt differently had she known Mr Bore had created her job in the first place only because she reminded him of a girl he had had a crush on at school. But she didn't know that. And so she felt exactly as she felt.

The two of them worked their way up the floors, and Timothy found himself getting progressively more frustrated with the whole thing. It wouldn't have been so bad if they had actually had a chance to hang about and explore each floor, but Sarah had the technique down to an art and could make her round in thirty seconds flat. In fact, they spent more time in the elevator, and that was only because Sarah had no control over the speed with which it rose through the building.

"What does MIO mean?" asked Timothy, pointing to a button as they rose steadily. He had seen it many times now and couldn't help asking about it.

Sarah nodded. "That stands for Most Important Offices. Top floor, in other words. But don't worry, we won't be going up there."

Timothy thought that, of all the floors he had visited, that one sounded like the least boring and the one he was least likely to "worry about". Just his luck it would be the one floor where they wouldn't be stopping.

"So what do you want to be when you grow up?" she asked as they stepped out on to the seventy-first floor, which was made entirely of soft rubber.

"Why do you care?" replied Timothy, carefully trying to balance himself on the squishy floor.

"Because I'm curious." Sarah tapped an employee on the shoulder as he was heading to the toilet, reminding him of his eleven-twenty-one meeting. They made their way back into the elevator.

"So?"

"So what?"

"So what do you want to be when you grow up?"

"A lamp post."

Sarah stopped questioning him after that, and Timothy silently continued to follow her as she notified employees of meetings for another three floors, before he finally threw up his arms. "This is stupid. Why couldn't someone just have sent a memo about these meetings?"

"I think memos are quite cold. I prefer the personal touch, don't you?"

"It's just a meeting, it's not like you're inviting people to a wedding or anything."

The doors of the elevator opened on to a floor where the walls and ceiling were made entirely of glass. Sarah sighed as she stepped through into the hall. She spotted a woman with short blonde hair and quickly ran over to remind her of her eleven-twenty-three meeting.

Timothy stayed where he was and looked down at the elevator buttons. He smiled.

"Come on, Timothy." Sarah was motioning to him from the other end of the hall.

"You know what? You go ahead. I'm just going to check something out, 'K? I'll meet you back at my dad's desk." Timothy pushed the MIO button and followed up quickly with the "Doors Close" button.

"Timothy, don't you dare!" Sarah ran back towards the elevator, sliding across the glass floor. She made it back just in time.

For Timothy, that is.

The doors of the elevator closed solidly, and Timothy grinned, leaning back against the mirrored wall. That was much easier than he had thought it was going to be.

THE THIRD CHAPTER

In which Timothy meets Evans Bore

When you are from a well-respected family, often-times you will have pressure to "live up to your family name". That is to say, depending on your family's reputation, you will have to live in accordance with that reputation so that other people keep thinking of your family in the way it is used to being thought of. If you come from a family of do-gooders, then it is important to do good. If you come from a family of investors, it is important to make lots of money. If you come from a family of plastic surgeons, you should know how to pick a nose. And if you do not live up to your family name, then possibly your family will disown you. Which really isn't a nice thing, but can happen.

However, Evans Bore? He had spent the better part of his life trying to live down his family name. Literally. You see, he had maintained his family's reputation by going to a prestigious university and graduating with top honours. And he had also become CEO of a very important company as all his forefathers and -mothers had. So he had indeed made his family very proud and maintained the same level of respect that all the Bores had achieved. But he had also, in being born into his family, been given the terrible burden of having to live with a truly unfortunate family name. As you may imagine, having the last name "Bore" comes with a whole host of jokes and insinuations, and if you indeed tried to live up to that name . . . well, it would be quite unlikely that you would have many friends.

Unfortunately, Evans Bore had tried so hard not to live up to his name that he had nonetheless managed to alienate most people with his complete desperation to please, his manic energy, and truly terrible sense of humour. No one ever spent any time with him unless they were one of his employees or they wanted something from him, usually money.

Which is why when the elevator doors opened on to the MIO floor and Timothy tentatively made his way down the long dark-wood-panelled hallway, he was grabbed rather unceremoniously by the elbow and dragged into a corner office.

"Well, hello, hello!" boomed Evans Bore. "Have a seat, and my secretary will make you some coffee! Janice!"

There was a silence.

"Where the devil has she gone to this time?" asked Evans Bore, more to himself than anything. "Ah well, no coffee for us, then, eh?" And he laughed heartily. Timothy watched him and wondered exactly what was so funny. "So, so, so, so, so!" said Evans Bore finally when his laughter subsided. "Who are you?!"

"Um, Timothy Freshwater. My dad works here. On the thirty-ninth floor," replied Timothy, casually looking for an escape route.

"Freshwater, eh?" Evans Bore leaned back in his chair and nodded a few times. Then he sat upright. "Ah! Freshwater! Who works on the thirty-ninth floor!"

". . . Yes."

"Never heard of him!" Evans Bore dismissed the thought with a wave of his hand. "Well, never mind that now, Timothy. What are you doing all the way up here? Any important messages for me? Any," and he leaned in towards Timothy hungrily, "invitations to fancy parties?"

". . . No . . . what? No."

Timothy watched as Evans Bore's face fell. "No one ever invites me to fancy parties. Why doesn't anyone ever invite me to fancy parties?" He looked at Timothy expectantly.

Timothy stared back. "Seriously? You expect me to answer that?"

"Yes. Yes, I do."

Timothy shook his head in disbelief. "Well, I don't know. . ." he said. "I didn't know people had fancy parties in the first place."

Evans Bore stood up abruptly and then sat back down with just as much force. "That's it, Timothy! People don't have fancy parties in the first place! Which is why I am never invited to any!"

"Of course, I mean, people have other parties, and, I mean, are you invited to any of those, though?"

Evans Bore sank low into his chair. "No."

"So, I'm guessing it may be because people don't like you or something," was Timothy's conclusion.

"You are right, Timothy. No one likes me."

Evans Bore sat quietly for a few moments looking wretchedly dejected.

And so Timothy got up and left.

It's funny how some things work out. You can start off with a pretty simple plan to do some exploring, break a few rules, and then, strangely, find yourself with an internship. You see, Timothy did leave – Bore's office at least. But he made it only as far as the elevators, which opened up to reveal Sarah. She was red-faced, which played more like pink on her pale skin, and she started to lecture him about something that he really didn't much feel like listening to and so didn't. Then she marched him back into Evans Bore's office to apologize for having bothered him.

Evans Bore, who clearly had not minded Timothy's presence a few moments earlier, nonetheless was clever enough to take advantage of a situation and insisted that Timothy be made to work as his intern (i.e., unpaid) by way of apology. How they had managed to involve Timothy's father in all this, what with Bore's secretary, Janice, still nowhere to be found, completely mystified

Timothy. Nonetheless, his father soon arrived at Bore's office with the saddest of expressions on his face and sat quietly while Evans Bore yelled and pointed at him.

And, as if the days had been folded one on top of the other so that it hardly seemed possible that everything that had just happened had actually happened the day before, Timothy found himself dressed and ready for work first thing the next morning. Without the faintest idea what the heck he was doing there in the first place.

THE FOURTH CHAPTER

In which Timothy experiences what it's like to be an intern, and meets Mr Shen

"Yay!" exclaimed Evans Bore as Timothy entered his office early the next day. Timothy felt stiff and uncomfortable and ridiculous in his new suit, bought second-hand at one of those late-night second-hand-suit shops, and he walked more or less as you would imagine a rusty robot would walk.

"Ha! You look stiff, uncomfortable and ridiculous!" Evans Bore clapped his hands in excitement.

"Thank you."

"Oh no, no, no, no. Don't be like that." Bore escorted Timothy over to his desk and sat him down firmly in the chair opposite. He then took his position at the other side of the desk, and pulling in his chair a bit too tightly, causing him to gasp for air, said, "Oh, this is going to be brilliant, having you here as my intern."

"Is it?"

"Yes. You see, what you were saying yesterday really struck a chord with me. Very few people like me. In fact, I would venture to say no people really like me. So . . ." and he pressed the intercom buzzer on his phone, "Janice, could you bring some coffee, please?" He smiled at Timothy. There was a silence. Bore looked down at the intercom. ". . . Janice? . . . Jan . . . oh, never mind. . ." He released the button. "Anyway, I was thinking maybe you could help me change my personality so I could get friends. And in turn, I could teach you the ropes to help you on your path to becoming the CEO of a major corporation."

"I don't want to be a CEO of a major corporation."

Evans Bore looked astonished. "But, then, what are you planning on doing with your life?"

"Well, there are lots of other jobs out there. I haven't really thought about it. Besides, I'm only eleven."

"Other . . . jobs. . ."

"Never mind. Look, exactly what would you like me to do?"

"Well, first of all. . ." Evans Bore stopped and looked down at his feet. His left foot sort of swung back and forth a bit over the ground.

"First of all?" Timothy was losing what little patience he had left.

Evans Bore looked up. "You have to be my friend."

Oh, for. . . Timothy sighed. "Fine. We're friends." Evans Bore smiled a huge smile. "Now what?"

"Now? Now we wait for Mr Shen."

Mr Shen, it turned out, was a small Chinese man with

white hair who worked in the post room. Typically, Timothy learned, it was Mr Shen's job to sort the post and send it up with different post-room boys to the different floors. But because Evans Bore was the CEO of the company, Mr Shen delivered the post to him in person. He treated the job soberly, placing each individual letter down very deliberately on Bore's desk. Then with a small wave from Bore, he would be off, returning at five o'clock in the afternoon to collect any outgoing letters.

When they finally had the post, Timothy and Bore would go through it. Most often it consisted of documents that needed signatures, or catalogues for office supplies, but Bore maintained a not-so-secret hope that someday he might be invited to a fancy party, and so he scanned the letters carefully for any invitations.

The rest of the day passed with Timothy pretending to listen to Bore offer CEO advice. Occasionally, Timothy, in his effort to fulfil his end of the bargain, would attempt to explain why certain of Bore's actions had been inappropriate or socially unacceptable. Bore would be astonished at every one of Timothy's revelations and seemed genuinely surprised to learn that laughing loudly at your own jokes was considered slightly self-centred. Of course, the irony wasn't exactly lost on Timothy that it was he, of all people, giving instructions on how to make friends, seeing as he didn't exactly have any himself. But that was a choice on his part. Unlike Bore, who simply was hopeless in the friend-making department.

And so the weeks went on like this. He sorted the

post, never once locating a party invitation, and took all his meals with Bore in his office. And, every day, Timothy would always be slightly taken aback when the silent Mr Shen would visit the office. He wasn't exactly sure what it was about the man that made him take notice. Timothy barely acknowledged Janice's existence, as the secretary was pretty good at making herself invisible. But Mr Shen . . . Mr Shen *meant* something.

When Timothy had had that thought initially, he had mentally rolled his eyes. It was a pointless phrase, "meant something". But the feeling had persisted, visiting him at the oddest times of day and even occasionally in his dreams, so that eventually Timothy had got used to it lurking in the back of his subconscious. So much so that he had begun to forget it was there in the first place.

And he might have got entirely used to the feeling had it not been brought sharply into focus a good two months on.

It was all his father's fault, Timothy would tell himself later, when he was in the most desperate of emotional states and his body was battered and bruised. None of this would have happened if his father hadn't gone on that stupid business trip. Yes, it was easier to blame his father than to think he had got himself into this mess on his own. I mean, he couldn't very well blame Mr Shen. Logically, though, Timothy knew that in the end, of all the people, it really had been all the post-room clerk's fault. No, it was easier to blame his father, you know, than his best friend.

THE FIFTH CHAPTER

In which we meet Sir Bazalgette

Timothy's father didn't typically go on business trips. This was because he was usually the only one at home to take care of his son, his wife being away on tour or at a spa or something. But when it did happen, it was a terrifying prospect for the man. Timothy was not exactly the easiest guest to contend with and, in short order, Timothy's father had worked his way through part-time family guardians much in the same way Timothy had worked his way through schools. None of their relatives would have Timothy now. And sitters kept raising their prices each visit, so it was pretty much a miracle when Sir Bazalgette, their neighbour at Number 16, actually made the offer.

Sir Bazalgette Bazalgette had been their neighbour for as long as Timothy could remember. A very respected architect in his day, Sir Bazalgette had become so famous that municipal governments would commission his work in order to "put their city on the map". To have a Bazalgette was a sign of having good taste. (Another sign of having good taste is a sign that you can wear around your neck with an arrow pointing up, above the words "Good Taste".) Not only was having a Bazalgette; a sign of good taste, however; it was also an excellent way of improving a city's tourism, as everyone wanted to see a Bazalgette. For example, people had come from far and wide to see Mrs Linus's outhouse, the architect's first privately commissioned and owned work. In fact, this is where the euphemism for visiting the toilet, "to admire a Bazalgette", comes from.

While his work was large and popular, the man himself was small and isolated. He had shrunk slowly over time, like one of his decaying creations, and a lifetime of sitting drawing plans and sketches had permanently bent his spine. He was now a good foot and a half shorter than he had been in his youth.

His isolation had come on just as slowly. In his heyday, he had been quite the popular fellow, extremely well-spoken and charming. The toast of the town, some called him. Some called him Frank, which was odd since that wasn't even his name. At any rate, he was desperate to maintain his fame and wealth, and knew that down the line some new hotshot architect would come along and he would cease to be the most intriguing man in the city. He decided that the only way to keep people interested in him would be to stay interesting. And so he decided to lock himself up in his studio and correspond with the outside world only through his housekeeper. This trick worked for many years, his fans desperately curious as to why the man no longer came out in public. But then the novelty began to fade, and soon mention of Sir Bazalgette began to fade. And even when the man decided to reappear, he was greeted with little fanfare.

Sir Bazalgette returned to his home, gave up the pursuit of fame, and settled into a simple domestic life. He married his housekeeper, had a son, and gave all of his attention to his family. Oh yes, there was some travelling, and the occasional art dealer would stop by the house. But the life he now led was far less grand than it had been. When his wife died and his son left home, this time Sir Bazalgette locked himself up from the world for real and was never seen in public again.

What happened to his son is another story altogether.

From the outside, you wouldn't have known that Timothy's father and Sir Bazalgette knew each other at all. But they did. They had met once at the fence that separated their gardens, exchanged a few words, and each had decided in his quiet way that he approved of the other. From then on, they would meet on occasion and just talk. And when Timothy's father explained his dilemma about leaving Timothy alone, it was Sir Bazalgette who had come up with the suggestion.

This was why Timothy and his father found themselves standing at Sir Bazalgette's front door that crisp autumn morning, the motor (and I am sure the meter) of a black cab running in the distance.

The two stared at the Number 16 plate in silence for a moment or two. And then, just before his father rang the doorbell, he turned to Timothy. He dropped down into a squat and held on to his son's shoulders. "Please," he said. "Please."

The desperation he saw in his father's eyes enraged Timothy. He threw off his father's grasp and pushed the doorbell. "Just go on your stupid trip, OK?" he said.

His father rose slowly. Timothy could feel his father staring down at him. It made his face get all hot. If his dad didn't leave soon, Timothy just knew he would explode. It seemed that his father understood this, because when Timothy finally looked up again, his father was gone, and the black cab was halfway down the street.

"Yeah, that's it, just go," Timothy said quietly after the cab.

"Welcome, Timothy. Why don't you come inside and I'll make us some tea?"

Timothy turned back to the door and stared at Sir Bazalgette. The old man was wearing a red smoking jacket embroidered with a Chinese dragon. The elbows of the jacket were covered in a soft black material, and around the architect's neck was a white cravat. Most startlingly to Timothy, or to anyone, I would imagine, as it isn't a common accessory, was the black eyepatch he wore over his left eye.

"You a pirate or something?" asked Timothy as he crossed into the foyer of the house.

"No," replied Sir Bazalgette. He led him through his home towards the kitchen.

Despite having been his neighbour all his life, Timothy didn't know that Sir Bazalgette was an architect. He had no idea how famous he was or that he was a genius. He had no idea that Sir Bazalgette was also rather proficient at dancing the foxtrot. But that didn't really matter because no one really knew that. And so as Timothy walked through Sir Bazalgette's home, he was entirely and completely shocked.

Though his neighbour's home ought to have looked exactly like the Freshwater house, only in reverse, the architect had done so many personal "improvements" to 16 Wither Way that it was difficult to recognize anything. Where Timothy's house felt dark and claustrophobic, Sir Bazalgette's was bright and cheerful. He had been an architect known especially for his use of light and reflection, and had created several dozen skylights, some visible, like the vast dome they were now passing under as they went through to the kitchen, some hidden, like the ones in the breakfast nook where light filtered down to them from somewhere above. Mirrors were everywhere. Their job was to reflect light and give a sense of depth to a space that Timothy knew all too well was just not quite big enough.

Not only had Sir Bazalgette improved on the existing home, he had extended it as well. He had created an indoor courtyard, lit by the extensive dome, and Timothy was amazed to see all the statuary and random bits of randomness that had been collected and displayed.

"Over the years, I've acquired a fair few artefacts. Worth a pretty penny, I have no doubt," commented Sir Bazalgette, noticing his young charge's expression.

No doubt, thought Timothy, carefully sidestepping a giant marble foot.

"I used to have more, but I was required to return them to their countries of origin. There was a time when you could take what you pleased for research and educational purposes. Now everything belongs to somebody, and evidently such practices have become illegal." Sir Bazalgette shrugged and began to walk again.

"So you were a pirate," Timothy said with a laugh.

Sir Bazalgette stopped short and looked at him.

"Such things are not to be joked about," he said simply. Once Timothy nodded, Sir Bazalgette turned and continued his way through to the kitchen.

Timothy had never been one to drink tea. It was decidedly unglamorous, a beverage consumed primarily by little old ladies and small girls who liked to pretend they were little old ladies. Timothy's drink of choice was coffee. Not that he'd really ever had coffee, but he knew someday he would be completely addicted to it. He planned on being one of those men who couldn't start the day without one. He'd drink it black. And have dark circles under his eyes. At midday he would get grouchy and snap at everyone around him, and people would whisper to each other as he passed, "He hasn't had his coffee yet this afternoon."

But it turned out tea wasn't that bad. Especially after two sugars and a lot of milk. And Sir Bazalgette didn't serve it with a teapot or anything; he filled individual mugs, and Timothy got to add whatever he wanted to it. He also enjoyed dunking biscuits in the tea. But that was something that was universally accepted as a necessary action and wasn't a question of being cool or not.

"Tell me about your mother, Timothy," asked Sir Bazalgette, making himself comfortable at the other end of the small wooden kitchen table.

"My mother? What does she have to do with anything?" asked Timothy, reaching for another biscuit.

"I've never met her, and your father mentions her only occasionally. I'm curious. I know that she's an actress."

"Well, there's not much more than that, really." Sir Bazalgette looked at Timothy closely with his one eye. Timothy rolled both of his. "Oh, for . . . I mean, she's an actress! That's it. She acts. She does plays and people pay to see her, and that's it." He took a bite of mushy biscuit. "And she's on the coast right now. Doing some pantomime or something. Whatever."

"Do you see her perform?"

"Yes. Well, I mean, not recently, my dad's been busy with work. When I was little, my dad used to take me to see everything. I just . . . she's actually not horrible at acting, but she's always cast in really bad stuff, and I guess that's what I hate. It gets her all sad, and if she could only get something good she'd be happier and she could stay in the city and we wouldn't have to sit through all the bad stuff and it wouldn't be as annoying, you know? And . . . and she's on the coast."

"You said."

Timothy felt his shoulders up around his ears. "Look, what's the point of this?"

"Small talk? Yes, small talk is rather pointless, isn't it. I think it's one of the reasons I gave up on going to parties. I was just not interested in small talk. We can discuss something else if you'd like. Or we could do something else. Is there anything in particular you'd like to do?" asked Sir Bazalgette, and he looked around the room as if something very interesting and worth doing might be hanging on the wall directly behind him.

"Can we just watch the telly?"

"We could. If I had one. But I don't. So we can't."

"What sort of person doesn't have a television?"

Bazalgette stood up. "Come with me," he said.

"I'm not done with my tea yet." *I'm not done with my tea yet?* Timothy couldn't believe he'd just said that!

"Bring it along."

Timothy rose and started to follow Sir Bazalgette down some stairs at the rear of the kitchen. "Where are we going?"

"To show you what it is I do."

The basement room had been modified, as all the rooms in the Bazalgette house had been. This tendency of Sir Bazalgette's had rather frustrated his late wife,

33

who considered it mere obsession and not artistic inspiration that made her husband repaint the interiors of all the closets a slightly darker shade of brown than they already were. Nonetheless. The modifications to the basement room had been absolutely necessary to Sir Bazalgette's work because it was here that he kept his most prized possessions.

The far wall was made of six large dark wood panels on hinges. On them were hung blueprints and watercolour renderings of various buildings he had designed, along with several landscapes other famous artists had painted. You could swing open the panel to reveal yet another painting on the reverse side, with yet another hinged panel beyond. There were three full layers of these panels and paintings before you reached the actual wall itself.

Lining the other three walls were shelves packed high and deep with yet more artefacts like the ones in the courtyard. These looked unlike anything Timothy had seen in any of his more tedious school visits to the museum.

"What is this place?"

Sir Bazalgette took a seat at the small table in the centre of the room. "Did you know I was an architect, Timothy?"

Timothy shook his head no. "But it makes sense."

"I was. And I travelled the world looking for inspiration. Many architects do that."

"Whatever."

"Of course, I couldn't help but collect artefacts as I went about. You saw several upstairs."

"Yup. And you said you had to return some of them."

"I did. Some. But there were some I couldn't bear to part with, and so I hid them down here. The ones down here are very rare. They are worth a lot." He leaned forward on the table. "A lot. I used to be very focused on collecting artefacts. It was just a hobby compared with the architecture, but it became a very big thing for me. Those pieces I wasn't interested in I'd sell off. I have to say the invention of the Internet was a marvellous help with that. And then one day, something else became my life's work."

Timothy suspected that Sir Bazalgette wanted him to ask him what, and, for that reason, he didn't.

Sir Bazalgette waited a moment and then, unfazed, said, "I have a friend coming over later tonight for a conference, and I was hoping you would join us."

Timothy shrugged. "Sure, whatever."

"Excellent!" Sir Bazalgette stood up. "Let me show you some of my favourite pieces."

The two of them spent several hours going through Sir Bazalgette's collection, and Timothy had to admit it was all rather impressive and started wondering if there was maybe a way he, too, could make money in a similar fashion.

Evening drew in before long, and they returned upstairs so that Sir Bazalgette could make some dinner for the "conference". He was in the process of mixing up some sauce when the doorbell rang.

"Could you get that, Timothy; I'm up to my elbows in hollandaise at the moment."

Timothy stood and shuffled his way slowly through the darkened house to the front door. He turned on the hall light and unlocked the door. Then he opened it and stared open-mouthed at the man standing in front of him. He definitely could not have thought of a more unlikely person to be facing in the doorway. But as he spoke, he realized that, deep down, somehow, he had expected it, though he had no idea why.

"Mr Shen?"

THE SIXTH CHAPTER

In which Timothy is told the first of two extraordinary stories

"Timothy?"

"What are you doing here?"

"I didn't know that you would be here tonight."

"Well, I am, OK?"

"OK." The two stared at each other. "May I come in now?"

Timothy stepped aside and Mr Shen glided smoothly past.

"Ah, you've arrived! Good, good. My dear Shen, look who is my ward for the week. Timothy Freshwater!" said Sir Bazalgette, joining the two of them in the front hall.

"Yes, so I see. How lovely!" said Mr Shen, taking Sir Bazalgette's hand and shaking it warmly.

"Mr Shen was the one who told me you were working with Evans Bore, actually. And I thought that was such a happy coincidence!" Sir Bazalgette beamed at Timothy, who just continued to stare at Mr Shen. "Well, come on, shall we have something to eat?"

Timothy followed the two old men through to the kitchen. He could not for the life of him understand how they knew each other. From everything he had learned about Sir Bazalgette, it seemed the man never left his home. So how on earth would he have met a little old Chinese man who worked in the post room beneath the Tall and Imposing Tower of Doom? Besides, what did a postal clerk and a world-famous architect have in common anyway? Wasn't it a bit beneath Sir Bazalgette to associate with someone like that?

Timothy sat down opposite Mr Shen at the kitchen table and began to eat his supper slowly. He didn't speak a word as the two men chatted happily through the meal as old friends. They spoke of the weather and politics and nothing of any real significance, and as the main course was served, Timothy was beginning to wonder if this "conference", as Sir Bazalgette had called it, was simply what Timothy would call "hanging out".

But once Sir Bazalgette cleared the plates and returned to the table, there was a definite shift in tone.

"Now let's get down to business."

"Let's!" agreed Mr Shen happily.

"You may be wondering exactly why I have invited the boy to join us."

"I am indeed!"

"The boy is still in the room, you know," said Timothy through his teeth. "And before you get to why I'm here, can you tell me what's going on? Like how do you guys know each other, and what are you guys up to? I think that would be the polite thing to do." Was it really the polite thing to do? Seemed like it. In any case, he hated feeling so out of the loop.

"You are right, Timothy. Of course. Well then." Sir Bazalgette stopped. He was thinking hard while looking at a spot somewhere just past the centre of the table. Then he focused his gaze on his friend across from him. "How on earth do I start this, Shen?"

Mr Shen shrugged. He too stared into the space before him in quiet contemplation. He then looked up with a smile.

"I know," he said. He turned to Timothy and with a broad grin announced, "I am a dragon."

Timothy just blinked back at him.

"Really, Shen, I was thinking about easing the boy into it."

Mr Shen turned back to Sir Bazalgette. "I do not believe there is any way of easing anyone into something like that."

"Yes, well, you were never the most diplomatic character, were you?"

"What was your idea, then?"

"I thought I'd start maybe with the story, put it into context. You know a bit of context makes all the difference."

"You may have a point. I still think it would be shocking."

"Wait wait wait!" Timothy held his arms up to stop

the conversation. Both men turned to look at him. "What was that thing you said?"

Mr Shen gave a quick glance over at Sir Bazalgette, who gave him permission with a sweep of his hand. Mr Shen smiled at Timothy sheepishly. "I said I am a dragon."

Timothy chewed on the inside of his cheeks. "You're a dragon."

"Yes."

"Well, that's the dumbest thing I've ever heard."

"You must surround yourself with extremely bright people, then," said Sir Bazalgette.

"Look, he is so not a dragon! Just look at him. Does this look like a dragon?" Timothy pointed at Mr Shen.

Sir Bazalgette shrugged.

"Dragons are, you know, dragons," continued Timothy. "They are big monsters, and they have wings and scales and stuff. They breathe fire. And they most certainly do not look anything like humans."

"If you say so," said Mr Shen.

"Oh, and, by the way, they are also fictional. You guys are crazy. You guys are nuts. I mean, you guys are seriously senile."

Timothy could feel himself getting really angry. He was so used to people thinking he was too smart that it enraged him that anyone would think him this stupid.

"I think I know the problem," said Mr Shen quietly. He leaned forward and looked at Timothy. "From what you have described, I believe you are thinking about the Western dragon. A breed of dragon that became extinct hundreds of years ago. But I am, as may be plainly obvious to you, a Chinese dragon. An Eastern dragon. Eastern dragons take human form all the time. It makes going to the movies a little less awkward." Mr Shen smiled.

Timothy made a face. "OK, fine, Mr Eastern Dragon. How come you aren't extinct too?"

"Because we aren't hunted like a prize. We are much more revered in our homelands."

Timothy threw up his hands. "This is stupid."

Sir Bazalgette looked over at Mr Shen. "I think the boy needs some proof."

"Proof?" said Timothy. "You've got to be kidding me." He rolled his eyes so violently he gave himself a head rush.

Mr Shen looked down at the tabletop. Sir Bazalgette made an apologetic gesture, but Mr Shen waved it away mildly.

"There was a time when asking someone like me to prove himself would have been considered really disrespectful. And now. . ." Mr Shen rose and walked around the table to where Timothy sat. "I am going to walk to the door and back. Watch my feet."

Timothy watched his feet. And had he been the same age as his two companions, he might have had a heart attack. Timothy had noticed unconsciously just how gracefully Mr Shen moved, with elegant small hand gestures and smooth motions as he sat and stood. He had also noticed just how effortlessly he had seemed to glide across the floor as he walked. But he hadn't taken any particular care to notice exactly why that was.

41

Mr Shen's feet didn't actually touch the floor. They floated two centimetres above it, and though the man walked as anyone else might, the ball and heel of his foot never actually touched the wood.

"He's speechless," said Sir Bazalgette. Timothy could hear a slight laugh in his voice.

"But that's impossible," Timothy said quietly.

"And yet it's happening."

"But it isn't possible! Scientifically, I mean."

"It is possible. And someday I am sure science will find a way of proving how. It just hasn't caught up yet."

That made far too much sense to Timothy, and he wondered if he was going senile too.

"OK, OK, let's say it's all true, which it so isn't, but let's just say it is . . . why don't you just turn into a dragon now, instead of the floating and stuff?"

Mr Shen sat back down opposite Timothy.

"I can't."

Exactly, thought Timothy. *You can't.* "Oh, come on, just for fun," he said with a slight edge in his voice. "I won't tell or anything, if that's what you're worried about."

Mr Shen looked at Sir Bazalgette.

"I think it's time we told the lad the story," said Sir Bazalgette.

Mr Shen nodded.

"Story? What story?"

Mr Shen leaned back in his chair with his eyes closed and thought quietly for a moment. Then, without moving, he started to speak.

"A very long time ago, I mean a considerably long time ago, I was, would you believe, young. And with being young came all the usual trappings: arrogance, pride and an incomparable energy. I very much enjoyed being a dragon. It is an exhilarating creature to be, you see. You get to fly, you are revered, completely catered to, given parties and gifts. You get to visit the very peaks and depths of the earth, and everywhere in-between. Who wouldn't, really, if they could choose, choose to be a dragon? But I was very silly also. I would get into all manner of trouble. I once capsized a vessel heading out to sea because I was so involved in creating my first tidal wave. Men who were fathers, brothers, sons all lost their lives because I could not see beyond my own ambitions."

"Dramatic."

Sir Bazalgette put a finger to his lips. "Shh."

"My behaviour did not go unnoticed, and the yellow dragon, king of all dragons, finally summoned me to his presence and told me I must change my ways or expect a grave punishment. I bowed, I apologized, I went home humbled. But the yellow dragon did not trust me and sent along one of his servants to run my household. I didn't know the servant had been sent by the yellow dragon, so I continued as I always had. I never cared much for my servants, and treated them as I thought they ought to be treated, with indifference and, at times, anger when they displeased me. It really hurts to tell of it now. At any rate, my behaviour, despite the warning, grew worse. I was a dragon, after all, for all intents and purposes a god. Who could truly challenge me? I took up with pirates and helped guide their ships with my ability to control wind currents. I visited the treasure troves of the world hidden deep underground and plundered them for jewels. I disguised myself as a human and gambled away fortunes. Finally, the yellow dragon called me to his side once more and told me that he had to punish me for my dishonourable actions."

"Well, yeah," said Timothy.

"He turned me into a human without any power or ability to return to the dragon I once was. He told me that, since I had abused my power so utterly and completely, and mistreated my servants in such a horrific manner, I would be doomed to walk the earth as a servant myself. That I would never be able to do anything without the permission of my master. He forged a golden key in the fire at the base of a mountain and threw it out into the night. Whoever picked it up would be my master, and I would serve him unquestioningly. After that person died, or chose willingly to give it to someone else, I would follow the key to the next person. The first man to find the key was a very poor farmer, barely able to clothe himself, let alone take care of a servant. When he passed on, I waited by his body until the son of a wealthy politician came by, saw the key glittering around the dead farmer's neck, and grabbed it greedily. And so I went from home to home, business to business, serving whoever got the key next."

"Seriously?"

"Seriously."

Timothy looked at Mr Shen sitting peacefully with his eyes still closed. He never would have put up with a story like this from anyone else, but even though it seemed a little more than far-fetched, Timothy had to hand it to the man that he made it sound oddly plausible.

"So, what," asked Timothy, "are you just going to do this for ever?"

Mr Shen opened his eyes and looked at Sir Bazalgette. Timothy was startled to see that they were shining with tears.

Sir Bazalgette took over the story. "No, no, he isn't. The punishment was to last until the one hundred and twenty-fifth year of the dragon. And during the fortnight of celebrations for that new year, he would be able to turn back into his true form, but only if he and his master passed through the Dragon's Gate by the end of the festivities. It is important that both servant and master pass through it together; otherwise he cannot return to dragon form. Even then he would not be released from his servitude unless his current master gave him back the golden key and set him free before that midnight. Otherwise he would remain a servant for ever to the keeper of the key."

"But this time in the most terrible form of service. This time, as a dragon," finished Mr Shen.

Timothy bit the inside of his lip and pretended to nod

sagely. Things were starting to sound a little far-fetched again. "Man," he said, "that's . . . that's rough. I've heard that being a dragon servant totally stinks. I think I saw a talk show about that once. 'I'm a dragon servant and I want respect' or something like that."

Sir Bazalgette sighed loudly and stood, carrying his bowl over to the sink. Timothy smiled to himself and turned to Mr Shen. Who was shaking with laughter.

Of course, because he was an old guy and everything, Timothy worried at first if he was having a fit. It was only when Mr Shen had calmed down and was wiping the tears from his face that Timothy understood that for some reason Mr Shen had really enjoyed the line about the talk show. Which just annoyed Timothy further, as the joke had been meant to annoy, not entertain anyone.

"That was quite humourous," said Mr Shen, accepting a tissue from a startled-looking Sir Bazalgette. "I had the best image of several dragons sitting on a couch crying into a microphone. . ." Mr Shen started to laugh again. "I'm sorry! I'm so sorry," he wheezed out. "There, there." He took a few deep breaths. "I'm fine." He took another breath and then hiccupped. "Oh, just great." And he hiccupped again.

"I think it's time for dessert anyway," said Sir Bazalgette and he left the kitchen for the pantry, shaking his head.

"You are terribly funny," commented Mr Shen, trying not to hiccup.

"Not really. I mean, not usually. You're just weird."

"That I am, that I am."

Timothy was feeling exasperated.

"Look, the point was this: what does it matter if you are a servant as a dragon instead of a servant as how you are now? What difference does it make?"

Mr Shen nodded. "It is not fun either way, but, you see, as a dragon my powers are much more . . . impressive, shall we say? Right now I'm rather limited. A bit of control over liquids and air currents. Hardly anything. But as a dragon, as a dragon I can command hurricanes. Imagine if that power got into the wrong hands."

Timothy shook his head. He still couldn't quite believe he was having this conversation. He examined the old post-room clerk. His face was lined with deep wrinkles, and his immaculate goatee was a perfect white, matching his eyebrows exactly, the thickest that Timothy had ever seen. Thick enough that they even curled at the top.

"What are you thinking about, Timothy?"

"You've got some impressive eyebrows."

And Mr Shen started to laugh again, causing the hiccups, which had only just subsided, to come back full force.

Sir Bazalgette re-entered at this moment with three small pieces of cake and handed one to each of them.

"Honestly, Shen," he said sitting back down, "what's got into you?"

But Mr Shen was laughing too hard to answer, and

instead all three of them turned their focus to eating their cake, giving Mr Shen a chance to calm down, and Timothy to feel even more confused.

When he finished, he pushed his dish away and slouched into his chair. He'd been waiting now for the men to continue the story, but since neither of them had bothered, Timothy knew he'd have to bring it up again. Man, he hated bringing things up. It made it look like, you know, he was interested.

"So," Timothy said as casually as possible. "Why are you telling me any of this stuff, then? Like I seriously couldn't care less about your issues."

"You care enough to ask questions, though," said Sir Bazalgette, which made Timothy flinch inwardly. But before Timothy could come back at him, he added, "Well, actually, the reason is rather straightforward. We could use your help."

Mr Shen looked at Sir Bazalgette thoughtfully.

Timothy felt suspicious. "My help?"

"Yes. You see, in case you hadn't already figured it out, we are quickly approaching the one hundred and twenty-fifth year of the dragon since Mr Shen was sentenced into servitude. And I have been working closely with Mr Shen to plan our trip to China. There is only one problem."

"What's that?"

"The key."

"What key?"

"The key I told you about."

"Sorry, what key was that?"

"The key, the key the yellow dragon tossed out into the night, the one that ties Mr Shen to his master. Honestly, Timothy, were you not listening?"

"Whatever, I forgot. There was a lot to take in."

Sir Bazalgette sighed hard. "At any rate, I can't possibly take Mr Shen to China without that key."

Timothy looked at Mr Shen, who was nodding slowly. "Why not?"

"Because Mr Shen will only obey whoever has the key. He can't do anything of his own free will. And more importantly, we need it so that I can become his master and pass through the Dragon's Gate with him, and then free him once he has turned into a dragon again."

"Who has the key?"

"You'll never guess!" said Mr Shen with a laugh.

Timothy thought hard. He knew he hadn't really been challenged to solve the riddle or anything, but how hard could it be to figure out that one? Someone had the key and was Mr Shen's master. OK, so who was in charge of him if it wasn't Sir Bazalgette? Well, it could be . . . "Mr Bore?"

"He got it!" Mr Shen clapped his hands together gleefully.

"Mr Bore is your master?"

"Yes."

"How did that happen?"

"It wasn't supposed to," said Sir Bazalgette. "It wasn't supposed to."

THE SEVENTH CHAPTER

In which Timothy is told the second of two extraordinary stories

Sir Bazalgette then began a story almost as strange as the one Mr Shen had told. He spoke of being a young architect and touring around the world, "collecting those artefacts we saw in the courtyard." Timothy nodded.

Along with him he had brought the teenaged son of a good friend as his personal secretary, as a favour, to show him a bit of the world. The son, as it turned out, was Evans Bore. Sir Bazalgette had made his way to China at the invitation of another very well known architect, Sir Walter Prism, an elderly man, close to death and wanting desperately to pass on some of his discoveries involving light and reflection before he died.

There they had spent several months in his company, and Sir Bazalgette had grown to become quite good friends with Sir Walter. Then one night, the old man was at death's door, and Sir Bazalgette was summoned to his side. He had thought that Sir Walter was going to explain to him in intricate detail the art of creating a perfect concave mirror, but to his surprise an elderly Chinese man was brought into his presence. Sir Walter explained Mr Shen's story and asked that Sir Bazalgette do one thing for him – that when the time came, Sir Bazalgette would release Mr Shen, and if something unfortunate were to happen, and he couldn't do it, to find another soul willing to. Sir Bazalgette promised and sat by the old man all night until the man died early the following morning.

Unfortunately, in his delirium, Sir Walter had forgotten to actually hand over the key to Sir Bazalgette, and Sir Bazalgette had been so tired from staying up all night that he had forgotten to take it. So it was that the young Evans Bore, completely oblivious to the previous night's events, when sent to take care of Sir Walter's remains, found the key, thought it looked interesting, and took it from around the man's neck. Instantly Mr Shen appeared at his side and bowed down low, and Evans Bore learned that he had suddenly become the master of a dragon. Sir Bazalgette hadn't been too upset by the action. After all, the youth hadn't known what he was doing. But it was when Bore refused to return the key that things got a bit bad between them. OK, really bad. So bad, in fact, that they had not spoken since.

"There's one thing I don't understand," said Timothy once Sir Bazalgette had finished. There was actually a lot more than just one thing that he didn't understand, like why these two old men were playing with his mind like this, but whatever. "How can Mr Shen be here with you if Bore is his master?"

Mr Shen smiled. "Well, Bore made an impulsive mistake once. I mentioned running into Sir Bazalgette while on an errand for Mr Bore in the city. I told him I was reminded of how we all first met, and then he said, 'Well, if you like Sir Bazalgette so much, you should just go and hang out with him!' And so I did!"

"Right, OK," said Timothy, not entirely convinced. "And even though you could probably go with him to China, you need the key to be freed."

"Yes."

"And I take it Bore isn't willing to take you to China?"

"He does not appear to wish it," said Mr Shen sadly.

"And again, what do I have to do with all this?"

Sir Bazalgette looked at Timothy closely. "Guess."

Suddenly Timothy understood why Sir Bazalgette had offered to watch him while his father was out of town. He sighed.

"Timothy, no one ever gets close to Evans Bore. Yet he's taken you under his wing."

"Yeah, but why does it matter? Why can't you just take the key?"

"The only way to pass on the key is for its owner to die, or for the key to be passed on willingly. You can't simply take it."

"So you want me to somehow convince Bore to give you the key?" Timothy thought that unlikely.

"No."

"Good." At least there was some sense in the man.

"I want you somehow to convince Bore to give you the key."

Timothy stood up, shaking his head. "There is no way I'm being that guy's master, OK?" he said, pointing at Mr Shen. "No way!"

Sir Bazalgette scoffed. "There is no way I would let you. No, you get the key from Bore, I get the key from you. Simple."

"Why not give the key to Mr Shen?"

"It doesn't work that way," replied Sir Bazalgette through clenched teeth. "Timothy. We need your help. You are a clever lad and I am sure more than intelligent enough to persuade Bore to hand the key over to you. But if you don't think you can do it. . ."

"I can do it," said Timothy, "I just don't want to do it."

"Please?" Mr Shen spoke quietly and yet his voice pierced the room.

Timothy turned to the dragon. Mr Shen wasn't looking at him in desperation, or fear, expressions Timothy was far more used to dealing with. Instead he was full of hope, almost happy. Timothy wasn't sure what to do with such a look. He didn't want to get involved in this weird, stupid mess at all . . . but. . .

"I'll do it, but it's got to be quick. I get the key, you get the key. And I don't want any responsibility if things go wrong." Timothy sat down again, crossing his arms.

"Thank you, Timothy," said Mr Shen, placing a hand on his wrist.

Timothy shrugged it off.

"Now that that is all settled," said Sir Bazalgette with a broad smile, "we simply must put our plan into action as soon as possible. Mr Shen is going to be staying with me as well so that we can leave for our trip the moment we get the key. Definitely start Monday, right away. We really need to get this key as soon as possible."

"Sure, whatever," muttered Timothy, who was still feeling somehow as if he'd been tricked into helping them.

"Also, we should talk about the ninja," added Mr Shen.

Timothy and Sir Bazalgette looked at Mr Shen.

"What ninja?" asked Timothy slowly.

"I'm being followed by a ninja," replied Mr Shen gravely.

"Repeat that?" This was getting to be too much for Timothy.

"I'm being followed by a ninja."

"What exactly do you mean by you are being followed by a ninja?" said Sir Bazalgette.

"Just what I said. Everywhere I go, coming here tonight, there he is, following me," replied Mr Shen with a shrug.

"Does this happen to you often?" asked Sir Bazalgette.

"Not particularly, no. I only noticed for the first time last week."

"But he is a ninja; it is possible he's been following you for longer than that."

"True, ninjas are pretty stealthy, but. . ."

"But. . ."

"I'm a dragon."

"That's your excuse for everything!" said Timothy in exasperation. "What does that mean anyway?"

Mr Shen smiled slightly. "It means that I know when I am being stalked by a ninja."

The conversation was going nowhere, and Timothy was getting fed up. "Fine. So if he's following you," he said, "he's probably somewhere outside the house right now."

"Probably."

"Well, why don't you show him to us, then?"

The reasonableness of this suggestion was not lost on Mr Shen, and so the three of them went upstairs to peer out one of the darkened windows of the second floor. Mr Shen scanned up and down Wither Way, and then with a sharp movement pointed towards the garden across the street. A dark figure, barely a shadow, moved abruptly from behind a rubbish bin and hid itself among the shrubbery.

"That reminds me. Timothy," whispered Sir Bazalgette, "don't let me forget to put the rubbish out."

Both Timothy and Mr Shen turned slowly and stared at the architect.

"Sorry."

THE EIGHTH CHAPTER

In which we meet a ninja

In fact, the ninja had been following Mr Shen for only six days, and the reason the ninja knew that it had been only six days was that the ninja had an uncanny sense of time. If you asked the ninja what time it was, for example, and you might have in the past, I don't know, the ninja would be able to tell you without looking at a watch, sundial, or even glancing up at the sky. The ninja had always had this strange ability, though why, the ninja had never really known.

This perfect sense of time had been the cause of much grief and joy in the ninja's life up until this point. Her name was Emily. She had grown up in Bearclaw, Saskatchewan. Her parents were first-generation Canadian. And her grandparents had moved to the country from Taiwan. Though English was her first language, she had been educated in Mandarin, both at home and at school, from a very young age, and so spoke the language fluently.

She had dreamt her whole life of becoming a classical pianist. This was where her uncanny sense of time had proven both an asset and a liability. She was able to keep to the strictest beat while she played, not wavering, not even needing a metronome. As a young child she had been much praised for this ability. However, as she grew, this perfect pace-keeping had begun to stunt any true musicality. So that while everyone at a concert could agree that she had executed *The Dancing Toad Sonata* to perfection, no one could quite explain why it had left them feeling rather cold.

When she finally graduated from the Conservatory of Musical Studies and Learning, she left without any prizes, accolades, or indeed any offers from agents or symphonies. And so her parents had suggested she take some time to rediscover her roots and sent her off to stay with her aunt in Taiwan.

The two of them toured the country together and then went over to China. And one day while she was dancing at a club in perfect rhythm to the classic R&B hit "I Ain't Got No Nothin'" played by a Chinese cover band, she found herself being escorted kindly over to a slender man dressed head to toe in black sitting at a table in the far corner of the room.

He was known simply as the TV Repairman, and he was a master ninja trainer, having brought the art form to China from his native Japan. His unfortunate choice of name came from him not fully understanding the art of coming up with cool names to impress people. This possibly had to do with the precedent set by his master in Japan, who had called himself the Fog Machine for no discernible reason. At any rate, despite his name, the TV Repairman's abilities and his school were, and are, legendary.

He had noticed how precise Emily's movements were, how she moved with a fluid yet very accurate grace, and he invited her to train with him and his other students. And because Emily had had nothing but bad experiences with her gift, and this was the first time anyone had been genuinely impressed with her abilities, she had to say yes.

And so she trained with the TV Repairman. And so she became one heck of a ninja, and his prize pupil. On graduation day, her parents smiled proudly from the audience and watched as their daughter received top honours in everything from stalking to "being mysterious", as well as earning the coveted "My Favourite Student Ever" award, which, oddly, was handed out three times a year.

Her parents had taken her and the TV Repairman out for a celebratory dinner after the ceremony. And everything had gone extremely well until Emily had enquired as to what the future held for her.

"Well, we were hoping you'd come home now and help with the store," her father said, surprised. "Hasn't that always been the plan?"

Emily sat there dumbfounded. "Well, surely not! I mean, I'm a really good ninja. Wouldn't all of my training just have been a waste of a lot of time and money?"

"Emily, dear, it isn't that we aren't proud of you. We really are. But be serious for a second. What sort of career can you expect from being a ninja?" her mother asked, taking a sip of tea.

"This is insane!" Emily turned to the TV Repairman. "There are plenty of things I could do as a ninja, aren't there?"

"Well. . ." said the TV Repairman in his careful English. "Not really. Ninjas really aren't all that hot right now. I guess you could teach."

"There!"

"But I don't have any positions for you at the school right now. I think it would be best if you went back to Saskatchewan," he concluded.

Emily stood up and slammed her fists on the table. "This isn't fair! I am finally good at something and everyone just wants me to forget about it! Well, I won't. I'm going to find someone out there who will appreciate my abilities and pay me a decent wage to use them."

And with that she stormed out of the restaurant, never to see her parents or the TV Repairman again.

She had stormed out so quickly that she never had the chance to read the little notice her parents had put in many of the papers in Taipei. She had never seen the picture her parents had chosen of her, beaming in her cowboy hat, with the prairie stretching out behind her. And she never had the chance to read the little blurb they had proudly written for the world to read: "Congratulations to our only daughter, Emily, who has just graduated top of her class at the Ninja Institute located in the province of Yunnan. We love her very much, and could not have wished for more from a daughter. She has made us the proudest parents in the world. We love you!"

No, unfortunately, she never got to read any of this.

But the Man in the Beige Linen Suit had.

So that was how she found herself on a darkened street in a city she didn't know, stalking what, for all intents and purposes, was a dragon. And how she found herself taking out a small black notebook and writing down in a very precise script: "169 hours and 36 minutes to go."

THE NINTH CHAPTER

In which Timothy tries to get the key

At first Timothy had imagined convincing someone as gullible as Evans Bore to give him a key would be a relatively easy task. But as the days passed, Timothy began to realize that bringing up the topic of an ancient golden key in casual conversation was going to be trickier than he had originally thought. He tried by asking Bore about his youth, but Bore went slightly too far back and started to enthusiastically share the tale of when his first bike had been stolen. Timothy also asked him whether he had ever travelled anywhere exotic, but apparently Bore had had a very bad experience with dysentery in the Caribbean and had been just dying to share all the most intimate details of it with someone.

And so it was that the week passed, and Friday suddenly came upon them, and as Timothy sat shuffling through the post looking for fancy party invitations, he started to wonder if he really was as clever as he always considered himself to be. He was also getting rather tired of returning every night to the house only to be interrogated by Sir Bazalgette, who was becoming more and more frantic.

"Anything?" asked Bore, setting aside the last of his post and looking over at Timothy.

"No," replied Timothy.

Evans Bore sighed. "How am I ever going to make friends if I can't practise everything you've taught me, especially those new jokes, at a fancy party?"

"Look, what do you want from me?" asked Timothy. "I'm trying, you know."

"I know you are, Timothy, I know you are," replied Bore hastily. "I don't mean to sound ungrateful." He attempted a weak smile. Timothy sighed.

Just at that moment Mr Shen entered the room, and Bore sat immediately at attention, casually wiping away a stray tear from his face.

"No post today, Shen," said Bore gruffly.

"That's not a problem, sir. Have a lovely evening." And without even glancing at Timothy, he left. Timothy stared at the space where the dragon had just been. He had a thought.

"What about Mr Shen?" he said slowly.

"What about him?"

Timothy was slightly taken aback by the sudden sharp edge to Bore's voice.

"Well, I mean, I'm not sure if you two are particularly

close, but he seems very loyal to you. Handles all your post personally, doesn't just send a boy to do it. And he's very friendly."

Bore bit his lower lip and looked down at his hands.

"I mean, that has to mean something."

Bore shook his head sadly. "No, it means nothing."

"What are you talking about?"

"He has to be loyal to me. He has no choice."

"Of course he has a choice; he could quit. Or . . ." Timothy leaned across the desk, "are you blackmailing him or something?"

Bore stood up and wandered over to the floor-to-ceiling window behind the desk. He then turned around to Timothy. "If I tell you something, will you promise not to tell anyone else?"

Timothy nodded.

Bore took a deep breath and released it as he spoke. "Mr Shen is my servant."

"Really?" Timothy tried to sound surprised. "Well, that doesn't matter; he still seems to like you."

Bore came around to Timothy's side of the desk and started to pace the room. "No, no, no, he's . . . he's more like a slave, actually. I don't pay him. I don't have to. He just has to do whatever I tell him."

"I don't get it."

Bore stopped pacing and looked down at Timothy. Then, as if someone had shocked him with a jolt of electricity, he whipped around, crossed the room and prised a painting off the wall. Behind it was a safe.

"Original place to keep that," commented Timothy with a roll of the eyes.

Bore paid no attention to Timothy, but unlocked the safe and opened it. He removed a small jewellery box that looked like it had once contained an engagement ring, brought it over to the desk and returned to his seat.

"What's that?" Timothy brought his chair around to the same side as Bore and stared down at the box.

"This is. . ." Bore opened the box. "This."

"This" was the key. Neither remarkable nor your average house key, it had that old-fashioned thickness to it, instead of being flat. It was around five centimetres long and a thin gold chain passed through a hoop at the top. And it was indeed gold.

Timothy almost forgot he was play-acting, but remembered at the last minute. "What is it, though?"

"This key gives me my power over Mr Shen. Whoever owns the key owns him."

"Really? That's cool." Timothy didn't feel a need to pretend disbelief, nor did he have the time. "So Mr Shen will do whatever you tell him to? No question?"

"No question."

Timothy took the opportunity to gaze in awe at the object in order to plot his next course of action. He glanced at the clock, it was already five-thirty. *Think!*

"So you see, he isn't really my friend at all. I'm sure if I wasn't his master he wouldn't spend any time with me." Bore laughed to himself. "I bet if he had a fancy party he wouldn't invite me."

Ah yes, because fancy party invitations are the benchmark of friendship. Timothy sighed. "Look, if you want a fancy party so much, why don't you just host one yourself? You can't expect everyone to. . ." Timothy stopped. He turned and looked at Bore. He smiled. "Why don't you?" He said it with much more excitement this time.

"What? Host my own party? No one would come."

"Of course they would. You're their boss."

"But they wouldn't be my friends."

Timothy wanted to grab the man and shake him. "Listen. They might come to the party as your employees, but then you'll prove to them at the party how great you are and they will leave as your friends."

Bore thought about this for a minute. "But I don't know how to organize a fancy party."

I know you don't. Timothy patted the man on the back. "That's OK, I can do it for you."

"Would you?!" Bore beamed.

"Sure!"

"Oh, this will be great!" Bore started bouncing in his seat, as he tended to when he got excited. "Ooh! We'll have to hire a very fancy hall, and get the best party decorations, and food! Oh, we have to have the best food! And dancing, with a DJ. No! A band."

"Wow, that sounds great."

"Doesn't it!"

"And like a lot of work."

Bore agreed with much head nodding.

"I could probably use some help." Timothy raised his eyebrows at the man.

"Of course!"

"Maybe. . ." *Here goes nothing.* "Mr Shen?"

Bore stopped bouncing. He stared at Timothy. Then pointed at him. "Excellent suggestion. That fellow will do anything."

Timothy nodded. "Great. Can I have the key, then?"

"The key?"

"Well, if I'm going to have to tell him what to do. . ." *Please, oh, please*, thought Timothy. There was a chance, a chance that Bore would be clever enough and suggest that he simply tell Mr Shen to do whatever Timothy asked of him. If he did that, then Timothy wasn't sure he'd be able to get the key any other way. He also would have to actually plan a fancy party.

Bore stood, picked up the key, and held it by its chain. It dangled slightly hypnotically in front of him. There was a long pause. "You promise to give it back?"

Thank goodness. "Yes, of course. I promise." *Just give me the key already!*

Slowly Bore extended his hand. Timothy held out his, and in a move that would change the course of Timothy's life in ways he would not comprehend even when they actually eventually happened, let alone in that moment, Bore dropped the key into his palm.

Finally. Timothy stood and put the chain around his neck, tucking the key inside his shirt. "Great, thanks. Now I really have to get out of here. We'll talk more

66

about plans on Monday. Bazalgette is going to freak out that it's so late."

Bore staggered backwards and fell back into his chair. "What did you just say?"

Timothy looked at the man with confusion, and his heart sank when he realized what he had said. What a stupid slip-up, totally beneath him. "Uh . . . I said I had to get home."

"No, you said Bazalgette."

"Did I?"

Bore brought a hand up to his forehead and pushed back his hair slowly. It was obvious the cold, harsh truth had dawned on him. "There isn't going to be any fancy party, is there?"

Timothy was starting to feel uncomfortable. "Look, I have to go." He turned around and opened the door.

"Timothy!"

Timothy stopped. He half expected the meek Evans Bore to lunge at him. Then again, unless Bore was willing to kill him, there wasn't much the man could do about getting the key; Timothy definitely wasn't going to give it back to him. He stood frozen for a moment. When Bore neither attacked him nor said anything else, Timothy turned to look at him. "I'm . . . I'm sorry about your party," he said softly.

"Never mind the party. Timothy. You have to promise me something."

"I. . ."

"You have to promise me you won't give that key to Bazalgette."

Timothy was taken aback: that request was not what he had expected to hear.

"It's very important. Promise me!"

Evans Bore looked smaller than usual, sitting there at his big desk in front of his huge window. He also looked utterly terrified.

"I. . ."Timothy turned away from the man once more. "I can't. I'm sorry, Mr Bore."

And he stepped though to the hall, closing the door quietly behind him.

THE TENTH CHAPTER

In which Timothy's suspicions are raised

When Timothy finally returned to Sir Bazalgette's, it was already rather late. He slowly made his way upstairs to the guest room. He flopped down on the bed and took the key from around his neck. He let it dangle above his head, glinting in the light. It was hard to imagine that dragons had supposedly forged this small, innocuous object. Well, it wasn't hard to imagine it, just more like really hard to believe it.

There was a knock on the door. Instinctively, Timothy put the key back around his neck and hid it under his shirt. "I'm getting changed," he called out.

"Just curious how it went today," replied Sir Bazalgette through the door.

"Look, when I get your stupid key, I'll tell you. It isn't that easy, you know!" Timothy really had no idea why he was lying.

Sir Bazalgette opened the door to the guest room.

"I said I was changing!" exclaimed Timothy.

"And you are obviously not." The old man sat at the foot of the bed. "You wouldn't lie to me, Timothy, would you?"

Timothy stood up, crossing the room to stare out the window.

"I don't like being lied to."

"Why would I lie? I already told you I don't want any part in any of this. When I get the key, I'll give it to you, OK?" Timothy leaned his forehead on the cold pane of glass.

"Fine, then." Timothy heard Sir Bazalgette stand up. "But get that key soon, Timothy. I need that key." There was the sound of footsteps crossing the room and the door opening and closing. Timothy glanced over his shoulder and found himself alone once more.

Returning to the bed, he changed out of his work clothes and into his jeans and a T-shirt. Then he lay down on top of the covers, hands behind his head. Right now he really wished he had a television to help get his mind off things. He was very much put out that his mind cared at all, but it did. And his mind was not exactly stupid. It knew something was up. Judging by what Bore had said, and now Sir Bazalgette's tone of voice, there was something just not right about the whole situation. And Timothy was caught in the middle of it.

He lay there, his mind wandering about this way for an

hour or so, until he heard the front door open again. Mr Shen was home. What would that mean? Timothy wondered. Could Mr Shen sense that he had a temporary new master? If so, what would happen when Sir Bazalgette found out Timothy had been lying to him? It was just one too many thoughts to add to the ones already floating about in his head, and Timothy found his body shutting down in response. Before he could protest, Timothy found himself in a deep, dreamless sleep.

"I believe there is a ninja in the house," said Mr Shen. He was standing calmly over Timothy, who had awoken in the exact same position as he had fallen asleep.

"What time is it?" Timothy scratched the top of his head.

"Three or four in the morning. But I am not sure why it matters."

Timothy shifted his body so that he was sitting upright, legs dangling over the side of the bed. "It matters because it explains why I'm feeling so tired. You know, because I should be asleep."

Mr Shen didn't seem to understand the sarcasm.

Timothy yawned. "OK, there's a ninja in the house. Why are you telling me this? Shouldn't you tell Bazalgette?"

"I was compelled to tell you first, because, well, you know."

Timothy looked Mr Shen in the eye for the first time. The dragon's expression was unreadable, but there was no doubt in Timothy's mind that he knew Timothy had the key.

Fine, then. "Where's the ninja now?"

Mr Shen cocked his head in an effort to listen to something. Then he nodded. "In the kitchen."

"Then let's go warn Bazalgette."

Timothy slipped on his shoes and grabbed his corduroy jacket for warmth. Then he carefully opened the door of the guest room and had a look around. He could see a light on in Sir Bazalgette's study, but this was nothing special; the old man tended to stay up late and fall asleep in his chair with the lamp still on. Timothy made to step out on to the landing, when he was pulled back into the room by Mr Shen.

"The ninja is on the stairs."

Timothy pulled the door towards him, keeping it slightly ajar, and stared through the crack. He noticed the door to Sir Bazalgette's study suddenly open and a dark figure pass through it before it closed again.

"What— Who are you?" Sir Bazalgette's voice was loud and surprised. There was a silence, or at least what Timothy had thought was a silence, but it obviously wasn't because Sir Bazalgette suddenly spoke again. "I don't know what you are talking about. Key, what key?" There was another silence as the ninja replied. "In this house?" Sir Bazalgette's voice was less panicked now, more thoughtful.

Timothy closed the door entirely. He wasn't sure what to do. It didn't seem altogether safe to leave Sir Bazalgette alone with a ninja. At the same time, when the ninja realized Sir Bazalgette didn't have the key, he would no doubt come in search of the one who did.

And that was Timothy.

Why oh why oh why on earth had he got himself involved in this mess? What normal eleven-year-old boy had to deal with ninjas and dragons and stupid magic keys? No normal eleven-year-old boy, that's who. It just wasn't fair.

He ran over to the window and opened it wide. It looked like it would be pretty straightforward to climb down to the iron fence one storey below.

"What are you doing?" asked Mr Shen, coming up to him.

"Just taking in some night air. What does it look like I'm doing?! I'm getting the heck out of here." Timothy threw a leg over the window sill.

"Oh." Mr Shen looked down out the window at the street. "What about me?"

"What about you?"

"Shall I wait until you return?"

Timothy stared at Mr Shen. The dragon was looking at him, eyebrows raised, waiting calmly for instructions. He seemed so trusting, so oblivious to Timothy's indifference to him. Trying to make the indifference a little more obvious, Timothy exhaled a frustrated breath and turned back to the window.

"Come along if you want, whatever, but just do it fast, OK?" he said, keeping his back to Mr Shen and sliding out the window.

In a few moments, he and Mr Shen were running down Wither Way towards the main street. Timothy checked his pockets. He had a bit of cash, enough maybe for a cab. A cab to where, though? He glanced over at Mr Shen, jogging a step back. What exactly was Timothy supposed to do with him? If only there were kennels for dragons. Who could he palm Mr Shen off on?

As they turned on to the main street, Timothy had a brain wave. He slowed his run to a walk and noticed Mr Shen following suit. Timothy smiled to himself. He knew exactly who deserved to be burdened with the responsibilities of taking care of a dragon.

"Hey, Mr Shen," said Timothy, "how would you like to catch a show?"

"That would be lovely. I've always been a fan of the theatre."

"Shall we take the train to the coast, then? That's where my mum's starring in a play."

"What fun!"

What fun indeed. Timothy couldn't help but laugh to himself. *Oh man*, he thought, *she's going to hate this!*

THE ELEVENTH CHAPTER

In which Timothy and Mr Shen have an unusual experience with local traffic

T he sun had begun to rise, and the day already looked to be a dull one. Overcast and cold. The sharp wind blew every so often, causing rubbish to fly about in a strange sort of musical chairs, so that one crisp bag would fly up to land where a gum wrapper had only just moved on from, and so on. Very few cars passed as the two trudged along. And even fewer cabs. Those that did were already occupied, and it seemed quite possible that the two of them would have to walk clear across the city to get to the train station.

"Man, this really stinks," said Timothy, pulling the collar of his corduroy jacket up around his ears. "This massively stinks."

Mr Shen, a perfect metre behind him, agreed with a soft, "Hmm."

They went back to their earlier silence, passing shop

after shop. Each was sealed off from its patrons by thick metal grates. Locked wooden gates to the occasional garden rattled in their general direction, and every café pronounced in slightly faded lettering that it was very much not open for business. It seemed as if the world just didn't want to have anything to do with them.

"A cab," said Mr Shen.

Timothy turned and watched as a black cab pulled to the kerb next to them and stopped.

"Where to?" asked the driver. He was dressed in a dark green pinstriped suit and had on brown leather driving gloves. He wore a fedora on his head.

"Central Station," said Timothy, climbing into the back. Mr Shen followed. It was super annoying the way he just always followed.

"Central Station," confirmed the cabby.

The black cab took off at a fairly reasonable speed, seeing as there was no traffic.

Timothy turned to Mr Shen. "OK, look," he said. "I think we've got to establish a few ground rules here."

"Of course."

"First, stop walking like right behind me. We don't want people to think you're my servant or something."

"But I am your servant."

"Yes, but we don't want people to think that. We just want to pretend we are two normal people. Though" – Timothy looked at Mr Shen hard; his appearance could not really be anything but extraordinary – "that is never going to be completely possible."

"I understand. It makes sense."

"And next, I really hate calling you Mr Shen all the time, like you're my teacher or something. What's your first name?"

"I don't have a first name," replied Mr Shen, scratching behind his ear thoughtfully. He seemed rather nonplussed about the issue.

"How can you not . . . oh, never mind." Timothy knew the answer would be something like "Because I'm a dragon", and he was getting really sick of that excuse. "Is there a first name you like, that you wouldn't mind being called? You know, just so we could blend in a bit more?"

Mr Shen sat thoughtfully for a second. Then he smiled brightly. "I have always rather liked the name Obadiah."

Timothy shook his head. "OK, never mind, we'll think of something later." He turned to stare out the window.

They had left the main street and moved on to the motorway. More cars joined them now, and the world started to feel slightly less foreboding. The tall towers of the city loomed in the distance.

"That's interesting," commented Mr Shen, who had followed Timothy's gaze.

"What's interesting?" asked Timothy, not turning around.

"From what I remember, Central Station was two exits ago."

Timothy turned sharply. "What do you mean?"

"I mean that we have passed the turn-off for Central Station. We could be going a different route, but the closer we get to the city, from what I recall, the further we are from the station. I must make a note of this route. It does not seem as if it would be faster, but obviously our cabby believes it to be."

Timothy leaned forward and knocked on the glass that separated them from their driver. "We're going to the train station, right? Central Station?" he shouted.

The cabby nodded. "Yes, sir, Central Station."

But as Timothy leaned back, he started to feel distinctly uncomfortable. They were now deep in the heart of the city, nowhere near the station, and despite Mr Shen's optimism, Timothy was not so trusting. Considering they were on the run from a ninja, it wasn't entirely out of the question that there might be other people out there just as interested in that stupid key. As the streets got darker and narrower, and their progress took them further and further away from the station, Timothy decided that they were, in fact, in a bit of trouble.

Of course, now that he thought about it, he realized that down deep he had considered that there was something suspicious about their cabby from the get-go. If not the expensive-looking leather gloves, then definitely the fedora had been a bit of a tip-off. But of course he had just been so relieved to have got a cab finally that he hadn't thought too hard about these signs. Now, of course, their oddness seemed so glaringly obvious.

"Mr Shen, we have to get out of this cab," said Timothy.

Mr Shen nodded and looked about. Then he pointed at a little red light in the door. "We are locked in," he said.

"Well, let's try the windows then."

Timothy and Mr Shen each took a window and started to roll it down. Instantly both windows went back up.

"Sorry 'bout that," said the cabby from up front, not even turning around, "got a bit of a cold, see."

Timothy and Mr Shen sat back again.

"Is there anything you can do? Anything at all?" asked Timothy softly to Mr Shen. "Anything, you know, dragon-like?"

"My powers are quite limited. . ."

"Could you make it rain so hard that he has to pull over or something?"

Mr Shen shook his head. "With the current state of my abilities, I need more water than just what is in the atmosphere. I require a puddle's worth at least. Even then I do not have enough strength to change the weather."

Timothy sat thinking hard. They were passing nothing but office buildings now. And it seemed quite obvious that there was no way they were heading for the station. He didn't know what was going on, but he knew the two of them had to get out of that cab immediately. Then he had a thought.

"Does it have to be water?"

"Sorry?"

"Does it have to be water? Can you work with something else? What about antifreeze?" Mr Shen nodded carefully, following his train of thought. "If you could make the antifreeze leak out of this cab, and I mean quickly. . ."

"It would overheat. He would have to pull over." Without another word, Timothy watched as Mr Shen's expression grew soft, almost peaceful. It was hard to tell if he was doing anything at all, but in a few moments Timothy noticed steam rising from the bonnet of the car.

"What the. . ." said the cabby.

More and more steam poured out, almost completely blocking the view through the windscreen. The black cab began to make strange straining noises.

"Curse it," said the cabby, and he slowly brought the taxi to the kerb and turned off the engine. He opened his door to have a look under the bonnet, and when he did so, the little red light indicating the doors were locked went out.

"Go, now, Mr Shen!" cried Timothy.

Mr Shen and Timothy dived out of the car and ran as fast as they could down the pavement. They took a sharp right and found themselves facing a thick crowd of office employees all pushing against each other to get to work. Why they were so keen on getting somewhere they had no desire to be, Timothy couldn't understand. But he really didn't have the time to philosophize.

Quickly he gestured to Mr Shen and they darted down a narrow alley.

"I think we are safe," said Mr Shen as Timothy looked frantically around him.

"What?"

"I don't think that driver followed us at all. I mean, his car was out of order."

Timothy looked at him closely. He felt his breath get more regular, and he nodded.

"OK," he said. "Let's get out on to a main street and figure out where we are."

They hurried down the alley and out the other end. Timothy glanced up the street. Though it was a big street, there were very few people on the pavement here, thanks in part, no doubt, to some construction taking place on the façade of one of the buildings.

"I think we need to find a bus stop or something. They usually have maps." It was tricky going, as they stepped over some wet cement and carefully avoided an open manhole. Just as they passed through the construction site, they noticed a deserted-looking bus shelter on the opposite side of the street.

Timothy took a step off the kerb, but was pulled back fiercely by Mr Shen. Mr Shen, it seemed, was rather good at pulling Timothy back from things. In a roar, a black cab charged past, mere centimetres away from Timothy's face.

"Jeez, where did that come from?" Timothy's heart was in his throat.

They watched as the black cab turned the corner.

"That can't be the same one from before. There's no way he could have fixed his engine, right?"

"I shouldn't think he could have." But the dragon looked down the road to where the cab had just vanished and squinted.

Just as Timothy had settled his nerves and was ready to cross the street again, Mr Shen said, "No." He said it quietly, but in a tone that made Timothy freeze in place. He followed Mr Shen's gaze, and then, almost as if they had summoned it with their minds, a black cab slowly turned the corner and sat idling, facing them, about three buildings away.

"What's he waiting for?" asked Timothy in the same voice that Mr Shen had used only a minute earlier.

"I don't know."

Timothy's suspicions were raised. Slowly he took a small step off the kerb once more. The black cab stayed still, but not in the way an inanimate object like, I dunno, a rock stays still, but in the way a cat watching a piece of string dangle in front of him might stay still. Timothy took another step. Then another. Then for good measure, yet another one.

That's when the cat pounced.

With acceleration worthy of a Ferrari, the black cab went from zero to sixty in less than a second, and Timothy had to leap across to the other side of the street, a bit like the way a crazy person might leap across to the other side of the street if they, too, were in danger of being run down by a black cab.

"Are you OK?" cried Mr Shen from the other side of the street.

"Oh, just fine, thanks for asking!" returned Timothy. He was leaning against the wall of a parking garage.

Mr Shen made to cross the street, but Timothy raised his hand in protest. "Stay where you are!" He stood upright and focused his gaze down the street, watching for the cab to return. "Come on," he muttered to himself. "We're still here. You know you want to."

"Timothy!" called Mr Shen again.

Timothy looked over to the dragon, who was pointing in the direction from which the cab had charged him. He turned and looked. There it was again. Sitting quietly. Waiting for him to make a move.

"There's no way he could have made it round so fast," muttered Timothy, staring at it in shock. "Unless. . ."

Timothy turned again sharply. Facing up from where the first cab had vanished was another black cab. Or was it the original black cab and the one at the top of the street was the other one? Timothy looked left, then right, then left again. And then right one more time.

"OK, OK, Mr Shen," he said slowly. "Now the trick is going to be you crossing the street without being killed."

"That looks a bit difficult.

"Look, just do what I tell you – you have to!" said Timothy. He looked at Mr Shen's frightened expression. "You can do it, just cross the street!"

Mr Shen nodded. He looked both ways. It's funny, when you look both ways before crossing the street, typically it's to double-check that no car is going to hit you. To make sure that nothing is coming. In this case, however, it seemed to be an altogether unnecessary action, considering there was no doubt that Mr Shen was about to be, in theory, run down.

Timothy watched the dragon think carefully. He desperately wanted Mr Shen to speed things up a bit, but he could kind of understand why he was hesitating. Mr Shen looked back towards Timothy with a puzzled look on his face. Just as those bushy white eyebrows furrowed together, Timothy realized that the purring engine from one of the cars had got louder somehow. He looked at both of them. They were still some distance off and didn't seem to have moved closer. Odd. The sound was getting louder, inching up on him. Inching up on him, Timothy realized suddenly, from behind. . .

There was a relaxed moment of dead calm that washed over Timothy as he slowly turned and stared down deep into the black depths that was the parking garage behind him. Two bright lights stared at him coldly from the dark. An engine revved and Timothy backed away slowly, his heels dangerously close to the kerb. One of the cars in the street revved in reply.

As this third black cab emerged from the shadows, Timothy could see the driver clearly. Like his cabby from the ride in, the man wore a fedora that covered his eyes, a pinstriped suit and leather gloves. The hands inside the gloves tightened their grip on the wheel, the knuckles rising slightly.

Timothy stared down the driver. "What do you want with me?" he yelled. He turned and looked down the street. "You really want me? Seriously?" He turned to the other one. "You want me?! Or maybe," he pointed at Mr Shen, "you want him!"

The cab in front of him responded by moving closer, so that Timothy's shins were touching its bumper.

"Come on!" he egged on the driver and slammed the palms of his hands hard on to the bonnet of the car. He stayed hunched over, arms bent at the elbow, and palms hot from the engine of the cab. Timothy looked up at the driver.

Then he spun around.

And ran.

In an instant, all three black cabs were speeding their way towards him. Timothy didn't look at any of them, just maintained eye contact with Mr Shen, who had his hand outstretched in his direction. He jumped to grab it, narrowly missing the front bumper of the black cab coming from the right. The front bumper coming from the left, however, hit his shin square on. Fortunately it sent Timothy flying towards the pavement, a few metres down from where Mr Shen had been waiting. The last black cab that had charged him from behind went flying straight into the wall where the dragon would have been standing, had he not rushed over to help Timothy to his feet.

"We must get out of here," Mr Shen said, propping Timothy up with his shoulder. Timothy tried to put some weight on his leg, but it buckled under him.

"Well, I obviously can't run now, can I?" Timothy scanned the street. The remaining cabs had both made remarkably tight three-point turns and were preparing for the charge again. The injured one was backing slowly away from the wall, shards of glass from the headlights sticking to the bonnet. "There!" said Timothy. He and Mr Shen moved as quickly as they could back down the pavement, retracing their earlier steps, and limped towards the construction site and its open manhole.

They stared down. It was dark. And smelly. A strange mist rose up from its depths. "After you," said Timothy with a grimace.

"Actually, I think in this case, it's more like after you," replied Mr Shen.

Timothy sighed and with much effort sat himself down, resting his legs over the edge. "I don't know if this is such a good idea," he said, looking up at the dragon. Mr Shen shrugged and then Timothy noticed beyond his shoulder the large shape of the third black cab bearing down on them. It was driving along the pavement itself, bits of glass and metal flying off it in all directions. The decision had obviously been made for them. Despite concern for what was below and his injured leg, Timothy launched himself down the manhole.

Man, he thought as he fell, *this is really going to hurt.*

THE TWELFTH CHAPTER

In which Timothy and Mr Shen discover something unexpected in the sewer

There were two sets of sewers that ran beneath the streets of the city. There was the sewer sewer – you know, the one where all the . . . stuff goes . . . and . . . stuff. . . That sewer had never been considered all that interesting to go down and visit. This, despite the mayor's somewhat unfortunate attempt to show it off a decade earlier to the Olympic Commitee for some reason that has never been made quite clear. Then there was the other sewer. An antiquated version of modern plumbing that had been started by the Romans and completed by the Victorians. And virtually forgotten about by the current residents.

Nevertheless, the point to all this is that, as Timothy fell, he didn't fall through the access tunnel to the left that the construction crew had been working on. Instead, he fell through the one on the right towards the old sewers, which led him, rabbit-hole-like, much deeper than he had anticipated and caused his fall to be drawn out longer than expected. It also meant that the water waiting for him at the bottom was not full of . . . stuff . . . and . . . stuff. Instead, it was relatively clean because of an underground river. Which was a bit of luck considering that water was exactly the right thing for someone like Timothy, with the state his leg was in and everything, to land in. And so you shouldn't feel icky that it was water in a sewer. That was my point.

Unfortunately, however, Timothy didn't fall into the water. He fell on to the bank right next to it. Hard. With his injured left leg bent underneath him. So I guess all that explanation was sort of pointless, really.

Timothy lay there in silence. The pain was excruciating, and he just had no way to convey that thought. Yelling would have only increased the amount of pain he was in. And, of course, Timothy wasn't exactly much of a crier. So he waited silently until his dragon floated down next to him.

"You can float?" asked Timothy through clenched teeth.

"Yes," replied Mr Shen, sitting softly beside him. "Air currents, remember."

"Why didn't you make me float then?"

"You did not ask."

Timothy looked at the dragon hard. He could easily imagine doing something unpleasant to Mr Shen, and so instead he focused on the pain in his leg.

"Well, help me with this, would you?" he said, trying to sit up.

Mr Shen held on to Timothy's arm as the boy sat upright. Then, gingerly, the dragon unfolded Timothy's leg and laid it out straight before him.

"Let's see now," said Mr Shen, and he felt the shin carefully. "You are lucky, nothing is broken. Just a sprain."

"That's lucky, is it?"

"Yes, very. Shall I tend to it?"

"Please."

Mr Shen undid Timothy's shoe and took off his sock. He tied it tightly around Timothy's ankle, took careful stock of his handiwork, and stood back. "There," he said. "That should help you put a bit more weight on it."

"That's it?" asked Timothy.

"What did you expect? I am a dragon, not a doctor."

Timothy opened his mouth to answer, but thought better of it.

"Let's try it, shall we?" Mr Shen extended a hand to Timothy. Putting all his weight on his right leg, Timothy rose slowly. Then he carefully tried to use the left one. A sharp pain caused him to spontaneously yell out. He tried again, and while it hurt a heck of a lot, he was able to hobble about somewhat with Mr Shen's help.

"Man, this stinks," he muttered to himself.

"It certainly does 'stink', doesn't it? How do you propose we get to the train station?" asked Mr Shen, sitting Timothy back down.

"I don't know! Stop asking me questions. Why don't

you figure it out for once!" snapped Timothy, instantly regretting it. He looked up at the dragon, who had turned to stare quietly down the river. "Look," Timothy said with a sigh, "I don't know what those black cabs were after, but it must have something to do with you. And . . . I don't know. You think they'll follow us down here?"

"I doubt they will fit."

"Not the black cabs!" Timothy threw his hands into the air. "The drivers, man, the drivers."

Mr Shen shrugged.

They both gazed silently out at the water. Timothy didn't know what to do any more. Not that he had known what to do in the first place. It wasn't fair. Why was any of this happening to him? He should be at home watching telly or something. Or at least going in to work and hanging out with Bore. Not looking after some stupid dragon. Maybe he had been wrong about Sir Bazalgette. And, you know, even if he had been right, what did it matter to him? Why hadn't he just handed over the key and got out of this whole mess when he had the chance?

Timothy shook his head. He'd done it again. Somehow he had created a whole big mess, just as he always did at school, and this time, this time no one was coming to pick him up to drive him home.

"Whatever," he said so quietly to himself he wasn't sure if he'd actually said it at all. But Mr Shen turned and looked down at him with a sad look on his face. "Whatever," Timothy said more loudly right at Mr Shen, and then turned and looked back out at the water. "Well, we can't go back up there. We'll have to find our way down here for the time being."

Timothy looked to both sides and finally just sighed and chose to go left. As he hobbled along, Timothy found himself getting used to the pain in his ankle and eventually even able to walk without Mr Shen's help. They walked down through the dark sewers, keeping close to the wall. They wandered aimlessly for a while in the darkness. Though Timothy did attempt to match the streets above in the sewers below, after a few forks they became disoriented, and it eventually became impossible to tell which direction they were going.

"I am getting hungry," announced Mr Shen at that convenient moment.

"Well, there's not much I can do about that right now," replied Timothy, trying to peer into the dark ahead of them.

"I dislike being hungry."

Timothy shoved his hands into his pockets. He drew out a mint, covered in fluff. *I wonder how long that's been here?* he asked himself as he passed it over to Mr Shen.

"Oh no."

Timothy turned around. "What? What's 'oh no'?"

"There it goes." Mr Shen pointed back up the sewer from where they were standing.

"Mr Shen, did you drop the mint?"

"Sorry."

Timothy watched Mr Shen watching the mint float

away, though he himself couldn't see it. Then he had a thought.

"Come on, Mr Shen." It was so simple it was almost stupid. Most things were, actually, thought Timothy as he turned around. Obviously it would make the most sense if they simply followed the flow of water out of the sewers. Eventually it would have to lead them to some kind of exit. Timothy only wished he'd thought of the idea sooner.

They wandered back along the way they had come, beneath the entrance from the manhole, and along in the opposite direction they had originally taken. The water was moving more quickly now, and even though there was no need to catch up to it, Timothy found himself picking up speed, despite his injured ankle.

"We have to be getting to an exit soon," he called over his shoulder.

And they did, very soon. However, the exit they finally came across proved less than satisfactory.

"Oh," said Mr Shen, looking over Timothy's shoulder.

They found themselves in a dead end, the water rushing by them now at quite a speed and disappearing through small pipes dotted along the wall before them.

Timothy hit his hand against the wall. "This is so idiotic!"

He turned around and stared at the blackness behind him and then in a fury charged back into it, not even caring if the dragon was following or not. He felt angry and reckless and was hardly paying attention now to the current or where he was going. It was only when he came across a quiet, still pool lit from a small grate many metres above that he finally realized he was lost.

He sat down on the ledge in a huff, as if to prove to someone or something that he had had quite enough, thank you, and he was going to teach everyone a lesson by sitting down.

"I believe we are lost," said Mr Shen, joining him.

"You think?" Timothy rubbed his face with his hands, pushing them up back through his hair. He stared at his feet, dangling just above the water. It was hard to tell how his ankle was doing from this angle, with so little light and a sock around it. Timothy only knew that it hurt, a lot. Again.

Suddenly something large and orange came bursting up from the water and disappeared back into it just in front of him.

"What the heck was that?" Timothy scrambled to his feet in an instant, flattening himself up against the wall.

"Looked like a shark," replied Mr Shen calmly, peering over the edge to take a closer look.

"Mr Shen, get away from there!"

Mr Shen pulled back just as the whatever-it-was leaped out of the water at him. Timothy saw a bright orange flash again, and the animal vanished back into the water.

"I no longer believe that is a shark," concluded Mr Shen.

"I don't care what it is, we have to get out of here."

Just as he said it, the orange blur launched itself at him again, this time grabbing Timothy's arm with its mouth. It wasn't painful, as the creature had no teeth, but it was enough to send Timothy off balance and topple him into the water.

Timothy splashed and flailed about as the creature repeatedly attacked him. Well, not so much attacked him, but sort of head-butted him. Timothy tried to swim away, but the creature was faster, swimming around him and blocking his escape. Timothy dived under and watched through the now churning water as the creature came zooming right for him. As he came to the surface, Timothy saw a pair of rubber boots appear in his line of sight. He brought his whole head above the water and looked.

"Down, boy, down!" growled a loud voice. Timothy watched as a tall, sturdy man hit the water in front of him with a large staff. The creature tried to swim towards Timothy twice more, each time being blocked by the staff. It eventually gave up and, almost sulking, started to swim aimlessly around the now calm pool.

Timothy bobbed in the water in shock. It took him a moment to realize a hand had been offered to him. He grabbed it and was helped back up on to the ledge. The man came up beside him and towered over him. Then, removing his hat, he spoke: "Howdy, gents. Hope he didn't startle you. Frank's got a pretty playful nature. But he wouldn't harm a fly, that one. Name's Leopold." He held out his hand. "Leopold Blyth, fish herder."

THE THIRTEENTH CHAPTER

In which Timothy learns how to herd

"Fish herder?" said Timothy, taking Leopold's hand and shaking it.

"Indeed. And who might you be?"

Timothy appraised the man. He was dressed kind of like a fly-fisher, with rubber waders up to his waist and a plaid shirt. He had a leathery-looking face with deep lines around the mouth. And his thick head of greying hair was slicked back with either grease or water.

"Uh, I'm Timothy. And this is Mr Shen. Fish herder?" he asked again, hoping for a better explanation.

"Howdy," said Leopold, shaking Mr Shen's hand.

"Howdy," replied the dragon.

Leopold turned back to Timothy.

"Never heard of fish herding, then, eh? Wouldn't blame you. I think I may be the only fish herder in the whole world. Don't do it for money, son. Don't need to. I'm an accountant most of the year."

"Accountant."

"But then the fish herding season comes along, and that's when I take my two weeks. Doesn't take that long to herd 'em, but it does for the smell to go away!" He laughed loudly at that. Then stopped. "No, seriously, it takes that long for the smell to go away."

Timothy could understand. Despite the strange odours from the sewer itself, the man's stench stood out. Kind of smelled as if he'd kept a piece of anchovy in his pocket for one day too many.

"So that would make Frank a fish, then," concluded Timothy, looking down into the water, where the outline of the creature could be seen swimming back and forth, stalking him carefully.

"Yup. Frank there is a bona fide eight-month-old *Carassius auratus*."

"What?"

"Goldfish."

It was Timothy's turn to laugh. "Yeah right. That thing is huge! That thing is the size of a big dog!" He stopped laughing when he saw Leopold's serious expression.

"Well, son, lots of stuff gets dumped down here in the sewer. Dare say Frank's grandma and grandpa were. Flushed before their time." Was there a tear in the man's eye? "You drink a little cough syrup that's also found its way down here, and your genetic code goes all funny. But it ain't no laughin' matter, son. It's a tough life being a sewer fish. That's why I take as many as I can find and herd them out to sea."

"What do you mean, 'to sea'?"

"The sea. This here old-fashioned sewer empties out to the sea. I herd them along to their freedom. Oh, it's sad sayin' our goodbyes, but it's always worth the pain. Always been a fan of fish, see, have since I was little. Then one day I read an article about all them lost souls down here in the sewers, and I felt an obligation, you know? Hate to see such beautiful creatures trapped underground for ever. So, once a year, like I says, I help them find their way out."

"Can you take us with you?"

The man scratched his head for a moment, and then replaced his hat. "Don't see why not. Could use an extra pair of hands, actually. Dang near impossible to handle them Siamese fightin' fish once they get goin'." He turned around and whistled at Frank, who followed obediently.

Timothy smiled at Mr Shen, who seemed mildly satisfied that he had found a way for them to get out of the sewer.

"Don't you see?" said Timothy to the dragon as they followed Leopold and Frank away from the still pool. "We were heading for the coast anyway. The motorway runs along the coastline, so this way we can catch a bus or something from a rest stop and get to Sharpton."

"Yes, so I gathered," replied Mr Shen.

"Well, you don't seem all that excited that I got us a

way out of here." Timothy was starting to feel angry again.

"Oh, I am happy, but I am not surprised. I was completely confident you would find a way."

Timothy wasn't sure what to say to that. It was quite possibly the first time anyone had ever had faith in him. So he decided not to say anything.

"All right, lads. Mr Shen, was it?" asked Leopold when they'd made their way back into the tunnels.

Mr Shen nodded.

"Mr Shen, would you mind takin' hold of this here netting? I'll wade through to the other side and hold it there."

Mr Shen looked at Timothy.

"Help Leopold, please, Mr Shen," said Timothy, still not used to giving orders.

Mr Shen picked up the netting. Timothy watched as Leopold waded into the water to the other side of the tunnel. It was only then that Timothy looked down and noticed the schools of fish, all different shapes and sizes, swimming aimlessly about just below him. The net Leopold was talking about was strung across the water from one side of the tunnel to the other, preventing any of them from swimming back up the sewer.

"Normally I have to walk in the water behind them, but this will be much more efficient," said Leopold climbing up on to the opposing bank. "Won't lose a single fish with the two of us holdin' the net. And if you, Timothy, would walk a ways ahead, makin' sure they are all behaving themselves, we should make it out of this here sewer in no time!" He tossed his staff over the water to him, and Timothy caught it deftly in his right hand.

Timothy moved up a little way along the bank. He couldn't help but stare at the strange fish below him. Some were typical household pets, but there were others, some with three eyes or two tails, and some like Frank that were far bigger than was natural. He couldn't help but feel for them. "The rejects," he said to himself. Then he rolled his eyes. *They're just fish*.

"All right, lads, here we go. Yee haw!"

And so the fish herding began.

They moved along at a pretty steady pace, the fish more than content to keep going forward. Of the three of them, though, Timothy thought he'd been given the toughest job. Where Leopold and Mr Shen just had to slowly keep pressing forward, Timothy found himself constantly stopping to poke and prod at the fish, trying to keep things in order. As Leopold had suggested, the Siamese fighting fish were a particular nuisance, constantly picking on one school of guppies. But the catfish were no easier to handle either, with their sudden stopping to clean the sides of the sewer. And then of course there was Frank, who had obviously taken a liking to Timothy, and who would continually jump out of the water at him, startling Timothy to the point where he was ready to serve the creature up with chips.

In this way the three of them herded fish. And herded

fish. For hours, they kept herding fish. And just as Timothy started to realize how strange the whole situation actually was, almost as if he were waking very slowly from a dream, the walls of the sewer began to grow lighter, and he could feel a slight breeze on his face. Timothy gazed ahead. He felt awed by the concept of natural light.

"By gum, lads, we made it! And I believe in record time too! Fortune was smilin' on me today!" Leopold let out a whoop. Mr Shen let out a whoop as well.

Timothy just shook his head.

Soon the river emptied out of the sewer and into a small bay at the edge of the sea. The fish could obviously sense their freedom upon them, and in a frenzy started to swim off in all directions.

"You too, Frank," said Timothy to the massive goldfish next to him. "Come on." The goldfish seemed reluctant to leave his side at first, but then he slowly made his way into the bay, and with the salty water on his face swam quickly out to sea.

"Sorry to see this lot go," said Leopold, coming up to join Timothy. "Good bunch."

Timothy wasn't sure exactly how long he'd be forced to stand in the water staring out after a bunch of sewer fish. He hoped it wouldn't be for too much longer. Judging by the light it was probably close to noon, and he and Mr Shen still had a way to go before they'd be in Sharpton. Fortunately, though sentimental, Leopold was pretty practical.

"Well, that's that, then! Nothin' more to be done. Now to return to the missus and start the de-stenchifying process. You lads all right here?"

Timothy nodded and passed the staff back to him. "Thanks for the help."

"Any time, lads, any time." With that Leopold Blyth turned back towards the sewers, pulled up the netting and slung it over his shoulder, and, with his staff in hand, made his way back into the dark. Then, with one final salute in their direction, he disappeared into its shadowy depths.

THE FOURTEENTH CHAPTER

In which Timothy and Mr Shen
visit a local rest stop

Timothy and Mr Shen made their way to the small rocky beach and took stock of their situation. They were standing directly below cliffs that towered above them. The sea could be seen just beyond where the small bay drained into it, and waves broke mildly against the shoreline.

Mr Shen seemed utterly transported, staring out at the vast water in front of them.

"I truly cannot remember the last time I saw the sea," he said. He was visibly moved.

"Eh, whatever, it's just water," Timothy replied, reaching down to tighten the now damp sock around his ankle. It helped soothe the pain a bit. A very little bit.

"Yes, I suppose it is." Mr Shen turned to Timothy sadly.

"I mean, not that the sea isn't cool and everything," back-pedalled Timothy. Man, this dragon was easily hurt.

"I just mean. . ." Timothy sighed. "I don't know what I mean. I'm sorry. I'm sure by the time you get to China and everything you'll be pretty sick of the sea."

Mr Shen smiled. "That would be nice."

"OK," said Timothy, clapping his hands together. "Right now we really need to get to that bus stop. Come on."

Mr Shen nodded and turned to follow him.

In short order they were on their way, moving along the beach towards a steep path leading up to the top of the cliffs that Timothy had noticed earlier. It seemed pretty climbable, though annoyingly steep, especially considering his still-aching ankle. Just as Timothy was about to start the long climb, he turned to Mr Shen. "Hey, how about we make this a general order, 'K? How about if you ever see me fall anywhere or anything, you make sure that I float down using your air currents and stuff."

Mr Shen nodded. "I will do my best to the degree that my diminished powers allow."

"Thanks," replied Timothy. "Well, I guess we should just start climbing, then."

As it turned out, Mr Shen's limited powers concerning air currents, which, oddly enough, is also the title of a reference book I used once in physics class, were completely not necessary at this moment in time, as neither he nor Timothy found themselves in a precarious position. The fact was that the path leading from the beach was pretty much meant to be an easy route, and so this particular part of the story is wholly uneventful.

They eventually made it to the top of the cliffs and wandered down the motorway to a rest stop a half-mile down the road. It wasn't particularly special-looking. Several eighteen-wheeled lorries were parked in a large lot at the back, and several cars of the smaller variety were in the front. And as they entered the small diner, everything had that strange rest-stop-like feel – slightly foul to the senses, and yet oddly heavenly at the same time.

Timothy sat Mr Shen down at a table and then approached the young woman at the counter.

"We were told we could get a bus from here out to Sharpton," he said.

"You were told right."

"So?"

The woman stared at him blankly.

". . . Where would we find the bus?"

"Oh, sorry, the bus doesn't run today," replied the young woman, and she turned away from him, rubbing a dish towel absent-mindedly across the counter.

Timothy stared at her back for a moment. Then he returned to join Mr Shen. "Great, just great," Timothy muttered, taking a seat. Mr Shen was concentrating on sucking a milkshake through a straw.

"Where'd you get the milkshake?" asked Timothy.

"I don't know. It was just here."

"OK," sighed Timothy, grabbing the milkshake from him. "Eating someone else's rubbish? Not cool, 'K?"

"But it was enjoyable!" Mr Shen reached out for the drink.

"Hey, who's the master here?"

Mr Shen withdrew his arm. "You are."

"While I would agree that on most occasions, other people's rubbish is not exactly the healthiest of comestibles, I would request that you not lump all trash into the same heap," said a deep voice.

Together, Timothy and Mr Shen turned and looked over at the neighbouring table. A burly man with long wild hair and a beard to match, wearing a plaid shirt and worn jeans, was watching them carefully through squinted eyes. Emanating from him was such a foul smell that it caused even Timothy, who had just spent several hours in a sewer, to flinch.

"Whatever," replied Timothy, turning his attention back to Mr Shen.

"Pay attention to me!" said the man, pulling his chair abruptly over to their table.

"OK, Mr Shen, time to move," said Timothy, standing. Mr Shen rose to join him, and they found a table at the other side of the room. Timothy took the few crumpled notes from his pocket and looked at the food on the counter. No, he had to save his money for the bus. He put it away.

The man appeared once more at Timothy's side and grabbed his arm. "I haven't had anyone to talk to for so long! Let's talk rubbish!"

Timothy attempted to shake the man off, but his grip was ridiculously strong. "I don't want to. Let go!"

The man stared at Timothy with clear blue eyes. It

was difficult to read what exactly was going through his mind. After a few moments, the man let go of Timothy and sat in the chair opposite.

"No, well, I guess you don't have to," said the man as Timothy adjusted his jacket, pulling at the collar. "But you do need a lift to Sharpton, don't you?" He gave Timothy a sideways glance. "I could give you one in exchange for a good old-fashioned discussion about rubbish!"

Accepting rides from strangers was strictly against the rules. Then again, since when had Timothy ever cared about the rules? The guy was obviously crazy. But then again, that said nothing about his character. And, of course, there was the man's hygiene, which would make for a very unpleasant ride. But waiting for the next day's bus could mean that eventually he would be sitting next to someone even more unpleasant.

The final analysis of the situation came out with no concrete conclusion, and Timothy was ready to walk out on the man, when out of the corner of his eye, he spied something distressing. Through the window of the diner, Timothy noticed something that spurred his mind to decisive action – the arrival of a very familiar vehicle.

"Do you think maybe they put some sort of tracking device on our persons, surreptitiously?" said Mr Shen, noticing the black cab at the same time as Timothy. "Surreptitiously." Mr Shen said the word again, rolling it around in his mouth.

Possibly. Or they were psychic. Whatever the reason,

Timothy could just not believe his eyes, and so it took a moment before he finally turned to the crazy man. "OK, we'll listen to you if you can give us a ride to Sharpton, like, now." The crazy man looked at him with a smile. "No. Like, now!"

The crazy man nodded that he understood, or maybe just nodded because he liked the sensation of nodding, and stood quickly.

"No problem, no problem at all!" he said, bouncing on the spot.

"Is there another way out of here?" asked Timothy, watching as another ominous vehicle drove up and parked itself next to the first.

"Sure thing! Follow me!"

THE FIFTEENTH CHAPTER

In which Timothy and Mr Shen
follow the crazy man

Timothy and Mr Shen followed the crazy man towards the counter of the diner, and then beyond it through to the kitchen. They ran past a startled sous-chef and a very depressed-looking dishwasher, and practically barrelled right into the delivery man carrying two tons of raw bacon. Timothy noticed Mr Shen eyeing the meat hungrily. "Leave it," he warned, and grabbed Mr Shen by the shirt, dragging him out into the back car park.

"Come on, chaps!" said the crazy man, running faster than ever.

The running was starting to really hurt Timothy's ankle, and as he and Mr Shen caught up with the crazy man, he asked, "Why are you running so fast?"

"Why are you?"

"Because you are . . . oh, never mind!"

"There she is," announced the crazy man, pointing ahead of him. Timothy and Mr Shen stared ahead and saw the man pointing at a giant purple eighteen-wheel lorry. "I call her Daisy."

"Hi, Daisy!" said Mr Shen, patting the door as the crazy man unlocked it for him.

Timothy just shook his head. The beast of a lorry was massive. The wing mirror was bigger than his head.

Timothy waited for Mr Shen to clamber into the cab of the lorry, and as he followed suit, noticed, now that his head had moved out of the frame of the mirror, a third black cab had turned the corner around the diner. The alpha cab. The one that had barrelled out at him from the parking garage and chased them along the pavement back in the city. He didn't quite know how he knew – all the cabs looked pretty much the same – but he just did. And he started to seethe with rage.

"Come on, come on!" called out the crazy man, who had taken his position in the driver's seat.

Timothy found himself mesmerized by the black cab. He knew at any minute it would charge, and that really he shouldn't be wasting time playing chicken like this. With his left foot up on the step and right arm holding on to the underside of the roof of the lorry, Timothy watched the black cab rumble quietly.

And then, just a moment after Timothy thought it wouldn't bother, it charged. Timothy watched the cab grow bigger and bigger in the wing mirror. It was aiming at Daisy as if it planned to sideswipe her. The crazy man started Daisy's engine, and a loud growl emanated from her bowels. And still the black cab charged. Timothy wouldn't move. *I dare you*, he thought, *I dare you*.

"Up we go!" said the crazy man. Mr Shen jerked Timothy up on to the seat next to him. A mere second after that, the black cab shot by, taking the passenger door with it. "And there goes the door!" said the crazy man with a laugh. With the man's foot jammed hard on the gas, the lorry barrelled through the car park, practically tipping over as it fishtailed around to the front of the rest stop.

"Yee-haw!" sang the crazy man as they flew down towards the slip road of the motorway. "Man, I am just loving this!"

Mr Shen nodded in agreement, but Timothy felt slightly sick, grabbing hard on to his seat and feeling the rush of air on his side, the road a grey speeding blur just next to him.

"Now there's three of them!" announced the crazy man.

Timothy leaned over and looked in the wing mirror.

"Can you shake 'em?" he asked, not really wanting to put himself through such an activity, but realizing there was very little choice.

"I can give it my best. Fasten your seat belt, boy, it's going to be a bumpy ride!"

With much effort to prevent his falling out of the side of the cab and thus being squished beneath at least eight massive tyres, Timothy managed to fasten his belt. "I'm ready!" he called out.

"Here we go!"

The crazy man spun the wheel and drove directly into oncoming traffic, passing two sports cars and a van before pulling back into his own lane out in front of a Rolls Royce, the startled driver of which honked his horn as a means of pointing out the fact that Daisy had pulled out into oncoming traffic and then had almost run right into him, in case the crazy man hadn't realized what had happened.

"This isn't working!" shouted Timothy over the roar of the wind and traffic. The cabs were much smaller than Daisy and could weave through the cars with much greater ease. One was racing parallel to the crazy man, and another was inching its way up next to Timothy's exposed side.

"You're right!" The crazy man slammed on the brakes. There was a loud screech and the smell of burning rubber as the lorry spun sideways to a stop. Two air bags popped open helpfully, as Timothy, Mr Shen and the crazy man were flung forward and then back as their seat belts braked. The sound of the rushing wind stopped instantly, as did the roar of traffic, and was replaced by a symphony of honking horns, each expressing a different emotional state, from slightly put out to angry to the point of white-hot rage.

The black cabs, who had not anticipated this sudden change in the chase, had flown past, and were now regrouping a mile down the road and starting to head back their way once more.

Timothy turned to Mr Shen and the crazy man with a look of utter shock on his face. He was completely speechless. Though he attempted to say something, all he could make was a small *ip* sound.

The crazy man fiercely nodded his wholehearted agreement with this sentiment, and then added, as he popped off his seat belt and rose in his seat, "Quick, everyone! Into the helicopter!"

THE SIXTEENTH CHAPTER

In which Timothy learns that looks can be deceiving

There are certain phrases you never really expect to hear. And because you never really expect to hear them, you can't really say what those phrases might be until you do hear them. But of course when you do hear them, you are somehow totally certain that that phrase is something you never expected to hear. Despite not knowing that you hadn't expected to hear it.

"Quick, everyone! Into the helicopter!" was definitely one of those phrases.

Timothy did not quite know what he should make of the crazy man's order, and so instead decided not to make any decisions on the subject and just follow him. Crawling around behind where Mr Shen was sitting, the crazy man pushed open a small door that led from their cramped cab into the large trailer that it dragged behind them and stepped inside. Mr Shen followed, and then

Timothy, who took one final glance out the window to see the black cabs fast approaching.

"Let's not dawdle now," said the crazy man, flipping a switch. Instantly the trailer was filled with light, except for the places that were in shadow due to a large purple helicopter sitting, minding its own business, in the centre.

"Look, a helicopter!" pointed out Mr Shen, turning to Timothy.

"Really? Where?" said Timothy drily. As Mr Shen looked at him with a puzzled expression, Timothy walked past and approached the crazy man, who was already inside the flying machine. "Who are you?" he asked.

The crazy man looked up at him. "About time you asked that, don't you think?" He looked down again and fiddled with a few instruments. "All right, get in, you two!" he called out.

Timothy and Mr Shen climbed into the helicopter and each put on a set of headphones passed to them by the crazy man. Suddenly there was a loud crashing sound from outside and the trailer of the truck lurched to the side.

"Seems like those black cabs of yours have caught up with us again," said the crazy man, his voice slightly mechanical through the headphones. "We're ready, so everyone hold tight!"

The crazy man reached up and pushed a large purple button. There was another loud crashing noise, but this one came from within. The sides and roof of the truck flopped open, like the panels of a cardboard box, and they suddenly found themselves sitting in the sunlight with a host of startled drivers staring up at them. The crazy man pushed a few more buttons and the blades of the helicopter started to spin. Slowly the whole machine rose into the air, and the crazy man reached for the intercom.

"Ladies and gentleman!" he announced, his voice flooding the area. All the drivers and their passengers looked up at the helicopter. "I am so sorry for any inconvenience we may have caused. As a way of apology, please accept this small token from me, Daniel Fiberman!" He motioned to Timothy, who looked at him, confused. Covering the mouthpiece with his hand, Daniel Fiberman whispered, "The bag, over there, dump the contents out of the helicopter!"

Timothy moved towards the back of the helicopter and grabbed a large duffle bag and looked in it. There, stacked neatly in front of him, were piles of hundred-pound notes grouped together in small bundles in vacuum-sealed plastic bags. He looked up at Fiberman in surprise. The man gave him a quick nod in return. Timothy shook his head. Carefully sliding open the side of the helicopter, Timothy took one final look at the contents of the bag. He took a bundle for himself and stuffed it in his pocket. Then he turned the bag upside down and emptied it out into the air.

The crowd below got very excited and started to

jump up to catch the falling money. "I love you, Daniel Fiberman!" a young woman called up.

"And I love you too!" replied Daniel into the loudspeaker. "Thank you so much for your patience, and remember, one man's rubbish is another man's treasure!" He went to replace the mouthpiece when he had another thought. "And don't forget to buy a copy of Willomena Brown's debut single, 'Love is a Four-Letter Word', which comes out this Friday!" Then he hung up the mouthpiece and sat back in his seat. Mr Shen was looking at him quizzically. "We're producing her first album," explained Daniel.

Mr Shen continued to look at him quizzically.

Timothy returned to his seat, and they all sat quietly for a few moments, watching as Daniel eased the helicopter away from the motorway and out over the water. Mr Shen watched quietly through the window as the sea passed beneath him, and Timothy kept a steady eye on the shoreline.

"So," he said finally. "You're Daniel Fiberman."

"I am," replied Daniel Fiberman.

"I didn't recognize you with the beard."

"Yeah, I figured you didn't."

"You're the guy who became rich going through people's rubbish."

Fiberman smiled. "No, I became a billionaire going through people's rubbish."

"Fine, billionaire. Why are you dressed like this, then, and driving a big lorry?"

"And spending time at rest stops?"

"And spending time at rest stops."

"Well, I thought it might be a bit of a blast to drive across the country in a big rig."

"Is it?"

"It's not bad," replied Daniel, turning the helicopter parallel to the coast. "Not as thrilling as I thought it would be. Kind of lonely. That is, until I met you guys!" He laughed brightly.

"Yeah, well, thanks for helping us out."

"Hey, no problem. Say, what does the cab company have against you guys, anyway?"

Timothy shook his head and glanced over at Mr Shen, who was still completely occupied gazing out the window. "I don't really know. I don't really care. All I do know is that they really make me angry."

"They been following you a long time?"

"Not a long time, but I think the fact they are following us at all is kind of annoying enough."

Fiberman nodded.

They sat in silence for the next little while. Fiberman focused on flying the helicopter, and Timothy took the time to nurse his throbbing ankle. He couldn't quite believe he was in a helicopter with a famous billionaire, and so instead decided he would just consider it the most normal of situations. It made his brain hurt less.

Then about half an hour later, Fiberman pointed straight in front of him.

"And there's Sharpton!"

THE SEVENTEENTH CHAPTER

In which Timothy and Mr Shen
arrive in Sharpton

Timothy leaned over to look out the window. He'd been to Sharpton several times over the course of his life. Each time except one was to see his mother in some show in the only big theatre in town. The one other time had been an attempt at family bonding that had failed miserably, when he and his father, and even his mother, decided to spend a day at the beach. First of all, the day had really not been conducive to swimming. It was grey and especially windy down by the water. Secondly, his father had spent the entire afternoon sitting in his swimming trunks on a faded yellow towel surrounded by spreadsheets and inputting furiously into a calculator. His mother was utterly miserable with the wind and the spray ruining her hair and make-up. She was then made even more miserable when a pair of Italian tourists came up to her and asked for her autograph, something that on its own would have thrilled her, except that they had mistaken her for Tafty Doberman, the star of the hit medical drama *Sick It to Me*. Timothy had spent the afternoon waist-deep in cold water, trying to avoid both parents, and wound up stepping on a broken beer bottle hidden in the rocks.

Oddly, it was the evening that followed in the hospital, as doctors tried to extract the glass from his foot, that had been the most pleasant experience of the day. His mother had sat with him, holding him the whole time and telling him silly stories from when she was on tour to take his mind off things, and his dad had kept fetching him different kinds of chocolate bars.

So Timothy was pretty familiar with the city. It consisted mostly of faded white buildings that were separated from the sea by a long, grey, rocky beach. It was entirely the wrong season for Sharpton. Sharpton was a summer town, though recently even in the summer months the city had lost the glamour and appeal it once had, and no one of any note had summered with any seriousness there for at least three decades. The pier still hummed along happily, possibly more to entertain itself than anyone else. It jutted into the sea like a butter knife, dull but persistent. The Ferris wheel and roller coaster at the far end were dangerously out of date, and the Hall of Mirrors just downright creepy.

The candyfloss, however, remained relatively edible.

Parallel to the current pier, down the beach a couple of miles, was the pier from Sharpton's glory days. Now stripped bare, it was a skeleton structure that looked more freaky than anything, despite the mayor's insistence that it was a historical monument and not to be touched. The waterfront would have benefitted greatly from its removal, as several construction companies had been interested in building holiday homes on the beach opposite, but couldn't persuade any buyers that the dilapidated structure was more akin to the ruins in Greece than to a haunted house.

Fiberman glanced over at Mr Shen. "So, where am I dropping you lads?"

Mr Shen awoke from his daze, and turned to look at Timothy expectantly.

"Uh, I don't really know," said Timothy, watching the white buildings grow taller as the helicopter lowered itself. "My mum is performing in *Peter Pan* at the Royal."

"The Royal it is, then!"

Timothy wasn't quite sure what Fiberman meant by "The Royal it is, then." After all, the theatre was located down a rather narrow street, with no really convenient place to land. Unless, of course, when Daniel had asked where he was dropping them off, he meant. . .

"OK, so here we are!" announced Fiberman, as they hovered over the old Victorian theatre. "I'm just going to toss out the ladder, and you two can climb down to the roof. Makes the most sense, I think!"

Timothy stared out the window. "Are you crazy?" Yes, the roof wasn't that far down, but the wind from the blades was whipping about dangerously.

"OK, so slide open the door again, and – see that bundle over there? – that's a ladder, just toss it over the side!"

Timothy looked at Fiberman and then at Mr Shen. "You remember what we agreed on," he said to Mr Shen.

Mr Shen nodded and stood next to Timothy as he opened the door. Dust from the roof of the theatre flew into their faces. "Of course, with my limited powers concerning air currents. . ."

Timothy picked up the ladder and looked at Mr Shen. "Just try, OK?" he said as he tossed it out into the air. The ladder unfurled and the end grazed the rooftop for a moment, and then rose a metre or so.

Timothy approached Fiberman, who was working hard to keep the helicopter steady.

"Thanks for the ride," he said and offered his hand. Fiberman took it and shook.

"No problem," he replied. "And if you ever need anything, here's my card."

Fiberman passed over a bright purple card with his name embossed in black on one side.

Timothy nodded and placed it in his pocket with the cash he had grabbed earlier. He then returned to where his dragon was staring down out the door.

"All right, Mr Shen," said Timothy, also looking down, "after you!"

Mr Shen nodded and lightly slipped over the side and on to the ladder, which was now blowing about fiercely. In a matter of a few moments, he was on the roof of the theatre, looking up at Timothy with a smile.

With a deep beath, Timothy sat down at the edge of the helicopter, his legs hanging out over the side. He looked at his left ankle, which had started to throb in rhythm to his heartbeat. *OK*, he thought, *just do it. You can't let some ancient dragon upstage you like that.*

"You'd better get going. The wind is picking up," announced Fiberman loudly.

Placing his right foot a few rungs down on the ladder, Timothy turned and clambered out of the helicopter. Putting as little weight as possible on his left foot, he started to ease himself down. It wasn't going too badly, actually.

Of course, thinking those sorts of thoughts, especially without knocking on wood or anything afterwards, leads to the inevitable result. Suddenly the helicopter lurched upward. Then downward. Then slightly to the right. Timothy, holding on for dear life, was starting to feel a bit like a marionette being jerked about. He looked down at Mr Shen. The roof was farther away now, though not impossibly far down.

"Jump!" called Mr Shen. His voice was faint against the noise from the blades.

"Jump, yeah, there's a smart idea, I'll jump," said Timothy, rolling his eyes. "Are you crazy?!" As he said it, the helicopter tried to shake him off again. His head snapped back, then forward again, like the lid on a water bottle. *OK, maybe I'll jump*, he thought, and let go of the ladder.

He fell slowly at first. Which was a strange sensation, and Timothy was grateful that he had instructed Mr

Shen to help him. And then, without warning, things started to pick up, and he began to plummet towards the roof.

"Oh my, that must have been painful!" said Mr Shen after he had watched Timothy brace for his fall and land on his hands.

Timothy rolled over on to his back and stared up at the helicopter. It swerved wildly in the sky for a few moments, and then, as if it had been stung by a bee or something, it suddenly took off, rising high above them and disappearing behind the buildings.

Mr Shen sat down next to Timothy.

"So what happened there exactly?" asked Timothy quietly, looking at his hands, which were studded with gravel.

"Well, you see, I tried, but it was extremely demanding keeping control, there was so much wind . . . and my powers are so limited. I am so sorry!"

"You're sorry." Timothy picked out a pebble from his palm.

"I deeply regret it. But it was . . . really difficult and I really did try very hard." Mr Shen shook his head and gave him a sad look.

"Did you? Did you really?" Timothy's voice was still very soft. He started to massage his right wrist, and noticed that it burned rather painfully. "I don't see why you should feel bad. I mean, you tried, right? That's all that mattered. So what if I could have landed the wrong way, and, you know, broken my neck or something? The point is you tried. You tried very hard. Well done, you!" Timothy pushed himself up to a sitting position and looked Mr Shen in the eye.

"I said I was sorry!" Mr Shen broke eye contact and looked down.

"I don't care how sorry you are, it doesn't change the fact that I was depending on you and you totally let me down!" Timothy slowly stood up. "And now I am in considerable pain!" He staggered slightly. "Like, I mean, considerable pain!"

"I said I was sorry," repeated Mr Shen softly.

Timothy shook his head. He didn't actually think it was Mr Shen's fault that he had been hurt. He was just really angry and felt like he needed to blame someone. Of course, now he was feeling guilty for taking it all out on Mr Shen. He sighed.

He had a look around the roof. He knew there was an entrance into the theatre up there somewhere, having sat with his mother and her cast watching fireworks several times in the past – one of the few decent memories that got in the way of the general unpleasantness that was his life. Finally he spotted the door, hidden behind an old flat decorated in pastel flowers that had belonged to the set of *An Ideal Husband* a season earlier, and wandered over to it. Knowing their luck, Timothy fully expected it would be locked. But it wasn't. And Timothy pulled it wide open.

"Come on, Mr Shen," said Timothy looking back towards the dragon. "Let's just get on with it."

THE EIGHTEENTH CHAPTER

In which Timothy is reunited with his mother

The Royal Theatre was a lovely decrepit mess. Still relatively well used, it was the one shining jewel in a crown of faded ones. It was possibly the only thing that kept the tourists coming to Sharpton, and possibly also the only thing that wasn't laughed at behind its back. Many of the major shows either began or ended their tours at the Royal, and a good review from the *Sharpton Gazette* was almost always a sign of a sure-fire hit. Once the summer season, which was their most profitable, finished, other prepackaged shows would rent the space.

And, of course, beginning late autumn and straight through into the new year, the annual pantomime would entertain kids and "kids at heart". Timothy's mother had starred in these pantomimes for two decades now, taking only a brief hiatus when she finally got her big break as the lead in a short-lived soap opera, *Sweet Pretensions*. It had run all of two seasons, to some of the most terrible reviews ever garnered in the soap-opera industry. Not only had the writing and film quality been atrocious, but instead of creating scandalous characters and situations, the plotlines had been surprisingly tame. Once an entire week's worth of episodes had been devoted to a misplaced set of car keys.

Both Timothy and his mother had found the whole thing a deep embarrassment. So had most of the viewing public. It was so terrible, it wasn't even famous for being terrible. And so, mercifully, the show and her participation in it had vanished quietly into the ether.

Anyway, for two Christmases Timothy had had his mother at home, which had been kind of interesting, in fact, and, though both were loath to admit it, kind of fun. Then she returned to the Royal and had been in every pantomime since.

Timothy and Mr Shen made their way carefully down the flight of rickety wooden stairs that led from the roof directly into the flies above the stage itself. It was dark, and it took some time for his eyes to adjust, but it was obvious from the sounds below that the matinee had already begun. They descended past lights and rigging, until eventually he and Mr Shen landed on the main catwalk. They stopped for a moment, or rather Timothy stopped because both his ankle and wrist were being annoyingly painful, and Mr Shen joined him in staring down at the stage far below them.

There were several actors onstage, from Timothy's vantage point all looking like furry blobs, and he presumed some scene with the Lost Boys was going on. They were in the midst of a sing-along with the audience.

"What is all this?" whispered Mr Shen.

"Have you never been to pantomime before?" asked Timothy. It seemed odd for a dragon who had been living in the country for decades not to have encountered a pantomime even once.

"Never. It looks like a great deal of fun, though!"

Timothy scoffed. "Yeah, if you're, like, five."

"How old are you?" asked Mr Shen, turning to examine Timothy carefully.

"Eleven." Mr Shen continued to appraise him. "That's more than twice five! You can't tell me you don't know the difference between five years old and eleven!"

Mr Shen shrugged. "I tend to perceive time more in centuries. Six years' difference, that means very little to me."

"You know what. . ." Timothy couldn't think of anything to say, and it seemed pointless to try anyway. "Whatever," he offered up instead.

Mr Shen returned to staring down below them. "So explain a pantomime to me."

"A pantomime," sighed Timothy, crossing his arms on the railing of the catwalk and resting his chin on them, "is a play, usually about a very popular story, like a fairy tale. In this case they are doing *Peter Pan*, but they aren't doing the real version of *Peter Pan*. They are doing a little kids' version, so they add in all these songs where the kids can join in and stuff. And then there's the whole 'look behind you' gag, which is so stupid."

"What's that?"

"It's when someone dressed as a giant cat or something walks across the stage and the other actors pretend they don't see it, and the kids yell out, 'He's behind you!'"

Mr Shen smiled broadly. "Oh. That does sound like fun!"

"It is so not fun."

"Can we go down there now?" The catwalk had started to vibrate, and Timothy noticed that Mr Shen had started to shake slightly with excitement.

"There's no point in going down yet. They're still in Act 1. We'll have to wait for the interval."

Mr Shen sighed, looked at Timothy, and then decided to imitate his posture, so the two of them stood side by side, arms folded, watching.

"What are we doing here anyway?" asked Mr Shen.

"Well, I didn't really know what to do with you and everything, and my dad's out of town. I dunno. I thought maybe Mum could help." He looked at Mr Shen sideways. "Not that she's much good at stuff, but, I mean, she is totally way better suited to take care of you than me. I mean, she's a girl. They have natural instincts that way."

"I'm confused. I thought we were going to China."

"Well, you're going to China. But, I mean, there's no way I'm doing that. I shouldn't be doing any of this. And after everything we've already been through, there is nothing that's going to convince me that going on a long journey to the other side of the world is just the thing I should be doing." Timothy rubbed his wrist absent-mindedly.

"But how am I going to get to China?"

"I don't know!" said Timothy loudly. He winced as he heard the sound echo around the flies. "I don't know," he whispered. "I don't care."

Mr Shen laughed. "Of course you care! That's just absurd!"

"No, no I don't. I really don't." Mr Shen started to speak, but Timothy interrupted him. "No, Mr Shen, you have to believe me. OK, so I didn't want to see you killed, but my plan was to get on a train and get you here and hand you over to my mum. Things went a little wrong that way, but we finally made it. I've got a life, man, I've got stuff and . . . stuff."

"Yes, stuff's really important," said Mr Shen with a frown.

"Don't try to guilt me. It won't work." He looked at Mr Shen, who was rubbing his nose against his arm sadly. "It's not that I don't like you or anything, but, man, I'm just not the right person to take care of you. I'm. . ." Timothy stopped.

Mr Shen looked at him. "You're. . .?"

Timothy stared out into the black of the flies in front of him. Then he shook his head and gave a small laugh. He turned back to Mr Shen. "I'm a kid."

"Poor Wendy!" a high-pitched, girlish voice from a little way below suddenly called out. Though it was hardly threatening, it caused both Timothy and Mr Shen to jump slightly, a third voice being wholly unexpected up there with the two of them. Then there was a loud noise, and the ropes directly in front of Timothy and Mr Shen began to move.

Timothy looked up and saw a set of motorized winches unwinding the ropes, and he and Mr Shen moved off the central catwalk and on to one that ran perpendicular to the stage. Three metres below them, a woman with long blonde hair, wearing a fraying white nightgown, was slowly being lowered to the stage. Her right hand was holding an arrow to her chest, and her left flailed about dramatically, waving her distress to the audience. Which must have been considerable considering the manic way her hand was flapping about. She was meant to be floating gently to the ground, but it came across as significantly less delicate – more, in fact, as if she were an infant being lowered into a bath by its underarms. The ropes jerked for a moment, briefly getting caught in the groove of one of the pulleys, and then the process continued. Finally the woman made it to the stage, and with one final, "Poor Wendy!" collapsed to the floor, taking careful concern to splay her hair out beneath her in a dramatic fashion.

Mr Shen, who was staring, mouth open wide, at the spectacle, turned to Timothy and asked, "What was that?"

Timothy did not return the look. He watched as the woman lying on the ground was eventually hidden from sight by a dozen brown furry blobs. With a rage that would only be suppressed so long as he didn't open his mouth too wide, he said through clenched teeth, "That, Mr Shen, was my mother."

THE NINETEENTH CHAPTER

In which Timothy Freshwater and
Kathryn Lapine face off

"Does your father know you're here?!" Kathryn Lapine whipped off her long blonde wig angrily, revealing a skullcap through which her short auburn hair was starting to show.

"Why would he?" replied Timothy. He was sitting on a faded red love seat playing with the bandage on his wrist, the stage manager having tended to and bandaged it and his ankle nicely. Opposite him sat his mother at a small mirror framed at the top by three lights, the central one of which had begun to flicker slightly.

She stared at her son in the reflection of the mirror and then, with more vigour than was necessary, she started removing the thick coat of make-up from her face.

"Well, we'll just have to call him," she said.

"Yeah, that makes sense," scoffed Timothy, crossing his arms and slouching low into the love seat.

His mother spun in her seat and stared at her son. Her cheeks were smudged with the black that had encircled her eyes, and her lips still had a pale ring of pink that went from mid-chin to just below her nose.

"Don't give me that attitude, young man. I've just finished a show, have another one in three hours, and I've just discovered that my eleven-year-old son has decided to take it upon himself to come visit Mummy when he should be in school! Anything could have happened to you along the way! You could have been hurt, or kidnapped, or. . ."

"I was expelled from school," replied Timothy, "not that you would know about that."

His mother furrowed her eyebrows. "When did that happen?"

"A while ago. Dad was supposed to write to you. I guess he didn't. He's such a chicken."

Timothy's mother turned back to the mirror and stared at herself for a quiet moment. She reached up and peeled off the skullcap. She teased out her hair. Then she grabbed another baby wipe and finished removing the last of the make-up.

"Well, right now, I need some food. Are you hungry?" she asked quietly.

Timothy didn't say anything.

His mother stood up and looked down at him. "Come on," she said, "we'll go to the pub."

She walked towards the door and opened it. Mr Shen

was standing, waiting patiently, on the other side and gave her a small bow.

"Hello, I'm Mr Shen," he said.

"Hello, Mr Shen," replied Timothy's mother. "I'm afraid I'm not in the right frame of mind for autographs at the moment."

Mr Shen laughed. "Ah, no, I'm waiting for Timothy, actually."

"Really?" His mother looked over her shoulder at Timothy, who had risen and was standing a few feet behind. "Why?" she asked, looking back at Mr Shen.

"I'm his."

Kathryn Lapine smiled. "His? His what?"

"His dragon, of course."

Timothy's mother looked at Mr Shen carefully and bit her bottom lip. Then she turned around fully to look at her son, crossed her arms over her chest, and raised an impressive eyebrow as she did so.

"Hey, you didn't ask," replied Timothy, walking past his mother. "Come on, Mr Shen, Mummy's taking us out to eat!"

"Oh, good," replied his dragon, turning to follow him, "I'm famished."

They didn't have far to go. The Curtain Call, the pub that was frequented by the theatre folk, was directly across the street from the Royal, as it is a well-known fact that theatre types don't much care about the quality of the pint, as long as it is nearby. In fact, the sure-fire way to judge if a pub is close enough to be frequented is the costume-change test. If an actor can walk off the stage, leave the theatre, grab a pint, return to the theatre as well as put on a new set of clothes, all within one five-minute costume change, the pub passes the test. Simple, really.

Timothy's mother led her son and his dragon through the main room of the pub, smiling at the few audience members who had just come from the show, and through into the back room where the rest of the main cast was already into their second round.

Timothy knew them all well, as the casting never changed, despite the different plays. There was Shirley Lemondrop. Not, of course, her real last name. She always played the male lead. Known for her vibrant, almost manic energy onstage, she was fairly docile in real life, almost to the point of being comatose. There was Douglas Pepper, a cheerful round man with a mop of curly red hair, now going faintly grey. He played "the dame", which meant he played large ridiculous women varying from matriarchs to housekeepers. And perhaps it was because he spent most of his time pretending to be a woman that he had become infamous for his skirt chasing. Timothy disliked the man intensely.

Then there was Arthur Montgomery. Or rather Sir Arthur Montgomery. A tall, slender man with silver hair and a black goatee, Sir Arthur had joined Shakespeare's Men, the highly respected theatre company, directly out of theatre school. He had played minor roles with the company for a decade without much acclaim, and was due to be kicked out the following year, when something very strange happened. He was confused with the well-known explorer and archaeologist Arthur Mortimer and was summoned by the Queen to receive his knighthood. It wasn't until our Arthur had risen from his kneeling position as Sir Arthur that anyone realized the error. And this was only because at the very moment he had stood upright, the large gold encrusted doors to the chamber had flown open, and the small, frantic figure of Arthur Mortimer, sweat pouring down his brow, came bursting into the room with a long and echoey, "Noooooooooooooooooooo!" Sir Arthur Montgomery returned to the company, where he was immediately cast as Hamlet. And while he promptly butchered the part, he was now a knight, and so audiences adored him anyway. Years later he was asked to play the villain in *Aladdin* at the Royal and to be the titled actor over the marquee. The pay was excellent, and the pub very close by, and this year he was playing Captain Hook.

Lastly, there was Nicholas Wren. Some distant relation of the architect Christopher Wren, possibly – or possibly not. He was a lovely man, with wispy white hair and a pleasing disposition. He had no fighting spirit, though, so while he was by far the most nuanced and talented of the performers, he had not made much of a name for himself. But he didn't ever seem to Timothy to mind much. This year he was playing Nana. The dog.

"Look, everyone, it's young Timothy!" called out the red-headed Douglas Pepper as they entered the back room. "Timothy! Come sit by me, lad!" Douglas pulled a chair from another table up right next to him.

"I'd rather not," replied Timothy, but Douglas just burst into hearty laughter and took hold of Timothy, firmly pushing him into the space next to him.

"What will the lad have to drink, then!" Douglas spoke loudly right into Timothy's face and Timothy recoiled slightly. Douglas's breath smelled like a blanket you might find down a dark alley.

"I don't care. Orange juice."

"Orange juice! That won't put hair on your chest!" Douglas accosted the waitress by pinching her on her bottom. "Molly, bring the lad a whisky!" The waitress rolled her eyes at him and walked off. "That'll put hair on your chest."

"Who's this then?" said a low smooth voice.

"That, Sir Arthur, is my son's dragon. Nice, isn't he?" said Timothy's mother, looking at Mr Shen with a fixed smile on her lips.

Timothy gave his mother a dirty look, but had to admit to himself he hadn't exactly explained to her that the whole dragon thing was a secret. Still, she should have known better.

At that extraordinary introduction, everyone suddenly turned to look at Mr Shen, who was standing calmly in front of the table. There was a long silence. After they had all had their fill of staring at Mr Shen, Sir Arthur spoke thus: "Well now, Timothy's dragon, why don't you sit and join us?"

"I am perfectly content to stand," replied Mr Shen with a smile.

"You aren't frightened of us, are you?" said Sir Arthur with an oddly threatening laugh in his voice.

"Oh, no. No, you are some of the least frightening people I've met."

No one at the table really knew whether to be insulted by this, and they sat silently for a moment trying to make a decision on the subject.

"Mr Shen, just sit down, please," said Timothy, standing up and giving his seat to the dragon, then taking another one for himself. This move also served to distance him from Douglas, which had also been the point.

Sir Arthur seemed intensely fascinated by Mr Shen and scratched his goatee thoughtfully. "Now then, what exactly does it mean that you are Timothy's dragon?"

Mr Shen looked at Timothy. Timothy looked at all the actors and found himself unsure of what to do. In fact he had been feeling unsure of what to do for quite some time now – from the moment he saw his mother lowered ungracefully down to the stage. He had made up his mind what felt like ages ago to hand Mr Shen over to his mother. He hadn't really given the plan much thought, though. Sure, on the surface he'd relished seeing the look of shock on her face when he showed up with a dragon. But, he grudgingly realized, deep down he'd kind of hoped she'd also fix everything. After all, she was a mum, and weren't mums supposed to help get their kids out of jams and stuff? But now it seemed like a really stupid idea. What could she do with him, really? Then again, what could Timothy? All this was just not fair. He never should have been dealing with any of this in the first place, and now, well, what now? He felt completely stuck.

He supposed he could just tell the actors the story, get Mr Shen to walk about a few centimetres off the floor and such, but what could the actors do about him? I mean, they were actors.

"Come on, I want to hear about this dragon stuff!" said Douglas, who now had grabbed tightly on to Mr Shen's arm.

Timothy sighed. *At least the good thing about actors*, he thought, *is that they are unlikely to be any kind of threat.* "Sure. Fine."

As the food was served, Timothy launched into the story, starting with Sir Bazalgette and ending with landing on the roof of the theatre. He focused primarily on Mr Shen's journey to China and the need to cross through the Dragon's Gate. For some reason, though, he decided to keep the key and the master/servant-connection stuff a secret.

The others sat and listened, at first with bemused expressions on their faces, but once Mr Shen did his levitating thing, and demonstrated his limited powers concerning air currents by making a coaster fly around the room, the expressions turned from scepticism to awe.

"Now I say, that is just about the most fantastic story I've ever heard!" Nicholas beamed. His speaking was a departure for him. He usually remained quietly thoughtful when everyone was at the pub. Then he frowned suddenly and said, "Not that I don't mean it isn't very sad and all. I am sorry about all that's happened to you."

Mr Shen nodded in gratitude. Then he said, "Yes, but I also deserved it."

"This is utterly fascinating. I find this truly very fascinating," said Sir Arthur, who seemed by far the most mesmerized by the tale. "And you need to get back to China, you say. What was your plan, exactly?"

"I do not have a plan. This is Timothy's plan." Mr Shen turned to Timothy.

Timothy sat chewing on his lip, as all attention turned on him once more. "The plan," he finally managed, "is. . ."

And that was all he could say. It actually seemed like a pretty good answer to him, kind of deep, and philosophical. On an exam it might have been followed up with, "Since the plan is, does its existence depend on its execution? Discuss with references to Fowler's treatise on the 'Impermanence of Everything'."

The cast, however, was still waiting for him to finish his sentence.

"I bet I know what the plan is," said Timothy's mother, reclining in her seat luxuriously. All eyes turned to her.

She was expecting these eyes. They were part of the reason she was reclining in her seat luxuriously.

"The plan is to let Mummy deal with it, isn't it, Angel?"

Man, he hated it when she was right. "Yeah, like you'd know what to do with a dragon." Timothy glared at her.

"Actually, Timothy, that was your plan, remember? Up in the flies? That is exactly what you said," said Mr Shen helpfully.

"Thank you, Mr Shen," replied Timothy loudly.

Timothy's mother smiled triumphantly. "Told you so." She leaned forward to look at him. "And how exactly did you think I'd get him to China?"

Timothy stood up. "Look, I don't know, OK? I just thought maybe you would be able to help ... somehow."

Timothy's mother sat upright. "Timothy, what on earth can I do? Honestly, you never think anything through, do you? You are such a smart boy, and yet you are constantly making a mess of things!"

"No I'm not!" He could sense his voice getting louder. But he couldn't help it, he was angry – at his mother, but mostly at himself. After all, it was true: he always made a mess of things.

Timothy's mother stood up to face him. "Then why have you been expelled from every school in the city? Why have you run away from home? Why have you brought me some dragon-man-person who needs to get to China when, for one thing, I am in the middle of a run, and, for another, have no bloody idea how to possibly get there! What other possible reason could there be?"

"Oh . . . shut up!"

"Don't you dare tell me to shut up. I'm your mother!"

"Then act like one. Oh, I forgot: you're bad at acting!"

Timothy could feel a strange tightness in his throat, and a burning in his eyes. *No. No! I am not going to cry*, he told himself fiercely. *I won't give her the satisfaction.* He made eye contact with his mother and could see the pain in her face. He felt horrible. After all, she might not be the perfect mum, but she wasn't some pantomime villain either. And he had put her in an impossible situation.

"I didn't mean it," he said quietly.

His mother's eyes had welled with tears by this time.

"I try," she said softly. "I try my best."

Timothy felt so confused. On the one hand he wanted to lash out. On the other, he wanted to hug her. He also felt extremely tired. It was a terribly confusing group of emotions to put up with.

He felt a hand on his shoulder.

"Timothy," said Nicholas softly. "Why don't I take you back to the theatre? You could have a lie-down in the stage manager's office. You've had a pretty long day so far."

Timothy knew Nicholas was just trying to calm things down, but he did really want to get away. He nodded numbly.

"Come on, Mr Shen," he said.

"If it would be all right," said Sir Arthur, rising, "I would love to just sit a bit and chat with him some more. I find him," Sir Arthur gave Mr Shen an unfathomable look, "very interesting."

Timothy looked over at Mr Shen, who didn't seem to mind staying with Sir Arthur. "Sure, whatever, have a nice little chat," he said.

He and Nicholas left the pub and crossed the street back towards the Royal. They entered through the stage door and passed through the backstage area, arriving at Nicholas's dressing room, and stopped.

"You want to talk at all?" he asked.

Timothy looked at the little man with the wispy white hair. He looked slightly elflike. "Nah," he replied. "But I think I will lie down for a bit, if that's cool."

"No worries," replied Nicholas. And with a small smile, he passed into his dressing room, closing the door behind him.

Timothy made his way down the corridor and entered the stage manager's office. It was a tiny room with a desk and a computer and a small cot in the corner. He wandered over to the cot and lay down, staring at the peeling paint on the ceiling. He closed his eyes. He felt suddenly very free. For the next few hours he wouldn't have to think, to plan, to do anything. He didn't have to worry about exactly what he was supposed to do next with a stupid dragon. He could just sleep.

And so he did.

THE TWENTIETH CHAPTER

In which Timothy wakes to something unusual

When Timothy awoke a few hours later, he was utterly and completely confused. He stared out at the black in front of him and had no idea where on earth he was. He lay perfectly still, his body deciding between fight or flight, and was about to bolt upright when he suddenly remembered everything. He muscles relaxed and melted back into the cot, and he turned to his side.

The office had become very dark, obviously because the sun was no longer in the sky, and the small square window above his head was pitch black. He had a look at his watch. It was a quarter to nine.

Timothy sat up, getting a bit of a head rush as he did so, and blinked a few times. He rose slowly, suddenly very much aware of each bruise and sprain on his body. His ankle seemed extra tender and his wrist called itself to his attention with a quick, sharp stabbing feeling. Not only that, but all his muscles were aching. Walking seemed close to impossible as the stiffness in his upper legs practically prevented him from bending his knees.

Eventually he made it to the light switch and instantly regretted turning it on. The light blinded him and caused spots to swim in front of his eyes. To steady himself, Timothy leaned against the closed door that led out to the backstage area. He rested his forehead against it and closed and opened his eyes a few times so his pupils could adjust to the change. Finally, he could see again. And he tested his recovered vision by reading the note that he discovered taped on the door directly under his nose.

Dear Timothy,

I have done a lot of thinking, and I have realized that I have been nothing but a burden to you. I am sorry that I have caused you so much grief. Please accept my apologies. I have decided to go to China by myself, so I just wanted to say goodbye, and thank you for everything.

Your dragon,

Mr Shen

Timothy ripped the note off the door and turned around to lean his back against it. He reread the letter. Then he read it again. He read it a fourth time. And then a fifth. Finally, by the sixth, Timothy understood the thesis of the note. Mr Shen had decided to go to China by himself. OK. That seemed to be an odd choice for him to make. *There is something odder still about this*, pointed out his brain.

It was during the seventh reading that finally his brain caught up to his senses. . .

"Mr Shen couldn't have left this note," said Timothy aloud slowly, "because I didn't order him to." *Which means*, he thought to himself, *which clearly means . . . there is no way in heck he went to China either*.

Timothy swore sharply. Spinning around and flinging open the door to the office, he ran out and looked up and down the hall.

"Mr Shen!" he called out.

"Shh!"

Timothy turned to see a stagehand place her finger to her lips. He stopped and listened. There were loud sounds coming from the left. *Of course*, realized Timothy, *the play*.

He turned left down the hall and continued along towards the stage. Timothy was furious with himself. He remembered the way Sir Arthur had been so eager to keep Mr Shen with him. And that look he'd given him, that stupid unreadable look. He totally would have paid attention, too, if he hadn't been so mad at his mum at the time. It was all his mother's fault, distracting him like that. It always ended up being her fault. Man, he hated her.

He continued to fuel his rage by going through a list

of everything his mother had done wrong over the course of his life. This then boiled over into a list of everything he hated about actors in general. And as he approached the backstage, he decided that everyone everywhere was just really pointless and stupid. And that he hated all people.

Now the sounds from the stage had turned into coherent speech. Timothy charged through the stage-right wing, all the way to where the stage itself began. On it was the set of a pirate ship.

The fellows who always played fellows, or in this instance the Lost Boys, were all quietly tied up around the base of the mast and being rescued by Shirley as Peter Pan, which the much larger evening audience were having a blast pointing out loudly. And standing downstage, arguing with a ridiculous amount of pomp with his mother, was Sir Arthur wearing a long curly wig, large red hat, and costume to match.

Timothy seethed as he observed the scene. Sir Arthur looked out to the audience.

"What did you say? Did you say Peter Pan?"

"He's behind you!" screamed the shrill voices from the crowd, mixed with hysterical laughter.

"What? Where?" Sir Arthur turned and looked over his left shoulder, where Shirley clearly wasn't. There was more laughter. He turned back. "Oh, he's there?" He looked over his right shoulder. He continued to do this until Shirley suddenly jumped in front of Sir Arthur with a triumphant, "Here I am!"

There was a large round of applause as Shirley posed for the audience and started to bow. Sir Arthur grabbed Shirley from behind and growled at her. Then with one large motion he "threw" her off into the wings. Shirley overacted her throw with wide-open eyes and mouth, and, once she was back in the wings, quietly made to cross to the other side of the stage and walked right into Timothy.

Without a moment's pause, Timothy grabbed the sword from her hilt, nothing more than a fencing foil, and charged out on to the stage. Sir Arthur, who was waiting for Shirley to reappear stage left, didn't notice him until a sudden hush fell over the audience and actors alike. He turned and stared at Timothy. There was a pause, one that probably wasn't all that long but seemed to last for ever in the spotlight onstage. Finally, Sir Arthur took control of the situation.

"I say!" he said loudly. "Who are you, then, and what are you doing on my ship?!"

Timothy shook his head angrily at Sir Arthur. "Where's my dragon!" he said, brandishing the sword. He had no idea why he was brandishing the sword. He had never brandished a sword in his life, nor did he think it was much of a threat to Sir Arthur, who, for one thing, would probably not be remotely hurt if the sword hit him since he was wearing so many layers, and, for another, had learned stage combat at drama school and was far more experienced with weaponry. But Timothy was really angry, and even he knew he wasn't quite thinking straight.

"Dragon?!" continued Sir Arthur loudly for the audience's benefit. "I know of no dragon, sir! Perhaps you are confusing it with my crocodile." He said the last word turning out to the audience, and they made tick-tick sounds back at him. Then without turning back to face Timothy, he grabbed him by his arm, pulling him close. "What the heck do you think you are doing?" he whispered fiercely into his ear.

"What have you done with Mr Shen?" returned Timothy just as fiercely.

"Stop, stop, it's unbearable!" cried out Sir Arthur loudly, placing one hand over his left ear and recoiling as the audience continued to tick at him. Turning as if in great pain, he led Timothy upstage.

"What the devil are you going on about!" said Sir Arthur, violently wrenching Timothy about to look at him.

"It didn't work, your trick. Mr Shen wouldn't just go to China like that."

"And I repeat, what the devil are you going on about!"

"This!" Timothy held the note right up to Sir Arthur's face. He watched Sir Arthur's eyes dart back and forth as he scanned the page quickly. "Well?" he asked when Sir Arthur shoved it back towards him.

"Well, obviously whoever wrote this didn't know about the key" was Sir Arthur's reply.

Timothy took a step back in shock. "How do you know about that?"

"Your dragon. We had a nice long chat after you left.

I felt there were some holes in your story, so he kindly shared that information with us. Is that it?" Sir Arthur indicated the gold chain that was peeking out from under Timothy's collar.

Timothy didn't answer the question, but just stood speechless.

"Look, he was with us when we came back to the theatre. That was the last time I saw him."

"Dark and sinister man, have at thee!" called out a loud voice. There was a massive cheer as Shirley swung in from stage left on a long rope, holding another fencing foil in her hand. She landed in front of the two of them and took another bow to the audience.

"Get off the stage now!" hissed Sir Arthur, and gave Timothy a shove.

Timothy nodded weakly and wandered off the stage to a smattering of applause, which his subconscious found slightly offensive, and stood in the dark of the wings one more time. He looked back out onstage as a large fight scene ensued. Everyone was fighting with everyone else; even some of the Lost Boys were fighting with each other. The only one who wasn't involved in the activity was Timothy's mother, who was standing, arms crossed across her chest, glaring at Timothy. He turned and sat in the chair belonging to the stage manager, who was deeply occupied being Tinker Bell with a large flashlight.

If Sir Arthur hadn't kidnapped Mr Shen, then who had? Or was it true that he had actually decided to go to

China on his own after all? But wasn't that, you know, impossible?

He puzzled this way all through the scene on the ship, and then through the manic set change, where his mother stood next to him, ignoring him. But that was OK because he was ignoring her too. He watched all the actors move to the upstage wing quickly for their entrance, and as the stage manager ran by even more frantically than before. This time instead of working Tink, she was wearing the bottom half of a dog costume. She ran right next to him and spoke into a headset dangling by his ear, "LX 137, go!"

Man, thought Timothy, as he watched her shove the head of the dog on and go out on to the stage, *she really has a lot on her plate. Surely they could have hired a few more people, she doesn't have to do ALL that. First Tink, now this dog, and she still has to run the whole show. . .*

Timothy jumped upright. His heart was pumping fast and adrenaline was coursing through his body. What was the stage manager doing in a dog costume?

It suddenly made perfect sense. Or at least, only some kind of sense, since he had no idea what on earth the motivation behind it was. If Sir Arthur was telling the truth, which it really seemed he was, then everyone in the cast now knew about the golden key, because Mr Shen had happily told them all about it at the Curtain Call. Everyone except for one person, who hadn't been there at the time.

Nicholas Wren.

Who was now conspicuously absent, his role being awkwardly played by the stage manager.

This time when Timothy swore, he swore so loudly that he could hear a few gasps from the audience as he ran back with a slight limp, through to the backstage area along the hall with all the dressing rooms. He charged past the same stagehand who had shushed him earlier, and he skidded to a stop, retracing his steps.

"Have you seen. . .?"

She put her finger to her lips again.

"Have you seen Nicholas?" Timothy tried again quietly.

The stagehand thought for a few moments. "Not since he went for his walk a few hours ago. Why?"

"Do you have any idea, any guess, anything at all, as to where he may have gone?" Timothy felt he was this close to going down on his knees to beg.

"I'm sorry, I don't."

"Does he have a car?"

"He doesn't drive."

"You can't tell me anything?"

The stagehand shook her head and looked at him apologetically. "I'm really sorry."

Timothy nodded and turned to continue down the hall.

"Wait!" said the stagehand. She seemed surprised her voice was capable of getting that loud. Timothy turned back to her. "He does have a boat!"

"A boat?! He does? Where is it?"

"There's a small marina by the old pier. Do you know it?"

Timothy nodded. He actually knew it really well. In fact, now that he thought about it, he remembered being dragged along on a cast outing in a boat that had been launched there. He realized now that it must have belonged to Nicholas.

"Thank you!" he said. The stagehand smiled, and Timothy returned to running down the hall.

I bet I'm doing permanent damage, thought Timothy, desperately trying to ignore the pain in his ankle. But it didn't seem like he was going to be allowed to stop all the running any time soon. Seriously, why all the running?

THE TWENTY-FIRST CHAPTER

In which Timothy seeks out Nicholas Wren

Timothy burst through the stage door and out into the night. He stopped for a brief moment. Once he had oriented himself, he turned to the right and ran down the street, turning left at the corner. The whole city sloped towards the sea, so it was pretty easy to find your way around.

He wasn't really much of a runner, or really one for exercise in general. Fortunately, he seemed to have an inexhaustible supply of adrenaline at his disposal. And so Timothy ran steadily and quickly, despite the aching muscles and sprained ankle. As he reached the boardwalk, the pain in his foot was slowly becoming actually unbearable, unmanageable. He wasn't sure exactly what he was going to do about it.

Timothy joined all the late-night joggers and dog walkers along the boardwalk and felt a bit like he was a human car, dodging human traffic, passing, weaving in and out, and nearly colliding with the pedestrian version of a lorry – a large baby carriage.

The moon was out now, and full, which might have accounted for why so many people were about despite the cold night air. It lit up the sky above the sea and reflected on the water, producing so much light it was almost shocking. Timothy ran past the new pier, the lights of which were bright and welcoming. Music from the Ferris wheel floated out over to him, and suddenly he found himself sorely tempted to take a break and go for a ride. He stopped for a moment to catch his breath and stared at it, far out at the end of the pier. Why on earth was he putting himself through such physical agony? Wasn't the point of coming to Sharpton to get rid of Mr Shen? So his mother wasn't up to the task; he never really thought she would be. But obviously Nicholas wanted Mr Shen for some reason. Why not just leave it to him?

The key, thought Timothy, *that stupid key*. He pulled the chain from around his neck and stared at it. *I could just throw it out to sea*, he thought, looking out at the churning water in front of him. But then that would mean Mr Shen would never be free. Even if someone found the key years from now, it would be too late. The small window of opportunity would have passed. *Who cares?* thought Timothy angrily. *Who really cares!*

Timothy stared unblinkingly ahead of him. Then he gave a long, quiet sigh. Slowly he put the chain back around his neck, tucking the key under his shirt. He looked out past the new pier and out towards the old one, its skeletal frame highlighted by the light from the moon.

Evidently I care.

With a deep breath, Timothy began to run again. Then, turning off the boardwalk, he slowed down and made his way down the rocky beach. The old pier loomed up before him, looking extremely threatening despite the fact that it was an inanimate object. He continued past it to where the rocky beach slowly came to an end and large cliffs started to rise once more.

A few metres along the cliff, a small little-used dock was being tossed around quite violently by the waves. There were three ships moored – well, three boats, more like. Timothy instantly recognized Nicholas's. It was a large white motorboat with a red stripe that ran around its hull.

And there was a light on in the window.

Timothy approached the docks carefully, not really sure if he should try to hide or not. But then he realized he was too tired to be sneaky, so he just walked down the path and on to the dock.

As he approached Nicholas's launch, he heard the sound of someone crying, and as he moved to the rear of the boat, behind the cabin, he saw a sad-looking Mr Shen sitting bound and gagged on the floor in the corner, quietly sobbing to himself.

"Mr Shen!" whispered Timothy, lightly stepping on to the craft, taking care not to make it move.

Mr Shen looked up and stopped crying instantly. A

broad smile crossed his face, or at least attempted to cross his face, the gag sort of preventing his mouth from making the shape.

Timothy quickly unbound the dragon, pausing slightly before undoing the gag, but then undid it as well.

"Timothy, I am pleased to see you," said Mr Shen. "I missed you."

Timothy shook his head. "You missed the key. Trust me, I doubt you missed me at all."

"Not true, not true! I missed the way you are always slightly annoyed at everything, especially me, and the way you like to turn up the collar of your jacket. . ."

"Uh . . . right. Whatever," said Timothy, shrugging. "We need to get out of here."

Mr Shen nodded and stood up carefully. Timothy didn't really think they'd be getting away that easily, but it was worth at least the attempt. Sure enough, just as they were about to step out on to the dock, Nicholas Wren burst out at them through the small cabin door.

"So, finally you stopped crying," he said to the spot where Mr Shen had been. When he realized he was speaking to a spot and not a dragon, he spun to face Timothy and pulled out a gun from the back of his trousers.

"Whoa, Nicholas," said Timothy, raising his hands, "that is so not necessary."

"Give me back the dragon." Nicholas's hand was shaking, but his eyes seemed pretty focused.

"Mr Shen, please go and wait for me down at the

beach," said Timothy. He tried to sound cool and calm as he spoke, but inside his heart was racing. He'd never looked down the barrel of a gun before. It was pretty freaky. Mr Shen slowly backed away and stepped off the launch. "Nicholas," Timothy took a step towards him, "please, at least tell me that is a real gun and not just some prop. I'd hate to think you just grabbed that off the set."

Without breaking eye contact, Nicholas shifted his aim and pointed the weapon towards the cliffs. A loud bang ripped through the still night like a gunshot, which is what it was, so really this sentence should read more like: "A loud gunshot ripped through the still night and a bullet ricocheted off the cliff face." Nicholas brought the gun down and aimed it at Timothy again.

"Oh, good," said Timothy.

"I want that dragon." It seemed like he really meant it.

"Yes, but why?" Timothy could think of nothing else to say, and to be fair, was genuinely curious.

"Why? You want to know why?" replied Nicholas, his voice rising in pitch. "I'll tell you why. Because Arthur Montgomery is a knight, that's why!"

Timothy thought about it for a minute. He thought about it a minute longer. "That makes no sense, Nicholas."

"Why is he a knight? He shouldn't be a knight, now should he? No, by all accounts, he should be wallowing in some two-bit regional theatre somewhere, not playing Captain bloody Hook!"

"Man, what's wrong with you? You were always so, you know . . . normal. . ."

"And nice? And quiet? And isn't Nicholas Wren such a reliable guy? Let's put him in a giant dog costume!"

Timothy was starting to get the impression that Nicholas had a few more issues than he had imagined. "You still haven't answered my question," he said.

"I deserve more than all this! I deserve to play the lead, and to do Shakespeare, and to be respected for my talent. I deserve to be knighted!"

"So be knighted."

"Give me your dragon and I will!"

The phrase rang out in the silence that followed. Timothy nodded slowly. "Oh, I see," he said quietly.

"I'll take Mr Shen to the Queen. It'll be huge. I'm bound to be knighted for that," he said, aiming the gun, which he had lowered during the explanation, once more at Timothy's head.

"Nicholas, put that away. You aren't going to shoot me, and someone could get hurt by accident." Timothy hoped what he was saying was true.

"No."

"Nicholas, this plan won't work."

"Oh yes, it will!"

"No, it won't, Nicholas." Timothy sat down carefully on the bench that contained the life jackets. "You don't know about the key."

"Key, what key?"

"The key you don't know about," said Timothy. "This key." He pulled it out of his shirt.

"What is that?"

"Mr Shen is a dragon. But he's been locked into servitude. Whoever has this key is his master. He has to obey my orders, and can't really think for himself, so you could kidnap him, sure, but what would be the point?"

"But. . ."

"Anyway, who wants a dragon that looks just like a human? You know the story of the Dragon's Gate, and if he doesn't get to go through that pretty soon, he'll never be dragon-like. Man, it's just not worth it."

Nicholas Wren shook his head and bit his lip. "No, there has to be a way," he muttered to himself. He looked up at Timothy and stared at him hard. There was a moment of perfect stillness. And then suddenly Nicholas lunged, going to grab the key around Timothy's neck. He moved so quickly that Timothy didn't really have time to react. Fortunately, he didn't need to do anything, as Nicholas's fingers slipped through the key as if it were a hologram, causing him to fall on to his backside.

Timothy shoved the key back in his shirt. "That was unexpected," he said, staring at Nicholas. "I didn't know that would happen, but I guess it makes sense. There are only two ways to get the key, man: if I give it to you or if I'm dead."

"Then I'll kill you!" Nicholas aimed his pistol once more at Timothy from his fallen position.

"No, you won't. Now stop this!" Timothy had had enough. He stood up and walked over to Nicholas. Reaching down, he took the gun from his hand. Then, without a second thought, he dropped it over the side of the boat. "I'm leaving. And you're going to have to deal with your issues or whatever. Hey, here's an idea: why not tell someone you want to have more interesting roles?"

"I . . . I don't like confrontation."

"OK, whatever. Dude, look, you can help yourself or not. But you can't have my dragon." And Timothy stepped up over the side of the launch and on to the dock.

"Timothy!" called out Nicholas. Timothy sighed. Why was it that people were always calling out his name just as he was leaving somewhere? He turned around. "Don't tell anyone about this, OK? Don't tell your mother."

Timothy laughed bitterly. "Yeah, like that would be something I'd do."

He made his way down the dock and back on to the rocky beach where Mr Shen was standing several metres into the shallow water staring out at the sea. Timothy walked to the water's edge.

"Mr Shen!" he called out. "Come here, we have to make some plans."

Mr Shen appeared not to hear him and remained still facing out towards the waves.

Timothy sighed hard. "Mr Shen, do you want to go to China or not?"

Mr Shen turned around and stared at Timothy. Then he smiled a huge smile, and started to walk back towards the beach.

THE TWENTY-SECOND CHAPTER

In which Timothy finds a way to get to China and has an interesting conversation with Mr Shen

"OK," said Timothy, "so how do we get to China?" They were making their way along the beach back up to the boardwalk, Timothy trying hard not to limp.

Mr Shen thought about it carefully. "I could show you if I had a map," he said.

"No, I didn't mean theoretically. I meant, how do we physically get ourselves to China?" Timothy rolled his eyes. Fortunately it was very dark despite the moon, so Mr Shen couldn't see and be offended.

"I don't really know. . ."

"Well, how were you and Sir Bazalgette going to get to China?" Timothy started at his own question: he hadn't thought of the architect in a long time. It made him wonder for a brief moment if he had been right to take Mr Shen away in the first place.

"We had been planning the trip for quite some time. I am fairly certain we were going to take a plane. That is really expensive, but Sir Bazalgette is rich."

"Yeah," said Timothy, shoving his hands into his jacket pockets.

"It would be easier if I were in my dragon form. Then I could fly us there. Of course, then we would not have to go in the first place. . ."

Timothy stopped walking.

"Funny how we sometimes have to remind ourselves why we are doing something, especially if we've been doing that something for a long time," continued Mr Shen. When he didn't get an answer, not even a sullen grunt, he turned to look where Timothy had gone. "What are you doing?"

Timothy had pulled two items out of his pockets. A business card and a vacuum-sealed bundle of cash. He looked at both objects and thought long and hard. Then he shoved the bundle back into his pocket and walked up to Mr Shen quickly.

"Let's get to a phone."

They walked to the boardwalk and looked around. There weren't that many pay phones left in Sharpton, though, fortunately, for the sake of the tourists, a few red ones had been kept (like the old pier, they too had been deemed historical). One was located a half-mile back towards the new pier, and as they walked down to it, they scanned the surroundings for loose change. By the time they arrived, they had found two ten-pence pieces and a fifty and also a piece of chewed gum that Timothy had to prise out of Mr Shen's hand just before the dragon had a chance to pop it into his mouth.

"OK," said Timothy, taking the receiver off the hook and pressing it to his ear. He put in the cash and looked at the card. Then he dialled.

It didn't occur to Timothy that it might be a bit late to be calling. And so he wasn't as relieved as he should have been when the line was picked up and a friendly female voice on the other end said, "Daniel Fiberman's office."

"Yes, can I speak to Mr Fiberman, please?" Timothy looked at Mr Shen, who smiled encouragingly.

"I'm sorry, he's busy at the moment. Who shall I say is calling? May I take a message?"

"Timothy."

"Timothy?"

"We met earlier today. Look, here's the thing: we really need his help."

"Oh? With what?"

"With. . ." Timothy stopped for a moment. It suddenly dawned on him just what he was asking. *Oh, whatever.* "With getting to China."

There was a pause on the other end of the phone. A long pause. Possibly the woman on the other end of the phone had covered up the receiver and begun to laugh at him hysterically. Possibly she had dropped the phone in shock. Possibly she was thinking hard as to what to say so as not to make him feel like a complete idiot. Man, the pause was long.

Then: "Mr Fiberman is wondering when you would be interested in leaving."

Timothy exhaled, which surprised him, as he hadn't realized he'd been holding his breath in the first place. "Well, like, tonight would be great."

There was another long pause. Mr Shen started to bounce from one foot to the other. Timothy covered the mouthpiece. "You have to go to the toilet?" Mr Shen shook his head. "Then stop it!"

"Timothy?"

"Yes, yes, I'm here," said Timothy into the phone.

"Mr Fiberman can't arrange for the plane to be ready any earlier than tomorrow morning. Will that be all right?"

"Yes, tomorrow morning would be great!" Timothy could not believe his luck.

"Excellent! So go to the Manfred Airfield, let's say around eight-thirty a.m.?"

"Manfred Airfield?"

"It's the small one just beyond the Fickle Estate. You know where that is?"

"Yes, yes, I do."

"See you tomorrow morning at eight-thirty then."

"Yup, eight-thirty!" Timothy hung up the phone. "So, Mr Shen," said Timothy as he stepped out of the phone booth, "we have a ride!"

But of course, as was always the case, and as Timothy expected was particularly the case in his case, first they had to walk. They had to walk clear across Sharpton to the large pink villa of the late-eighteenth-century Dutch poet and composer Wilfred Fickle.

There are many interesting facts about Wilfred Fickle, none of which I wish to expand on here.

At any rate, opposite the Fickle Estate was the Manfred Airfield, a small, underused airport for personal aircraft. It wasn't that it was poorly run or anything, just that the residents of Sharpton didn't own too many planes. There were enough well-to-do clients, however, to keep the airfield running, and they offered scenic tours as well, so it was really neither here nor there that it wasn't used to its full potential.

Timothy and Mr Shen arrived at the airfield just after two a.m. Both exhausted, and with Timothy's body screaming in pain, they collapsed on a small park bench that ran along the wrought-iron fence of the Fickle Estate. They sat and stared at the airfield in front of them, which, at this hour, was basically a big black hole of nothingness.

"Timothy, may I ask you a question?" said Mr Shen quietly.

"Go for it."

"Why are you taking me to China?"

Timothy leaned his head back against the wrought-iron fence, staring up at the moonlit sky and the few stars that hadn't been overpowered by its light. "Mr Shen, I have no idea. I have no idea about anything, why I do anything, what the heck I'm doing here in the first place. I just wind up places, you know? All the different schools I went to, all those different teachers, the Tall and Imposing Tower of Doom. They just sort of happen to me. You sort of just happened to me."

"And yet, you did choose to bring me here. You did choose to take me to China."

"It's better than going back to school."

"I do not believe that is the reason."

Timothy flopped his head to the side and looked down his nose at Mr Shen. The little old man was looking at him as he always did, that quizzical expression on his face. But deep down Timothy knew the dragon had a lot more going on inside than he let on. "Well, how else are you going to get to China, if I don't help you?"

"You could pass on the key to someone else."

There was a silence as Timothy rolled his head back to face the sky once more. "Why do you care?"

"I care because I find it interesting. I have had a lot of masters over the last thousand or so years. Most of them loved having a servant, someone to do their every bidding without the slightest complaint. Others could not deal with the responsibility, so they passed on the key to someone else very quickly. But you are, I believe, the first master I have had who did not want the key and yet kept it. So I am curious why, that is all."

"Well, I guess I just don't trust many people. And even the trustworthy ones are usually idiots. Seriously, who would I give the key to?"

"Why didn't you give it to Sir Bazalgette?"

Timothy sat up and looked at Mr Shen. "Like I said, I just don't trust many people."

Mr Shen looked at Timothy for a moment. "Sometimes I wonder if we should even bother going to China."

Timothy found this ever so slightly surprising. "What? Why?"

"I do not know. Should I really turn back into a dragon? Should I really be freed?"

"Why not?" Timothy was pretty shocked by the question.

"I have been a servant for so long, I don't know if I'll be able to make my own choices when the time comes. Do I even want to make my own choices? Also, what if . . ." he leaned into Timothy as if he were about to tell him a secret, "what if I just go back to my old ways?"

"You don't think you've learned your lesson?"

"I do not know. I mean, I feel that I have. I have seen so much of the world. I have seen real cruelty and heartlessness, and I would never wish to harm anyone through my actions again. But what if. . ."

"Look, man, you won't, OK? You just won't."

"But what if none of the other dragons like me? What if they remember who I was and they don't give me another chance? What if . . . it is just too late?"

Timothy scratched the back of his neck. It really wasn't his thing, comforting people, dragons, whatever. "You'll just have to prove to them you've changed. That's all," he said awkwardly.

"Yet it is still frightening." Mr Shen leaned forward, resting his chin on his hands.

Timothy tentatively reached out and placed a hand on his back. "It'll be good. It'll be OK. Heck, it'll probably be pretty fun. You'll get to fly again. Do whatever you want. And, yeah, it's scary to make choices, I guess, sometimes, but you'll get used to it again. And hey," he said with a pat, "at least your powers concerning air currents will be less limited."

"And my water control. I miss being able to make a thunderstorm. It is wonderful to make a thunderstorm." Mr Shen looked up at Timothy and grinned.

"When you're a dragon again you *so* have to show me that one," replied Timothy.

"Deal!"

They laughed a bit at that, the kind of laughter that isn't because something funny was said, but because they were both kind of happy and feeling better about their situation. Of course, soon there would be more challenges to face, and the whole issue of getting to China and everything loomed before them. But for right in that instant, in that release of laughter, both Mr Shen and Timothy felt that for some strange reason, despite the daunting task ahead of them, everything would be manageable – that in the end, you know, it would be OK.

THE TWENTY-THIRD CHAPTER

In which Timothy and Mr Shen fly in a plane

The fact that Daniel Fiberman was rich was just known. Just as you know you'll just miss the bus if you really need to catch it, or that the colour orange is . . . orange. He was seen everywhere promoting his brand. He had started out with a simple company that restored old pieces of junk and had grown into Daniel Fiberman, Incorporated. He had played himself in numerous guest spots in sitcoms and dramas. He was also quite a daredevil and could be found any given day jumping out of planes or scaling mountains, with the press filming every second of it. He advertised his many products himself in television ads and on billboards across the nation. And he had even written, produced and performed the number-one Christmas single three years previously.

So keeping in mind that everyone knew who he was

and, more importantly, how rich he was, you may find it a little amusing to learn that once Timothy and Mr Shen had made their way through airport security (Mr Shen looking slightly disappointed that the metal detector didn't beep on his way through), they were both extremely shocked to be escorted out to a fabulous, shiny, pure white private jet waiting for them on the tarmac.

"I guess I should have expected that," said Timothy, staring in awe.

Mr Shen just nodded like a little bobble-headed doll you put on the dashboard of your car.

They grinned at each other and approached the jet, where a woman, dressed perfectly for the trip in a long red Chinese dress with blue and green embroidery on it, was waiting for them. She bowed as they came up next to her, and smiled. In a slight Chinese accent, she said, "On behalf of Daniel Fiberman, we would like to welcome you, Timothy, and friend. Please come aboard and make yourselves comfortable." She extended a hand indicating the pristine white stairs that led into the plane, and Timothy and Mr Shen climbed up and in.

The inside was even more impressive than the outside. Decorated in purple and white, it was large and spacious. With Daniel Fiberman's penchant for jumping out of things at high altitudes, the interior had been fitted slightly differently from your average private jet. There was limited seating, as two large sliding doors ran along both sides of the cabin, allowing for easy access should one wish to skydive. And located at the end of each door were three large comfortable-looking purple leather chairs facing the captain's cabin. There was a gleaming, well-stocked bar just behind them.

Timothy took the window seat and Mr Shen the aisle, leaving one in the middle, and they both melted into the soft leather. The woman in the Chinese dress came up to them and offered an assortment of crisps and chocolate, as well as various beverages. She even provided an ice pack for Timothy's ankle. Then she walked into the captain's cabin, closing the door behind her.

"This is wonderful!" said Mr Shen.

"Yeah," agreed Timothy, tending to his ankle. "Who knew that getting to China was going to be such a piece of cake?"

"Ooh, cake. . ." said Mr Shen, his mouth full of crisps.

Timothy had to laugh at that. He looked down and focused on his ankle. "Not that we'll know what to do once we get there. . ." he said to himself quietly. It had been something that had been worrying him for quite some time. All he knew was they had to find the Dragon's Gate. Well, maybe he could ask around once they landed.

The engines of the plane started up, and at the same time the small monitors at their sides began to play a safety video, which Timothy didn't watch. There were only so many times you could hear about fastening your seat belt while seated. It was a strange rule, and something Timothy never quite understood, seeing as he imagined that if something went wrong with the plane, there was little a small buckle could do. Mr Shen, of course, paid careful attention to all the instructions, and fastened his belt precisely as demonstrated. In fact, he enjoyed the act so much that he did it three more times before Timothy leaned over and told him to stop it. They taxied along the tarmac until they reached the beginning of the runway, and, after a brief pause, began to roll along until suddenly they were taking off into the sky.

They spent a good couple of hours chatting and then watching movies and being served some more food by the woman in the Chinese dress. She was incredibly helpful and willing to bring them whatever they asked for, so long as it was in the plane. And she seemed to know almost instinctively when they needed her, appearing at their side to offer her assistance before once more disappearing into the captain's cabin.

And so they continued in this way until they both got bored and decided that the best way to deal with their boredom was to sleep. After all, it wasn't as if they'd had a particularly satisfying rest the night before. Mr Shen fell unconscious first. And then a few minutes later, Timothy reclined his seat until it was lying flat like a bed, pulled up the soft quilt that had been provided, and he too fell instantly asleep.

He didn't sleep for long. He didn't know he hadn't slept for long when he first woke up because he was feeling surprisingly refreshed. In fact, he had slept for only twenty minutes when he was jostled awake by a small bump of turbulence.

"Are you OK, sir?" asked the woman in the Chinese dress.

"Oh, fine, thank you," replied Timothy, and he laid his head back down on the seat, watching as the woman in the Chinese dress sauntered up to the captain's cabin and vanished inside. *She's quite pretty*, he decided, and closed his eyes.

But he had a bit of trouble falling asleep as easily this time. His brain started to poke him softly with a quiet nagging doubt. There was something that wasn't quite right about everything, it was insisting, and Timothy was really sick of his brain being so paranoid all the time. He opened his eyes and stared out at the chairs to his side, and through the windows to the sun beyond. Suddenly he bolted upright. He ran his fingers through his hair and thought hard. It had occurred to him what was wrong. Several times before he had fallen asleep he had watched the woman in the Chinese dress disappear into the captain's cabin, where he would get the briefest of glimpses of the equipment and the view through the front window, before she shut the door behind her. He had noticed it all unconsciously. But now it was clear to him – what his brain had noticed, but he had failed to see. The distinct lack of a person sitting in the captain's seat.

"That can't be good," said Timothy looking up at Mr Shen, who still slept awkwardly, with his chin against his chest.

Quietly, Timothy stood and made his way to the captain's cabin. He pressed his ear against it, but could hear nothing. Then, carefully and slowly, he turned the latch to the door and opened it.

Fortunately, Timothy was relieved to discover, there was someone actually flying the plane. The only problem was that it was the woman in the Chinese dress. She turned and looked at him.

"Can I help you with anything?" she asked with a smile.

"Uh . . . you're the pilot?" said Timothy, looking around the small space in case a co-pilot had managed to hide himself somewhere just behind the door or something.

"Yes."

"And also the flight attendent?"

"Yes."

"Is that safe?" asked Timothy. "I mean, you know, with only you and us. Is that standard practice?"

The woman in the Chinese dress pressed a few buttons in front of her and then stood to face Timothy.

"Of course, it's perfectly safe. Why don't you just have a seat again, and I'll bring you some coffee or tea?" She held the door open for him, and Timothy passed through uncertainly. He turned back to face her.

"See, I just don't think this is normal. I don't suppose there is any way I could talk to Daniel Fiberman at all?"

"Oh, I'm afraid you can't do that," replied the woman in the Chinese dress, stepping out of the captain's cabin to join him.

"Why not? There's a phone right there," said Timothy, indicating that indeed there was a phone right there. The woman in the Chinese dress escorted Timothy back to his seat, seating herself between him and Mr Shen and snapping her seat belt together as she did so. She placed a comforting hand on his shoulder and said, "There might be a phone, but I am afraid Mr Fiberman is bound and gagged at the moment, and therefore would be unable to answer your call."

THE TWENTY-FOURTH CHAPTER

In which Timothy is threatened in a plane

This was a surprising reason, and Timothy, for a brief moment, refused to believe that it had just been suggested to him. So he said nothing and just looked at the woman and blinked a few times when his eyes started to get dry. And then finally he said, "What?"

"I can see my plan isn't really going to work out as I had hoped."

"Who are you?" asked Timothy. Then he thought for a moment. "You don't happen to own a cab company, do you?"

The woman laughed. "No, no I don't."

"Well, who are you?"

"My name is Emily. I am a ninja by trade. I work for a very powerful man. He wants your dragon."

Timothy scrutinized the woman carefully. "You're the ninja?" He just didn't believe it.

"Yes."

"Why would a trained ninja want to do someone else's dirty work? Surely you have a lot of skills this guy doesn't. Unless he's a ninja too. Is he?"

"No. And I choose to work for him because he appreciates my abilities and allows me a lot of freedom."

"If you worked for yourself, you would have all the freedom you could want."

Emily's cheeks were getting flushed. "Never mind why I work for him. It pays the bills, all right?"

It was then that Timothy noticed her accent had vanished. "Fine, whatever. . . So who's this powerful guy then?"

Emily smiled. "Simply put, the Man in the Beige Linen Suit."

Timothy raised his eyebrows. "Yeah, that sounds threatening."

"He's the commander of a fleet of pirate junks. Maybe you've heard of them, the Fleet of the Nine Dragons?" At that Mr Shen suddenly woke with a start.

"Nope."

Emily shook her head. "Your ignorance is of little consequence to me. What is of consequence, however, is this." And she extended her hand and pulled his shirt collar to the side, exposing the gold chain.

"Well, you can't have it," replied Timothy.

"Then I guess I'll just have to kill you for it." She reached around her person and then winced. She turned to him and smiled. "Pity about airport security measures, eh?"

"No concealed weapons?"

"Unfortunately, no."

"Ah, whatcha gonna do?" Timothy said with a shrug.

"This."

She leaned towards Timothy and, for a fleeting moment, he thought she might straighten his hair or something, but she moved past him, reaching her free arm just above where he sat. Timothy turned to watch her pull a latch down hard. Instantly he knew what she was doing and grabbed for her arm. She neatly struck him across the face, knocking him to the side, and stars floated in front of his eyes.

"You open that door, you won't be able to close it again," was his final attempt at self-preservation.

"From what I understand, this plane was designed specifically so that Mr Fiberman could skydive in comfort. If I read the plans correctly, the door should close automatically in two minutes," she replied, reaching for the chain around his neck. "Don't worry. Your dragon and I will be just fine."

And with that the door was flung open, and as Emily's fingers slipped through the key in her attempt to grasp it, Timothy was sucked out through the side of the plane and into the air. Mr Shen and Emily remained buckled safely in their seats. Who could have predicted the safety video actually knew what it was talking about with all that seat-belt nonsense?

The freezing air was a bit of a shock. Not that Timothy hadn't expected freezing air at such an altitude, but a sudden blast of cold after one has been quite warm is generally a shock to the system. What was even more shocking was the wind as it rushed against his face. He could barely breathe as he fell, and the thoughts that rushed around in his head were inarticulate and highly offensive. He looked below him as the white clouds approached, and he dreaded falling through them, which he imagined would be a white, wet, claustrophobic experience. He continued to dread them for a little while longer as they seemed to take a bit too long to reach him. Man, they were taking for ever to reach him. And then it occurred to him that it might actually be the other way around, that for some reason he was taking for ever to reach them.

That's when he noticed the rushing sound of the air had lessened somewhat, and that the air pressure coming up against him had subsided to the point where he was able to move his arms and legs without much force against them. Eventually, as he began to float through the white, wet, claustrophobic clouds, Timothy realized what had happened. Mr Shen had finally pulled through for him. At last, Mr Shen's limited abilities concerning air currents had proven useful. Probably the best time for it to happen, really. He laughed out loud, calling out back up towards the plane, "Thank you, Mr Shen. Thank you very much!" And then he looked below him.

Appearing beneath him was the dark blue of the sea, stretching wide for miles in all directions without any land in sight. The momentary joy that he had felt knowing he wasn't going to die from his fall was gone, replaced by the imminent dread of drowning in freezing cold waters. *Great*, thought Timothy, *just great*. He now sincerely regretted not grabbing the conveniently located life jacket below his seat on the plane.

I guess, then, this is it, he thought to himself as the water gently rose to greet him. *What a way to go*. He closed his eyes and took a deep breath, and as he landed, the cold of the water searing its way up through his system, he uttered one last thought:

"Whatever."

THE TWENTY-FIFTH CHAPTER

In which Timothy contemplates his situation

T imothy was about to drown. The water was freezing, and he would be frozen soon. His heart rate would decrease. Eventually it would stop. And Timothy Freshwater would cease to be. It was in this precarious position that Timothy finally came to the conclusion that he was having a run of really bad luck.

It had begun from the moment he had agreed to take that stupid key. There was that whole ninja-in-the-house thing. Then the unfortunate coincidence of getting into one of only three black cabs on earth that were out to get him. He had continued this line of reasoning when his ankle had twisted beneath him in the sewer. Falling from a helicopter and injuring his wrist had only convinced him further, as had the kidnapping of his dragon. Still, Timothy had not been entirely convinced of his bad luck until he had been pushed out of a plane. That sort of confirmed the whole situation for him.

Funny how our minds work that way. We can utterly convince ourselves that something is a universal truth based solely on our one perspective. Yes, from Timothy's perspective he was being rushed at by cold salty waves. Yes, he was having trouble keeping afloat as his legs were getting sluggish. And, OK, yes, the sky and surrounding sights had all but been obscured from view because of his low eyeline in the water. Fine. From Timothy's perspective, he was having some bad luck.

But there are other perspectives in the world. Like maybe that of Mr Shen, who considered himself extremely lucky to have Timothy on his side. Or how about that of a sailor, bored and cold in a crow's nest staring out into the sea before him? Such a man would have the perfect perspective to notice a boy floating semi-conscious in the water and may even have the wherewithal to call out, "Man overboard!"

My point is, just because we think something doesn't make it so. Just because Timothy thought he had bad luck didn't mean he had bad luck. And just because he had convinced himself he was going to drown didn't mean that he was going to drown.

This realization only came to Timothy once he had been rescued. Not even then, because he was unconscious and had to be taken down into the surgery to be carefully tended. Actually, the realization didn't happen until after that bit, when Timothy slowly opened his eyes and realized he wasn't dead. Then he realized he wasn't going to drown. Because, well, he hadn't.

Timothy blinked a few times. The world was slightly out of focus, but he wasn't entirely sure if that was because of his eyes or the world. He blinked a few more times, and when the world around him eventually did sharpen, Timothy sat himself up and had a look around.

He was lying in a small bunk in a small wooden room. He was also completely dry. *How did that happen? Well, no sense panicking just yet. Keep taking everything in.* Timothy looked up. There were a few lit lanterns hanging from the ceiling and they were swaying slightly. He could see his jacket hanging neatly on the wall. It too was swaying. Then the sound of waves came into his awareness, and he leaned his head back against the wall. Yes, they were most definitely waves. So. . .

"Am I on a ship?"

"Yes, you are!" said an enthusiastic voice from the corner. Timothy turned to watch a small figure jump up and quickly run over to him. "You're awake!" it said.

"Obviously," replied Timothy. Instinctively, he felt for the key around his neck, but it was right where he had left it. He relaxed for a moment, and then out of the corner of his eye he saw a sudden movement. He sat upright again. "What the heck was that? Was that a rat?"

"Oh, no, it isn't a rat, though there are a few about. No, that was my cat, Giggles," replied the small figure, which came up beside him, hopping up on the bunk as

183

it did so. Timothy instantly recoiled. Clearly this person didn't have much sense of personal space.

"Who are you and why do you care that I'm awake?" he asked.

"I'm Alex, and I care because it was so weird finding you just floating in the middle of the sea with no sign of a ship or anything, and I wanted to know where you came from. Also I was worried you might die, and you being awake means you didn't." Alex stuck out a hand for a handshake. Timothy just looked at it. Slowly it withdrew.

"OK, whatever," he said. "Look, can I maybe talk to someone else? I don't mean to offend you or anything, though to be honest I couldn't care less if I did, but I really think I need to get some actual information from someone who knows something and not just some small boy."

Alex scrutinized Timothy carefully, then smiled broadly, and with a hearty laugh said, "You have no idea, have you? Well, why would you?" With a quick jump the small figure was off the bunk and sauntering over to the stairs of the hatch, where it picked up the bandaged cat that had been introduced to Timothy as Giggles. "I can go get someone else if you want, but I think in the end you'll really just want to talk to me." Timothy shook his head. There was nothing he hated more than boys his own age. They were invariably really, really stupid.

Alex turned and took a few steps up the stairs, and then stopped. Timothy heard a sigh and watched as Alex turned back around. "And I was going to have fun with you and not tell you, but you almost drowned and everything so I'll be nice." There was a quiet hiss from the cat. "I'm not a boy." She shrugged and headed up the stairs and out of sight.

Timothy stared at the retreating figure, and when it had vanished, lay back down on his bunk. *I take it back*, he thought. There was something he hated worse than boys his own age. Girls.

THE TWENTY-SIXTH CHAPTER

In which Timothy meets everyone

N o one came down to talk to him. Well, possibly someone would have come down to talk to him eventually, but after half an hour Timothy began to get tired of lying on his cot and waiting for something to happen. He also thought it was kind of rude that no one thought it would make sense to explain his current situation. After all, here he was, all alone, in a strange ship, and what . . . had everyone just forgotten about him? That really made him mad.

So Timothy launched himself off his cot, grabbed his jacket, which was still damp, and stormed up the same stairs Alex had left by. He was primed to give the first person he saw a good telling-off. But all the rage sort of evaporated when he found himself up on the deck.

Timothy had never been on a ship before. OK, he'd been on boats before, small crafts, and Nicholas's, but never a fully-fledged ship. And never one that looked quite as magnificent as the one he was currently aboard. She was a large brig, painted a deep black, and her red sails billowed full in the strong wind. There was something rather ominous about her appearance, and instantly Timothy's hackles went up, every hair on his neck standing at attention ready to fight the good fight, or at least blow in the wind menacingly.

There also seemed to be a rather small crew for such a big ship, and occasionally a sailor would run past Timothy with a look of panic on his face and then vanish behind a mast or up into the rigging. With trepidation, Timothy made his way to the stern of the ship and approached the helm. At the wheel stood a pleasant-enough-looking slender man with dark hair whose focus never veered from in front until suddenly he looked directly at Timothy with one quick movement.

"Well, I'll be!" he said. "You're awake, then!"

"Yes, I'm awake. Why is everyone so impressed that I'm awake?" Timothy could feel the tension in his shoulders caused by his concern replaced by tension caused by frustration.

"No one's impressed you're awake. They're impressed you're not dead," said a dry voice from behind him.

Timothy turned to see a second man – who looked, oddly, a lot like the man at the helm, though with fair hair – appraising him with arms folded across his chest.

"Whatever. I'd rather people just weren't impressed, period." At this point Timothy, too, crossed his arms.

"And I care what you think why?"

Timothy stared at the fair-haired man for a moment, masking his shock at the response by not blinking. "Whatever."

"Truly you have a dizzying intellect," said the fair-haired man. Stretching his arms above his head and yawning, he added, "I am responsible for saving your life, but I suppose that's of no concern to you either."

Timothy shrugged. "I never asked you to."

"Enough, you two!" called out the man at the helm, as he passed it over to another sailor and came to join them. "I'm Daniel O'Connell, quartermaster, and this here is Shakespeare, ship's surgeon."

"Shakespeare?" Timothy raised an eyebrow at the fair-haired man.

"Oh, like it wasn't obvious you were going to respond like that," replied Shakespeare, turning and walking towards the bow of the ship.

"And what's your name, then?" continued O'Connell with a quick glance at Shakespeare's retreating back.

Timothy wasn't exactly sure why he hesitated to share the information. "Timothy. Timothy Freshwater." This time he shook the outstretched hand offered him.

"Well, Timothy, I have to say it was a bit of a surprise to see you in the water there. I think we're all dying to hear the story, especially Alex, of course. You'll be wanting to share your story with Alex, I bet."

Timothy didn't respond. Just hearing her name made him feel really annoyed.

"Come on, if you're feeling up to it, let's go to the captain's cabin."

Timothy shrugged, but went along willingly. After all, the person most likely to give him answers would be the captain, of course. He followed O'Connell up past the helm and through the thick wooden doors of what he assumed was the captain's cabin. He noted, as he glanced at them briefly, that there was a skull carved deeply into the wood. OK, that didn't make him feel very comforted.

What he had expected to see and what was in front of him were not exactly well matched. After all the ominous clues dotted about the ship, Timothy had pretty much concluded that the captain must be at least a bit ferocious. But this proved very much not to be the case when a man with messy brown hair and a slightly nervous disposition rose to greet Timothy wholeheartedly.

"Why, hello, you're awake!" he said with a big grin.

Timothy took a calming breath. "Yes," he replied softly.

"Well, I'm Captain DeWit, and it is a great pleasure to meet you finally."

It took Timothy a second to understand exactly what the Captain had just said, the words had come out so quickly. When he realized an introduction had been made he replied, "I'm Timothy Freshwater."

"Pleasure, Timothy!" DeWit put a hand at Timothy's back and guided him to the moderately sized dining table, where yet another man, wearing an argyle sweater, was sitting. Timothy wondered how many more introductions were in store for him, as this was already his fourth in as many minutes. "This is Mr Underwood," said DeWit, gesturing towards the man. The man stood, pushed his floppy hair out of his eyes, and shook Timothy's hand. Timothy nodded in greeting and stared at the man for a moment. His skin was slightly sallow, and he looked as if he had lost a lot of weight recently. What the heck was going on?

"And, of course, you know Alex!"

Timothy looked to his side, and sitting right next to where he was standing was the girl, beaming. She stuck out her hand again, and because Timothy had taken each of the others', he shook it quickly. He then turned his attention to the captain. "Where am I, and what's going on?" He thought if he just asked it outright, he would get some sort of a straightforward answer.

"Long story, Timothy. Tim?"

"Timothy."

"Timothy. But I think right now, we are all just dying to know what happened to you."

Evidently a straightforward answer was too much to ask.

"No. I'm the stranger here. I don't know if I can trust you guys. I want an answer, and I'm not sharing my story until I get one."

There was a pause as each person sitting around the table thought about this statement for a moment. And then Mr Underwood leaned forward and said, "Fair enough." Timothy couldn't help but smile, and he relaxed back into his seat. He waited for Mr Underwood to start. "Alex?" said Mr Underwood, looking over at her.

"With pleasure," she replied. She gave Timothy a small look of triumph, which Timothy chose to ignore, bit her lower lip, and then launched into her story.

"It's a very long story, actually," she started, "and I don't think you'd care to hear it all. In fact, I have a feeling you definitely would not be interested in hearing it all. But basically what happened is that Mr Underwood here is the great-great-great-grandson of the Infamous Wigpowder."

"The pirate?" asked Timothy. He said it without thinking, realizing only when it was too late that it made him look like he was actually interested in what she had to say.

"Yes! You've heard of him."

"Everyone knows the story," he said with a shrug. "There was a feud between Wigpowder's son and the son of a man named Steele over Wigpowder's buried treasure. They killed each other because they were idiots, and then the families continued to fight and stuff. The treasure map was lost, and no one ever found it. I mean, everyone's heard of Pirate Captain Steele the Inevitable, the latest in the Steele bloodline, a pirate who is totally ruthless and who spends every waking minute of his life in search of the treasure."

"That's right!" replied Alex. "Except, of course, Pirate Captain Steele the Inevitable was a woman, but, yeah, that's pretty much it."

Timothy was starting to get tired of people he considered men suddenly turning into women. "Anyway," continued Alex, "Mr Underwood was captured by pirates from Steele's ship a few weeks back because the pirates thought he knew where the map was. He didn't. But, you see, I had found it, and so I went to rescue him. And that was a really crazy journey, I don't mind telling you." Alex laughed to herself.

"But I do mind you telling me. Get to the point."

Alex gave a look towards Mr Underwood and the captain. He couldn't tell what she was thinking, but it actually seemed as if she was trying to control a temper or something. "OK," she said slowly, "the point. The point is that, with the help of the HMS *Valiant* and Captain Magnanimous and his crew, I found Mr Underwood, rescued him, unearthed the buried treasure, and defeated Steele and her men."

It was Timothy's turn to look at the captain and Mr Underwood, who both nodded their agreement with the story. "Right. OK. So." Timothy wasn't sure exactly what to say. He didn't quite believe any of it, and yet he had to admit . . . would anyone believe his story either? "When did all this happen, then?"

"Yesterday," replied Alex simply.

Timothy nodded. He nodded for a while longer. He nodded to the point that he started to make himself feel slightly nauseous. Then he said, "So then, right now, I assume that you guys are returning home. . ."

"To Port Cullis. . ."

"To Port Cullis." He paused and thought for a moment. "But I thought you said your name was DeWit." Timothy looked at the captain.

"It is."

"But I thought the captain of the HMS *Valiant* was called . . . Magnanimous, was it?" He looked at Alex for confirmation. She smiled, almost as if she were indulging him. "Uh . . . yeah. Anyway, what's up with that? What happened to him?"

"He's still the captain of the *Valiant*," replied Mr Underwood.

"Well, where is he? Can I talk to him?"

"He's on the *Valiant* at the moment."

Timothy was starting to feel annoyingly confused. So of course again he said, "OK. . ."

Suddenly DeWit snapped his fingers. "I understand the confusion!" he said with a big grin. "You think this is the *Valiant*, don't you?" Timothy just stared back at him. "No, this isn't the *Valiant*." He laughed heartily and then pointed towards the window that looked out on to the sea. "That's the *Valiant*." For the first time Timothy noticed the view and stared out through the window at a blue-and-gold three-masted frigate following a few leagues in the distance, floating on what appeared to be giant orange water wings.

"Are those giant orange water wings?"

"Those are giant orange water wings."

Timothy turned back to DeWit. "OK then, if that's the *Valiant*, what ship are we on?"

There was another short pause. "Well, to the victor go the spoils," said Alex quietly. "We're aboard Steele's old ship."

Timothy looked at Alex hard. "Wait a minute," he said. "You're telling me we're on Pirate Captain Steele the Inevitable's ship?"

"Yes."

"Seriously?"

"Seriously."

"So you mean to tell me that we're on. . ."

"Yes," replied Alex with her first genuine smile since they had originally met. "Timothy Freshwater, you're aboard the *Ironic Gentleman*."

THE TWENTY-SEVENTH CHAPTER

In which Timothy tells his story

The *Ironic Gentleman* had always been something akin to the *Jolly Roger* to Timothy. Though deep down he knew that the *Ironic Gentleman* was a real ship, as opposed to the *Jolly Roger*, which was fictional, he had only heard tell of the *Ironic Gentleman* through story and legend, and therefore it seemed just as unreal as that stage set back at the Royal. To think he was on an actual pirate ship, though unfortunately woefully lacking in pirates, was a slightly overwhelming thought for him. It was also kind of cool.

And it also served to push any concerns or fear or anything for Mr Shen completely out of his mind, so that when Captain DeWit said, "And now I think you should tell us your story," Timothy had to think rather hard for an instant to remember it.

"Oh, uh, well . . . my story is pretty complicated," said Timothy finally after a moment's reflection.

"What story isn't?" replied Alex.

"There are complicated issues involving legends, and centuries, and dragons, and it's all become rather irrelevant now, seeing as they have him."

It was the first time since he'd awoken on this strange ship that that thought had occurred to him. With a short laugh, he shook his head and looked up at the ceiling. It had happened again. He ought to have predicted it. Once more he had utterly and completely failed. Just like with every stupid school he'd ever been to, he had been incapable of following through. It was why he never bothered trying, because, no matter how well things went, he'd always come across some sort of roadblock. And of course, this one time when he had given it a shot, this one time when he had thought that maybe he could make some kind of difference . . . well, this one time had proved to be just like all the other times.

"Who has who?" Alex said.

Let it go, thought Timothy, the rage swelling in him. He looked at Alex, who was doing her wide-eyed thing again. "Let it go."

"Who has who?" Alex repeated.

"They have Mr Shen, OK?! They have him, and I don't, and that's just how it is!"

"Who's Mr Shen?"

Timothy hit the table hard. That hurt his hand. Didn't much hurt the table, though. "Mr Shen is none of your business. Mr Shen is none of my business. Mr Shen . . . is on his way to China and will never get to be a free dragon again."

"What an interesting sentence," said DeWit thoughtfully. "Whatever does it mean?"

Timothy sighed loudly. "Mr Shen is a dragon who was sentenced to stay in human form as a servant until the one hundred and twenty-fifth year of the dragon. He can turn back into a dragon if he passes through the Dragon's Gate with his master some time after the new year is rung in, and before the end of the two-week celebration. But none of that matters, because in order for him to turn back into a dragon and then to be freed, his master has to be with him, and his master is only his master if he has the key. And Mr Shen needs to be freed, of course, within that same time frame because it would be too easy if it could just be done whenever. And you can't just grab the key or anything, even if you think the person's going to die a second later 'cause you've pushed them out a bloody aeroplane! Because you can only get the key" – he was standing now, shouting at the ceiling – "if the person gives it to you or if he's dead, not about to die, dead! So there!" He grabbed the chain with the key on it, pulled it from around his neck and held it up to the heavens. "You might just want to use Mr Shen and not free him at all, but there's no way he's going to do what you want without this!" He turned suddenly to Alex. "Try taking this from me."

Alex looked at Timothy with an expression of

concern, but reached up slowly to grab the key. And, just as it had with Nicholas and Emily, the key slipped through her hand.

"Oh my!" she said and looked over at Mr Underwood, who in turn looked at DeWit, who looked back at Timothy.

"OK, Timothy," he said, "I think it's time you explained everything to us, from the beginning."

"Give him some water; his face is completely flushed," added Mr Underwood.

Timothy looked at his companions and realized he was panting hard. His heart was pounding against his chest, and his whole body felt hot and feverish. But that wasn't the worst of it. The worst of it was that it appeared his face was rather wet. He reached up with his free hand and touched his cheek. Then he sat down slowly in his seat. He was crying. He was actually crying.

"Tell us your story, Timothy," said Mr Underwood, passing him the glass of water.

Timothy kept his gaze somewhere around his knees. He sat quietly like that for a long time. Until finally, and just because no one else was saying anything, he said, "Fine."

It took a great deal of effort to speak the first few words, as if he were dredging up some anchor wedged down deep inside his gut. But as he pulled and pulled at them, the words started to rise and, as they moved to the surface, more and more began to emerge until he was spilling the entire tale in one long wash of events – from the moment he had been expelled right up until his encounter with the ninja in the plane. All of it lying out on the table for the world to see. And when he had finished, he was left feeling like an empty shell. And not the least bit dizzy.

"Poor Mr Shen," said Alex after a moment's reflection.

Timothy nodded barely perceptibly in agreement.

"Well, we're just going to have to go to China then," she continued, and looked at Mr Underwood.

Timothy stared at Alex. She couldn't mean what he thought she meant by that.

"Alex," said Mr Underwood, "let's not get ahead of ourselves just yet. We have to think carefully about this."

Alex furrowed her eyebrows. "Don't be silly," she said. "You know that in the end we're going to go help Mr Shen, especially considering how much you guys have in common – you know, that whole kidnapped-by-pirates thing."

"I'm not saying his situation isn't bad and that we shouldn't try to help. But we can't just go off on a rescue mission without giving this some thought first. We are undermanned, and in not exactly top physical condition." Alex just shook her head at him. "For goodness' sake, Alex, I just finished taking on a whole pirate ship. I'm exhausted!"

"That was yesterday. You've had some time to rest. And anyway, it will take us a bit of time to get to China. I mean, surely you can sleep and stuff while we go."

"But. . ."

"We can't let Mr Shen become the servant of a ruthless fleet of pirates. Not only is it a horrible fate for a person, but it could also become incredibly dangerous for the rest of the world as well. A fleet of pirates that are able to command the air and water, well, they would eventually command the seas completely. Surely," Alex turned to DeWit, "Her Majesty's Navy would have a bit of an issue with that."

"Actually, don't forget that they would have no control over him without the key," interjected Timothy.

Alex turned to him quickly. "Oh, yes, and a fleet of murderous pirates aren't going to figure out their mistake and come and find you and kill you and take that key in a matter of weeks. Yeah, that's not likely."

Timothy hadn't thought of that before.

Alex turned back to Mr Underwood. "Timothy is in danger. Mr Shen is in danger. The whole world is in danger. And you don't want to do anything because you're tired?!"

Mr Underwood reached across the table and took her hand. "You know there is more to it than just that. You know that the last thing I ever want to do again is put you in harm's way."

Timothy watched as Alex lowered her gaze to the table. "I know," she said quietly. "I just don't think it's fair that this has to happen to Timothy, to Mr Shen. I just don't like thinking that there is nothing that we can do about it." She looked up again, tears shining in her eyes, but she didn't appear to mind. "I just hate feeling helpless and stuff."

Mr Underwood stood up and came around the table and kneeled down next to Alex. "I know you do," he said quietly. "I know you do." And he gave her a hug. When they pulled apart, he stood and looked down at Timothy, who was feeling slightly overwhelmed by all the drama going on in front of him. He was also feeling, he realized, a little afraid. It hadn't occurred to him that the pirates might come after him. He'd only been thinking about Mr Shen's safety. If these people refused to help him, well, he would be in serious trouble.

"Timothy," said Mr Underwood, "let's call it a day for now while we all have a bit of a think. We really ought to have a conference with Captain Magnanimous about all this anyway. He's really the man who can judge this situation best. I'm just a schoolteacher."

Timothy nodded. It did seem like the best course of action at the moment.

"All right," said DeWit, rising. "All of you are free to use the time as you see fit. I shall signal the *Valiant*, see if we can organize a meeting with the captain, or rather I mean, Captain Magnanimous. I think you're right, Mr Underwood."

He walked over to the door and held it open for them. Mr Underwood passed through, followed by Timothy and then Alex.

"I think I'll go have a chat with Shakespeare," said Mr Underwood, squinting in the sun. "Maybe you should take Timothy on a tour, Alex."

Alex smiled and watched as Mr Underwood walked

down from the helm and towards the hatches until he was out of sight. Timothy watched as the smile faded from her face.

"He keeps going to see Shakespeare," she said quietly. "I don't like that."

"What do you care if he sees him or not?" asked Timothy.

"He was starved and tortured by Steele and her men for weeks. I guess I'm a little worried that he's not doing that well, and the fact that he keeps going to see the ship's surgeon, Shakespeare. . ." She turned and shook her head at Timothy. "Honestly, you can't see why I might be a little worried?"

Timothy shifted his gaze. "Look, I didn't know that, OK? I just thought you didn't like that he was hanging out with that Shakespeare guy, not that you were worried he was ill."

"Yeah, I figured as much." He could tell she was still looking at him. "Just, I don't know why you had to be mean about any of it in the first place."

There was a pause as Timothy gazed out at the water. He wasn't particularly sure what he was looking at, but it felt oddly as if he was trying to look for something.

"Well, never mind all that now. Come on, you want a tour?"

THE TWENTY-EIGHTH CHAPTER

In which Timothy gets to know Alex

Timothy really didn't want a tour. He was feeling wrong somehow, though not in any way he could place. And not as if he was in any more pain than usual. In fact, the new bandages around his wrist and ankle reduced the usual throbbing significantly. He just felt . . . wrong.

"Sure," replied Timothy.

He followed Alex obediently around the ship, and he, in turn, was followed by Giggles the cat, who seemed more than suspicious about his presence. Timothy nodded and noted the sights, making the odd grunt in response to Alex's constant narration. When they finished with above-decks, they moved back down into the hold, wandered through the surgery, and came to a series of cells, almost like cages, lining the walls of the brig. "This was where Mr Underwood was for a long

time," she said, pointing to one. "And this one was mine."
She wandered over to the other side and opened the
door.

"This looks pretty unpleasant," said Timothy, going
inside.

"Yeah, it was. Though I didn't spend as much time
down here as Mr Underwood and. . ."

Timothy bent down and picked up a piece of crumpled
paper on the floor. "And?" he asked, opening it up.

There was a small silence. "And Coriander."

"Have I met Coriander yet?" Timothy squinted at the
paper.

"No. No . . . he died." Alex's voice was faint and a little
higher pitched, if that was possible, than usual. Timothy
turned his attention away from the paper and looked up
at her. She was biting her lower lip and staring into one
of the empty cages.

"Oh." He stepped out of the cage to join her. "I'm . . .
sorry."

Alex nodded, and he saw a tear rolling down her
cheek. Knowing that he personally would hate to be
seen crying, he quickly changed the subject. "What's up
with this?" he asked, handing her the paper.

Alex turned to look at it. A look of realization passed
over her face, and instead of coming out of her sadness,
for some reason, she started to cry harder.

"Whoa, relax!" Timothy didn't really know what to
do. "I didn't mean to. . . Stop it! I mean, OK, here, let's
sit down."

He guided her to the stairs leading out of the brig and helped her sit down. Alex was sobbing uncontrollably now. "It's all too much," said Alex softly. "Coriander, my uncle. I am such an idiot."

Timothy stared at Alex, with her face in her hands. She was so . . . tiny. "What on earth are you going on about?"

"I'm a horrible person!" She turned to him wide-eyed and brandished the paper in front of his face.

"Hey, put that down." He waved it away.

"You know what these are?"

"Not really."

"These are the 'pirate articles' that I was going to sign. I was so stupid that I was convinced that I should become a pirate! I gave up on my friends who were trapped down here, and I decided instead that I should join the enemy!"

"Yeah, well, but I mean, don't forget. . ." Timothy's voice trailed off. Alex blinked at him. "Well, pirates, they're kind of cool. I mean, on the surface and everything. They are pretty cool."

"Cool!" Alex stood up and sort of towered over him in her small way. "Cool?! They tortured my friend to death! They almost tortured me! They killed my uncle! They murder each other without a second thought! What pirates have you met who were so cool, then?"

Timothy raised his hands defensively and scooted a short distance along the step away from her. "OK, crazy girl. Calm down now."

Alex stared down at him and then shook her head. She took a seat a few steps up from him and sighed. "I'm not crazy, I've just been through a lot. And it's still really fresh. And even though it all ended OK, you know, it still stays with you. Like with Mr Underwood. It's going to take some time to get over all of this. I guess it's hard for someone who hasn't been through it to understand."

Timothy twisted his body to face her. With a smirk he said, "Well, I was just pushed out of a plane, you know."

Alex looked at him and gave a small laugh. "OK, fine. Maybe you do understand. And, hey, at least I'm out of danger. You, on the other hand. . ."

"Are right in the thick of it." And he started to laugh too. It was a bit weird, him laughing like that. But it was either that or his turn to start crying, and that was not an option. When they finally calmed down, Timothy took a breath and asked, "Do you think your people will help me?" He wasn't sure if he wanted the answer, and a small knot suddenly tightened in his stomach.

Alex glanced up the stairs as if to look for her "people". "Well, I could say that I don't really know, that it's a very complicated situation and everything, and you shouldn't get your hopes up." She turned back to Timothy. "But, yeah, my people will totally help you."

The knot in Timothy's stomach didn't exactly vanish, but it did loosen somewhat. "You sure?"

"Oh yeah. I mean, DeWit might be tentative, but Captain Magnanimous? Nah, there's no way he won't help you out. It's in his nature."

Timothy leaned back on his hands and stared out at the cages in front of him. "Wow. That's really weird," he said.

"What is?"

He leaned his head back and closed his eyes and saw the friendly face of Mr Shen float through his consciousness. Timothy felt a new sense of resolve. It was different from the old sense of resolve. This one was calmer, more assured. He opened his eyes and shook his head. "I'm getting a second chance."

THE TWENTY-NINTH CHAPTER

In which Timothy meets Captain Magnanimous

It is a very cruel thing to get someone's hopes up. I suppose it is equally cruel to bring someone's hopes down. In fact, toying with the hopes of another person is just, in general, quite dangerous, and I would definitely advise against attempting such an activity in the first place. So you may feel slightly concerned that Alex so easily answered for Magnanimous without having the actual facts before her. You may also feel concerned for Timothy, who, as we know, rarely opens himself up to anyone, and for whom this could all backfire terribly, so that he would never trust another living soul again.

But don't. Because Alex was right. Captain Magnanimous simply was not the sort of person to leave another sort of person in any sort of peril. He was simply too wonderful that way.

He was, of course, a captain, and an extremely

accomplished one at that. He hired his crew based on their talent, and not social status, and gave them each considerable sway and power when it came to decision making.

Most wonderfully, though, he nurtured their natural gifts, allowing his first lieutenant Francesca Giminiano, for example, to invent many strange and wonderful machines to help in the daily business of running a ship. Granted, many of these machines had kinks that needed to be worked out, but Magnanimous could tell the difference between true potential and a hopeless cause and kept his faith in her abilities.

And when she invented a method to inflate gigantic orange water wings in the event of a hull breach and ship sinkage, and the system was finally activated, and it worked . . . well, Magnanimous proved to the rest of the more sceptical navy that his practices were far from "ludicrous, offensive, and a turn-up of the nose to a fine established tradition".

The non-sinking of the HMS *Valiant* would turn out to be one of the least written about naval accomplishments on record, and the most gossiped about at dinner parties. The choice to ignore the amazing invention of Ms Giminiano would also always be considered as an incredibly sane decision by the Admiralty, and the stupidest move, like, ever, by the rest of the sailing community. Thus, while Her Majesty's Navy refused to have their ships outfitted with water wings, owners of private vessels queued up right away and paid very well for it, making Ms Giminiano a very rich woman indeed. However, none of this was to happen for quite a while still, as no one, aside from the crews of the *Valiant* and the *Ironic Gentleman*, knew of her amazing invention yet.

Right now, the *Valiant* was floating innocuously along in the *Ironic Gentleman*'s wake, and occasionally impressing the odd fish or bird. It also had impressed Timothy when he had finally been given the opportunity to look at the water wings close up from the longboat used to transport him, Alex, Mr Underwood and DeWit to meet Magnanimous.

"That's really crazy," Timothy had said, reaching out and touching one of them. "How does it work?"

"Don't ask me," Alex had replied with a shake of her head.

They met with Captain Magnanimous immediately upon their arrival. There was no pretending to be right in the middle of something and he'd be with them in a moment, or anything. And soon, Timothy found himself sitting around yet another table in yet another captain's cabin, this time joined by Francesca and Takeo Tanaka, second lieutenant.

Magnanimous listened to Timothy's story and nodded thoughtfully throughout. He was then presented with the current dilemma; namely, should they go to China to help free Mr Shen or not? There was silence as Timothy's attentive audience waited for the great captain to speak.

Then he did.

"Well," he said slowly, "before we can make the final decision, we are going to need one more piece of information."

"And that would be?" asked Timothy.

"Where in China."

"Where in China?"

Magnanimous nodded. "Exactly. China is a very big country. I would like to know where in China the pirates are planning on taking Mr Shen."

Timothy sat with his mouth slightly agape. He had never once asked that question. Not ever. He had taken on the task of bringing Mr Shen to China to pass through the Dragon's Gate without the slightest idea of where that would be. It could be. . . Timothy ran his fingers through his hair and swore inwardly at himself. . . It could be anywhere.

"I . . . don't know," he replied quietly.

Magnanimous nodded again at that answer.

"Well, let's think it through. You mentioned the Fleet of the Nine Dragons. You mentioned the Man in the Beige Linen Suit. So we have a pretty good list going here."

"But how do we find out where any of these things are?" asked Timothy.

Captain Magnanimous turned to him and smiled. "We know that we are looking at coastal towns, probably more like cities if a whole fleet needs to be supplied. There are certain ports known to be haunts of pirates. So we shall consult a map and make a few educated guesses. But mostly . . . we ask."

THE THIRTIETH CHAPTER

In which Timothy meets some other passengers
aboard the HMS *Valiant*

Magnanimous stood up and, with a gesture, invited the rest of the company to join him. As they walked out of his cabin, Magnanimous continued to explain to Timothy, "You know our story, of course, about the *Ironic Gentleman* and Steele, but perhaps it hadn't occurred to you that we are transporting many prisoners here aboard the HMS *Valiant*. Or haven't you wondered what happened to Steele's crew?"

Timothy had to admit that he hadn't. He hadn't really wondered anything in the way he ought to have done this whole journey. He should really look into fixing that.

"I think we are bound to find at least one pirate down there in the hold who can help us out. What do you think?"

"I think," replied Timothy, "that that makes a lot of sense."

Captain Magnanimous smiled and they all followed him down into the hold of the *Valiant*, where, in this case, the cells were completely filled with cut-throat pirates.

"And little old ladies?" whispered Timothy to Alex.

"Don't get me started on them," replied Alex, glaring at a group of five little old ladies in a separate cage who, in turn, glared right back at her.

"We have need of some information," announced Magnanimous to the pirates.

A small pirate in the front, with long lank red hair, answered, "Jack!"

Magnanimous continued, oblivious to the outburst. "Can any of you tell me where the Fleet of the Nine Dragons makes berth?"

There was much muttering at that request as the pirates began to converse with each other, occasionally eyeing their captors with deep loathing.

A nasal voice pierced through the din. "And why on earth should we help you?" Several pirates in the cage directly in front of Magnanimous moved to one side to reveal a slender man all in white sitting on a bench, his leg and arm bandaged tightly.

"Well, you don't have much of a choice, really," replied Magnanimous. "But you never know what good behaviour may get you in future."

The pirate in white laughed at this and stood up. Helped by one of his fellows, he limped his way to the front of the cage. "A likely story," he sneered. "The great

Captain Magnanimous making deals with pirates. A likely story indeed."

Magnanimous took a step closer. "Sir Geoffrey, you make a fair point. May I also point out, I have never been one to step outside the boundaries of proper punishment and fair trial. I would never, for example, hurt a foe without being directly threatened myself, or defending the safety of another. I am known for this. As a result, the guards of the prison in Port Cullis show me a certain respect by treating my prisoners with more compassion than might normally be expected of men who would not otherwise lose sleep over an unfortunate 'accident' happening to one in their keep. However, this whole affair with your captain has been a rather personal one for me. Many of my crew have been seriously injured. My ship, without the brilliant skills of my lieutenant, would be at the bottom of the sea. And the life of a ten-and-a-half-year-old girl has been put into serious danger. So, this once, I would be more than happy to release the jail guards in Port Cullis from their traditional loyalty to me."

Sir Geoffrey raised an arched eyebrow at him.

"Let me put this to you more plainly. If you don't help me out, then, by my word, I most definitely won't help you."

Sir Geoffrey stretched his mouth into a smile, lips tightly shut. "You make your threat very clear, Captain."

"I'm glad. Now, then, can you help us or not?"

He glanced at his fellow pirates. They looked at him

nervously, though they were secretly relieved that they didn't have to make this difficult decision. Then Sir Geoffrey gave the slightest of nods.

"Good," said Magnanimous heading back towards the stairs. "Bring him up to my cabin."

THE THIRTY-FIRST CHAPTER

In which we learn of Kaomai and plot a course to China

Sir Geoffrey was, while not exactly polite with Magnanimous and his friends, rather well-behaved, and had excellent manners, more so than you would expect of a notorious thief of the sea. And so Timothy found him rather puzzling. After all, he had only just met the pirate, much as he had only just met the crews of the *Ironic Gentleman* and HMS *Valiant*, and had no history with him or anything. In fact, had he not known that the man dressed head to toe in an absurdly flamboyant white ensemble was indeed a pirate, he would be hard-pressed to believe that this man really was such a thing.

Not that Timothy actually liked Sir Geoffrey. In fact, he had concluded that he actively hated him, but it wasn't because he was supposedly "evil". It had more to do with the way he carried with him a really obnoxious air of superiority.

For example, it took Sir Geoffrey a good fifteen minutes before he began to speak. First, he had to change chairs because the one he was in wobbled slightly. Then he had to get a glass of lemonade and then had to get another glass of lemonade when the first didn't have any ice in it. And then, finally, he stretched out his injured leg and leaned back luxuriously and said, "What was it you wanted to know again?"

Captain Magnanimous gave him a cold look in return.

"Fine, fine," sighed Sir Geoffrey. "The Fleet of the Nine Dragons. They make berth around the port of Kaomai." With a long slender finger, he pointed at the map in front of him. Instantly, everyone was examining the location carefully.

"That makes sense," said Magnanimous, putting on his glasses.

"Why?" asked Alex, turning her head so she could look at the map from his perspective.

"Kaomai is not a particularly large city, but it is extremely popular for its casinos and fan-tan houses."

"What's a fan-tan house?"

"Fan-tan is a form of gambling. It doesn't really matter. The point is that it is a city of a rather dubious pedigree. Perfect haunt for pirates."

"I didn't say they made berth there. I said they made berth around there," interrupted Sir Geoffrey. "The Fleet of the Nine Dragons isn't exactly a small one."

The company turned and looked at Sir Geoffrey.

"It's the third-largest pirate fleet in the China seas. It

used to be the largest, back when it was commanded by Duchess Rose. But those were the glory days. Pirates in China these days are having a bit of a rough go of it, in general."

"Why's that?" asked Timothy.

"Chinese pirates are pretty ruthless, and they work together in fleets, as you may have already guessed. Or maybe not." Sir Geoffrey appraised Timothy up and down.

"Whatever."

"The truly big treasures have long ago been found, and now they spend most of their time attacking small junks. With so many pirates, and so little wealth to go around, let's just say it isn't as lucrative a business to be a pirate in the south China seas as it once was."

"It would explain why this man you spoke of is wanting your friend," said Francesca in a thick accent. Timothy looked at her and nodded, noting how she carefully forgot to mention in Sir Geoffrey's presence the fact his "friend" was actually a dragon.

"I think we are getting a bit sidetracked," said Captain Magnanimous. "Geoffrey, if they don't make berth in Kaomai proper, where do they?"

"As if I'd know that," replied the pirate, examining his fingernails closely.

"Is there someone down in that hold who would?"

"Unlikely. Maybe he knows." Sir Geoffrey indicated Tanaka with his chin.

"I'm Japanese," replied Tanaka coldly.

"What's the difference?"

Magnanimous reached out a restraining arm towards Tanaka, who was giving Sir Geoffrey a look that suggested maybe he would just really hurt him and what would he think about that, and said, "Surely, if we made our way to Kaomai, we could find someone who could help us on our arrival."

"Surely," replied Sir Geoffrey, rolling his eyes.

"Are we going to go, then? Is that what that means?" said Alex, her eyes bright and shining.

"I think we should," replied Magnanimous with a smile. "Or rather I think you should."

Alex's expression shifted to one of confusion.

"There is no way I could possibly sail to China with a brig full of nasty pirates and strangely evil little old ladies. And, of course, while Francesca's excellent water wings have been truly a saving grace, I doubt that they would last us the journey."

Francesca nodded. "The *Ironic Gentleman*, on the other hand. . ." Magnanimous turned to DeWit. "What do you say, DeWit?"

DeWit nodded nervously. "I could do it. I could. Yes, I think we really should do it." He spoke with confidence, though slightly too fast. "I'd need more of a crew, however."

"Of course. Take Tanaka and a couple of other crew members of your choice. In fact, keep Shakespeare. I'd feel better knowing you had a decent surgeon on board. And keep O'Connell as well."

"Thank you, Captain."

"Ahem."

Without pause Magnanimous spun around to face Sir Geoffrey. "What? What is it you want?"

"I was just thinking that when you arrive in Kaomai, you may have a devil of a time getting information from anyone. Considering you are all not only foreigners, but members of Her Majesty's Navy."

"Your point?"

"Wouldn't it be better to have someone along that would be tolerable to other ne'er-do-wells? Who might . . . know his way around the city?"

"Like yourself?"

"I hadn't really thought that far. . ." Sir Geoffrey smiled his closed-lip smile at Magnanimous. "But that is a good idea, isn't it?"

"I hardly think that people find they can relate to you easily," scoffed Magnanimous.

"They would more to me, especially since I have a bit of a history with some of the individuals down there. Though I wasn't actually thinking about myself alone. You'll never believe it, but Jack Scratch speaks Mandarin."

"Ha!" laughed Alex. "Jack barely speaks English!"

"And he's certifiable. No, that's just absurd," added Magnanimous.

"Think about it . . . do any of you speak Mandarin? We know he doesn't" – he pointed at Tanaka – "because he is Japanese."

Tanaka closed his eyes for a moment, then opened them again and took a breath.

"I've been to China three times, and each time I brought Jack with me. Not only does he speak Mandarin, the locals find him terribly amusing. And do you know who just loves him?"

He didn't get an answer, but that didn't stop him from waiting. The silence was pointless and really just a power struggle over who would break the silence first. Hating all the games, Timothy shook his head. "Whatever – this is just stupid. Who, then?"

Sir Geoffrey glanced at Timothy and took a long sip of lemonade. "The Duchess."

"What? Who's the Duchess?" Timothy was starting to feel exasperated.

"Duchess Rose. Didn't I mention her earlier? I thought for sure I mentioned her earlier."

"You did," replied Alex and, turning to Timothy, explained: "The former commander of the Fleet of the Nine Dragons."

"Thanks for that. Still don't really care, though," Timothy snapped back, feeling like an idiot that he'd forgotten. Alex rolled her eyes and shook her head.

"I thought you would care." Sir Geoffrey arched his eyebrows in feigned surprised. "Seeing as she knows everything about the Fleet. Including . . . where they make berth."

This second silence was far more potent, and everyone turned to look at Magnanimous, who, they could all tell, was thinking hard. Finally he spoke. "And you are so interested in helping us with this mission because. . ."

"Because if I don't, it'll be right to jail. This way, well, I've got nothing better to do anyway."

Captain Magnanimous removed his glasses, carefully folded them up and placed them in his pocket. He moved around the table to where Sir Geoffrey was sitting and bent down low to speak into his ear. "I don't trust you."

"I wouldn't respect you if you did."

"You'll be watched every moment of every day."

"I have no doubt of it."

"And if you hurt a single member of my crew, I will have you strung up like the dog you are."

Sir Geoffrey turned to face Magnanimous literally nose to nose. "I'd like to see you try."

They stared at each other for a long moment, each not wanting to be the first one to break their gaze.

But eventually Magnanimous pulled away and stood upright again. "Very well," he said. "Someone fetch Jack Scratch."

The rest of the planning went much more smoothly. Jack and Sir Geoffrey were carted off to the *Ironic Gentleman* in handcuffs, and a course was charted to Kaomai by both captains. Timothy expressed some concern, considering the time constraints for freeing Mr Shen, but after some careful calculations it was determined they would arrive with two or three days left in the New Year celebrations. It wasn't a lot of time, but it was the best they could do in the circumstances. In all, things were settled pretty quickly, and they were ready to start their journey.

Timothy watched them part ways with the *Valiant* along with the rest of the crew of the *Ironic Gentleman*. But he stayed behind when the rest of them had returned to their duties, keeping his eyes on the horizon, long after the ship had vanished from sight. He didn't even notice Mr Underwood coming to stand next to him until he spoke. "How are you doing, Timothy?"

"Fine."

"Not a fan of adventures?"

"Not really, no."

Mr Underwood laughed. "Me neither. But they do just seem to sneak up on a person, don't they?"

"Whatever."

"Alex is truly amazing that way. She's fearless. Never gives the potential of real danger out there a second thought. Unfortunately, you and I have to fight back those negative thoughts, can't help but worry 'what if?'"

"Whoa," said Timothy, turning to the teacher, "I'm so not scared, if that's what you're saying. Alex may be fearless or whatever, but I, you know, have gone through a lot myself."

"I know that. I'm not saying you aren't brave, Timothy. But we're all different. We all live, learn, think in different ways." This last sentence was followed by a long pause. Timothy found the silence suspicious.

"What?"

"Timothy, do your parents know you're here?"

"I knew it. Look . . . whatever. It doesn't matter. And for the record, my mum does, OK." *Sort of.* "They don't care what I do anyway."

"I find that hard to believe."

"Well, believe it." It was hard for him to say it with much conviction, considering he didn't quite believe it himself. He knew his parents would be furious with him. But what else was new. "Just drop it, OK?"

"Look, I didn't mean to start anything. I'm sorry." Mr Underwood looked at Timothy for a moment. "At any rate, I just wanted you to know that if you felt like you needed to talk or anything, well, you know where to find me."

"Yeah, I do."

With that Mr Underwood gave him one last look and went off back down to the hold. Timothy stood rooted to the spot. He didn't really know what to feel, and even resorting to his usual rage seemed wrong. Instead he just decided to let it go and stare out at the grey water ahead of him.

So what if he was scared? It made sense, didn't it? After all, it wouldn't be too long before the pirates realized that they didn't have the key and came back for it. Of course, reasoned Timothy, looking up into the low-hanging clouds, he could just give them the key when the time came. The thought made him feel a little ashamed, and he glanced about to make sure that no one was reading his mind. *But it's true.* The little voice rang clear in his head. *It is true.* Not that he wanted to do something like that, but if it came down to a matter of life or death. . . And it wasn't like Mr Shen was going to be killed or anything – he'd just have to be a servant, something he was more than familiar with by now. Timothy didn't conclude the thought, though it was pretty obvious where it was going. He just let it be with a little, "Well, let's just see what happens." Then he emptied his mind completely and returned to staring blankly out at the deep dark waves.

THE THIRTY-SECOND CHAPTER

In which the *Ironic Gentleman* sails to China

N ow, you may be aware that spending several months at sea with a group of people you don't know quickly becomes several months at sea with a group of people you'd do anything to get away from. If even for a moment. But did you know it could also take just over two weeks to get the same result? Close quarters is close quarters. And time spent in close quarters with the same group of people can expand until it seems almost infinite.

Granted, it was only Timothy who was unfamiliar with these new people. Everyone else had sailed together for a while now. He found, however, that after forty-eight hours, he had got to know most everyone reasonably well, or as well as he really cared to, and the rest of the time he spent really trying to survive the company until their arrival in China. Not that Timothy disliked the company he was with. In small doses, they were perfectly tolerable. The captain had proved quite competent despite always seeming slightly ill at ease. And the crew had made every attempt to make Timothy feel welcome.

Then, of course, there was Alex.

Timothy just didn't know what to do with her. She wasn't particularly girly, which was a good thing, but she did have this energy about her, this constant "this could be rather exciting!" pulse she carried with her wherever she went, and it drove him crazy. Not all the time, mind you. There were days when she was downright moody and she and Giggles would sit by themselves in some secluded section of the ship. There were also days when he could not imagine how it was possible that this small girl had done all of the things everyone was talking about.

After several days together, Timothy had learned most of the details of her journey and still could not quite piece it together. He knew that she had come across some mad scientist guy who sucked souls out of people in order to make the bubbles in champagne. She had helped save both the acting career of an Extremely Ginormous Octopus and the fortunes of a hotel on the verge of bankruptcy. (*All in a day's work, no doubt*, Timothy had thought when the tale had first been recounted to him.) He had learned that the little old ladies over on the *Valiant* had been this group known as the Daughters of the Founding Fathers' Preservation

Society. They had held her prisoner in the same estate where she had found the treasure map, and, when she escaped, had chased her cross-country. He had learned, finally, that she had even been very nearly tortured down in the surgery by some of Steele's crew. She ought to have been, to Timothy's mind, just a little, you know, world-weary at least. It would have made her slightly easier to tolerate. But no, she was, for the most part, unfortunately perky. And whenever the two spent any time together, it seemed to become Alex's personal mission to get Timothy "to just get over himself", as she had explained to Shakespeare one night at the evening poker game.

The evening poker game had become a highlight for Timothy aboard the *Ironic Gentleman*. He'd never played the game before, but had watched poker tournaments on late-night telly several times. He always imagined he'd probably be pretty decent at it, being pretty good with numbers and having bluffed his way through most of his life. So when he had first been invited by O'Connell to join in, he'd accepted readily, thinking he could win some money without much effort. Evidently there was a bit more to playing poker than he had realized – the biggest lesson of all being that if he had a bad hand, he should fold.

"But what about bluffing?" In Timothy's mind, bluffing was the best bit in poker.

"Bad hand, fold," muttered O'Connell, shuffling the deck.

"Not even if. . ."

"Bad hand, fold."

Timothy didn't second-guess the instructions after that. There were many regular players, but it was Shakespeare and O'Connell who won most consistently and whom Timothy grew to admire wholeheartedly. And if they gave advice, well, Timothy was going to take it.

Alex was always there as well, but she watched, never played. She might not have come to every game – though she did seem to enjoy being a spectator – had O'Connell not considered her his lucky charm. She was dependable that way.

Despite feeling more comfortable in his situation, Timothy always had an undercurrent of panic flowing through his body. At the start of their voyage, he had just been so exhausted that thoughts of Mr Shen seemed slightly out of focus and not that urgent.

However, several days into the voyage something happened that jarred Timothy into a permanent state of unease. Timothy had been assigned to bring some dinner to the two pirates in the hold. He wasn't given the task often, but he'd been the only one free at the time. He'd brought the tray over and passed the food through the bars of their cages. Sir Geoffrey barely looked at his, though Timothy knew he'd eat it the second he was gone. Jack Scratch was always far more enthusiastic. He'd say a happy greeting of "Jack!", his greasy red hair falling into his eyes (which Timothy had finally realized were framed by no eyebrows) and take the food readily. This time, however, Jack had added, "*Xin Nian Kuai Le!*"

Timothy was so shocked by the strange explosion of sounds that he almost dropped the tray. "What the heck was that?!" he asked, knowing full well Jack would not answer him, aside from the usual "Jack!"

"That was Mandarin," replied Sir Geoffrey, in a surprisingly forthcoming manner.

"Really?" Timothy was still not convinced Jack could speak, well, any language.

"Really."

Timothy looked back at the little greasy pirate who was gulping down his stew in large leaking mouthfuls.

"What did it mean?"

Sir Geoffrey gave a disapproving glance over at his colleague. "Nothing really meaningful. He just said, 'Happy New Year.' I only know that because he always gets very excited around this time of year. Gives everyone little red packages and stuff. Oh the thrill. Yay."

Timothy felt his heart fall into his stomach.

"Well, whatever," he said, and left the brig.

When he was standing in the fresh air, he had to grab the deck rail to steady himself. It was the new year. It was now the hundred-and-twenty-fifth year of the dragon. It wasn't as if he hadn't been expecting it. He knew logically that the new year would happen while they were at sea. But the fact that it had happened so soon, the fact that it had happened at all, suddenly brought the reality home.

They had fifteen days – fifteen, that was it! – to find Mr Shen and get him to pass through the Dragon's Gate. No, that wasn't exactly true. They still had to reach China first.

This was insane! Timothy was officially panicking now. It wasn't going to work. They weren't going to make it in time. And even if they arrived in China when they had planned – two days?! That was all they had?! He couldn't do it. He just couldn't. Timothy tried to calm himself by taking slower breaths. Man, he hated feeling this way. Next time he went on an adventure like this, he was so not doing it by tall ship!

THE THIRTY-THIRD CHAPTER

In which the *Ironic Gentleman* reaches Kaomai

The fact that this journey was happening by tall ship not only had a bearing on Timothy and his timeline, but also on the general reception the crew and passengers of the *Ironic Gentleman* received when they finally began their approach to Kaomai along the coast. It wasn't the fact that the ship was a tall ship per se that caused all the small fishing boats and larger junks to scatter away at their approach, but the fact that this particular tall ship had red sails. Not that red sails weren't rather popular with the junks in China; it was just that red sails on a tall ship could only mean one thing. The *Ironic Gentleman* had come to town.

It's one of those strange things how news can travel. There are certain inconsequential bits of information – like, let's say, which famous celebrity has just got married, or which cheese has topped the cheese charts this week – that fly around the world at record speed. Then there are those bits of information – a small nation rising up and taking over half a continent or the discovery that life on another planet does indeed exist and that it is far more glamorous than the life here on earth – that only certain people get wind of, and then only months after the fact. Years, even. This, unfortunately, was the case with the *Ironic Gentleman*. The fact that one of the most infamous pirates this side of the equator had been vanquished hadn't yet become common knowledge.

"Do you think the *Valiant* has made it back to Port Cullis yet?" Tanaka asked DeWit, who was staring sadly at the retreating figure of a man in a small craft. He had waved happily at the man in the boat, but obviously the man had considered the action a threat to his very soul and had booted on out of there fast.

"They should have arrived at least a week ago. I suppose it's possible that the captain hasn't had a chance to debrief. Though with those prisoners of his, you would think. . ."

"It takes time for some news to travel," said Alex. "Besides, we're all the way on the other side of the world and everything."

"Still, I hate the way everyone runs away from us, though," muttered Timothy. How on earth were they going to find Mr Shen with everyone terrified of them?

So the new and very delightful crew of the *Ironic*

Gentleman, who were entirely the opposite of threatening pirates, stood silently watching the progress of their infamous ship through the large bay. The sun had just set, and the sky was a royal blue. The lush green hills that framed the bay were slowly losing their colour moment by moment. Lights from lanterns swaying on the small boats around them reflected in the black water, creating a confusing constellation of what was real and what was just an illusion. And then the *Ironic Gentleman* followed the coastline to the east and the city of Kaomai came into view.

"I thought we were going to China." Timothy said it feeling instantly like the biggest idiot, but he couldn't help himself. He had never been to China before, it's true, but he had seen pictures. He was expecting either to see a huge modern city with tall towers loom in front of him, or one smaller village with ancient temples and stuff. But Kaomai looked like neither of these.

What it did look like was a Chinese version of the Spanish Riviera. And that was just wrong in Timothy's opinion. Timothy knew that Kaomai looked like the Spanish Riviera because he had been to the Spanish Riviera once to visit his mother on set for a made-for-TV movie. So he recognized the different-coloured houses with the tiled roofs and the arched doorways and the stucco on the walls. And as they got closer, he could spot an honest-to-goodness Spanish cathedral, barely outlined against the blackening sky at the top of one of the many hills.

The reason for this strange appearance of European architecture was Kaomai had been a Spanish settlement up until only a few centuries earlier. With a beautiful harbour and lush foliage, it had been always considered the "garden of the East". The Spanish had even built a large fort high up on one of the largest hills. Of course, Kaomai was eventually reclaimed by China, which meant that over the following years the city had become a strange mixture of Chinese and Spanish architecture and an even stranger mixture of Chinese and Spanish residents.

Though it ought to have had serious identity issues, Kaomai had always possessed a rather straightforward personality, probably because early on in its history it decided it had rather a taste for gaming. It started off small – cards and fan-tan played in the streets, a daily lottery – but it grew and grew until large Hong Kong investors from large Hong Kong companies were building impressively large casinos further inland. The tops of these casinos could be seen from the water, and Timothy was now gazing at them in even greater confusion, as their flashing lights illuminated the surrounding sights.

The ship eventually dropped anchor and slowed to a stop, floating gently in the middle of the bay. With all junks and other seafaring vessels giving the ship a wide berth, it gave the appearance of having some extremely modern force-field protection device or invisible dome around it. DeWit sighed hard and called a meeting immediately in his cabin.

"Welcome to Kaomai!" Sir Geoffrey slid his bad leg delicately under the table as he sat in his chair. "Aren't you all just so popular!"

"What the devil did your captain do to the people here?" asked DeWit.

"Nothing out of the ordinary." Several eyebrows were raised in his direction. "For us. Really, really notorious pirates. The ordinary for us is rather reprehensible for most normal people."

"Let's talk about Duchess Rose," interjected Mr Underwood.

Sir Geoffrey shrugged. "What do you want to know?"

"How to find her would be a good start."

Sir Geoffrey frowned and gave the appearance of thinking hard. Then he looked up. "Haven't the foggiest."

And that comment might possibly have resulted in a bit of a brawl between him and DeWit had Jack, standing happily staring out the window, not said, "There!" And pointed in front of him.

Timothy moved over to where the greasy little pirate was standing and looked out the window. There, directly before him, was a large casino lit up bright pink, with a large open rose at the top in orange neon.

"Is that her casino?"

"Jack!" replied Jack with a smile.

"So we just go to the giant pink building with the rose on it? I mean, if that's all there is to it, why did we bring you guys along?"

Sir Geoffrey smiled and shook his head. "Duchess

Rose owns half the casinos in Kaomai. Jack was just not built to be useful. She never spends any time in them, of course."

"Of course," said Mr Underwood softly.

"Where does she spend her time?" asked Alex, who out of the lot of them had managed to maintain her composure best in dealing with Sir Geoffrey.

"Somewhere in the old city. Her original fan-tan house. Not hard to find, really, if you know where it is."

"And you know where it is."

"No."

Timothy was tired of Sir Geoffrey's games. He grabbed DeWit's sword, which had been lying unsheathed on the table, and pointed it directly under Sir Geoffrey's chin. "Great. Take us there!"

"As if that's any threat! Do you even know how to handle a weapon?" laughed Sir Geoffrey, looking down at the blade of the sword.

"OK, then," said Alex, calmly pointing her own sword at the nape of Sir Geoffrey's neck, "how about now?"

Timothy watched in utter confusion, and some resentment, as the pirate turned a pale yellow, and nodded faintly.

"Good," said Alex, moving the blade away. "So let's get ready, then."

Everyone else in the room seemed to agree with this suggestion and quickly set about getting themselves ready, whatever that entailed. For Tanaka, for example, it meant doing the splits, and for DeWit, carefully setting the timer on the lamp in the cabin to make it look like he was still on board when he really wasn't.

Timothy moved over to join Alex, who had put the sword down next to her and was now going through her rucksack. "What was all that, then? Why was he so scared of you?" he asked, leaning against the table to face her.

"Not that you really care or anything," said Alex, tying up her bag and placing it over her shoulders. "Giggles!" she called out. The cat ran up to join her.

"That animal is not coming with us, is he?" asked Timothy. He hated the way that cat appraised him as it did. What Timothy hated even more was that he had a sneaking suspicion that the cat's verdict was not in his favour.

"Of course he is!"

Timothy looked at the cat and could have sworn it stuck out its tongue at him. "Well, whatever." Timothy turned up the collar to his jacket. "So?"

"So?"

"Why was Sir Geoffrey scared of you and not me?"

Alex gave a small laugh and picked up her sword. "Well," she said, sheathing it with a smart ringing sound, "who do you think gave him those injuries in the first place?" And with that she walked by Timothy out of the cabin. But not before giving him a wink as she passed.

THE THIRTY-FOURTH CHAPTER

In which Timothy joins the others onshore

woman of mystery. That was how Timothy's father had always described Timothy's mother. Sometimes the description would be accompanied by a sigh when Timothy would ask why his mother had locked herself into her room. Other times, it would be followed by a hazy smile while his father stared at his wife across their crowded drawing room filled with her closest friends. And then there were the times when she would beat him at double solitaire, and then the phrase would be preceded by a jovial laugh of appreciation, which would totally drown out whatever television programme Timothy was attempting to watch at that moment.

Timothy really didn't understand why his father was so fond of that phrase. But now he couldn't help but have it pop into his brain as he stared at the back of

Alex's head while they were sitting in the longboat. Not, of course, that Alex was exactly a woman. *I mean, she's just a girl*, thought Timothy. And she wasn't mysterious or anything. She was pretty straightforward, actually. But she kept surprising him with these new hidden talents of hers. And that was, if not mysterious, deeply, deeply, annoying.

Alex explained it all to him while they prepared the longboat to go ashore. Mr Underwood, of all people, it turned out, was a fantastic sword master and had taught her while she was still in school. She, in turn, had become pretty darn good at the whole sword thing herself, and then in one final showdown on the ship, she had had to duel Sir Geoffrey.

"All in self-defence, mind you," added Alex hastily.

Of course in self-defence. Why would you do anything less than perfect and good? replied Timothy – but inside his head.

He sat quietly fuming behind Alex as Tanaka guided them through the maze of small junks that dotted Kaomai's harbour. Had Timothy not been quite so preoccupied with his own thoughts, he might well have noticed that the others sitting in the boat with him were also unusually quiet. It was only when a loud explosion split the silence that Timothy realized how hushed everyone had been.

Instinctively, Timothy ducked. He thrust his hands over his head (as if that would somehow protect him from a large falling piece of building). When he discovered that he had not been hit by anything but was starting to look a bit foolish, he sat upright again and followed the gaze of his fellow passengers.

"Fireworks," said Alex.

"Must be part of the celebrations," said Mr Underwood. "Possibly in preparation for the Lantern Festival."

"What's that?" asked Alex.

Great, thought Timothy, *now it's time for some learning. What fun to have a schoolteacher on an expedition like this. How useful!* He continued to point his gaze towards the sky, but still flinched when the next series of explosions erupted.

"The Lantern Festival takes place on the fifteenth day of the first month of the Chinese New Year. I've only seen pictures of it, of course, but our timing is pretty fortunate. It's quite beautiful, all these lanterns. . ."

"You mean there are *lanterns* at the Lantern Festival?" Timothy couldn't help himself.

"Yes," replied Mr Underwood, either not noticing Timothy's sarcasm or choosing to ignore it. "There are. And, of course, they'll be plenty of dragon dances."

"That's when people dress up as one long dragon?" asked Alex.

Timothy shook his head. Was there going to be a test at the end of all this?

"That's it exactly."

The conversation drew to an abrupt conclusion when the longboat arrived at a series of wooden docks all stitched together by a series of unsafe-looking narrow bridges. For a city known for its casinos and posh hotels, the harbour seemed very old-fashioned. Tanaka steered the boat beneath several low bridges until finally they made it to a reasonably solid-looking dock at the far end of the harbour.

With a bump, Tanaka brought the craft against the wood and jumped lightly on to the dock (doing a casual flip as he did so). Soon the longboat was moored to the dock and all passengers had disembarked.

"Jack," said Jack, thoughtfully looking around.

"Jack indeed," said DeWit.

Despite the bright lights they had seen from the ship, the harbour itself was very dark and, well, rather unfriendly in appearance. The casinos were all in the interior of the city, away from the water's edge where the ground was unstable, and the crew of the *Ironic Gentleman* were starting to feel distinctly unstable themselves.

"Right. Tanaka, O'Connell," said DeWit, "keep a good eye out. I don't like the looks of this place. Tanaka up front, I think."

There was a bit of shuffling about to create the most secure grouping. Timothy noticed even Mr Underwood had placed a hand on the hilt of his sword. Now Timothy wished he, too, had the hilt of something – you know, just in case.

"Don't worry, I'm with you," said Alex, coming up beside him.

242

"I . . . what? No, no, you are not my bodyguard, don't even talk like that," stuttered Timothy, feeling completely flummoxed and insulted.

"Sorry, sorry," replied Alex, raising her hands and backing away slightly. Giggles growled softly, but Timothy knew the cat was actually laughing at him.

"Now then," said DeWit, "Sir Geoffrey, if you would be so kind."

It was, of course, exasperatingly slow going being led by a pirate who, first of all, had no desire at all to lead them to begin with and, second of all, had an injured arm and leg. Even Timothy, who also had an injured arm and leg, thought the pirate was milking it a little much.

Eventually they made it up the small dark alley that led away from the waterfront to another small alley, this one lit by a few meagre home-made lanterns hanging on lines connecting from one window to the other across the street.

It was then that Timothy noticed their party had started to grow in number. They were first joined by a gaggle of children, who all really should have been in bed by this time, but probably weren't because of the festivities. Some teenagers considered joining next and followed for about a block, but they eventually gave up and turned away, as the "cool factor" for teenage activity is a short-lived thing in any corner of the world. But, eventually, grown-ups began following the group. Young and old. Quiet and very vocal. And in the end it felt very much as if they were leading a parade through the narrow streets, O'Connell having a devil of a time keeping the crowd at bay behind them.

"Ever felt like you were being watched?" Timothy whispered to Alex, who let out a short laugh. Timothy smiled in spite of himself and in spite of his concern for their present situation.

Then, just as quickly as the crowd around them had gathered, it was gone, coincidentally vanishing just as DeWit had turned down a dark, ominous-looking street. *This can't be good*, thought Timothy, just as Alex whispered the same thing. They gave each other a look.

The street was almost pitch-black aside from a faint light glowing around the edges of a closed window some paces in front of them. Possibly there were people in the shadows, possibly not. There was no way to tell. Instinctively their group got tighter.

As they approached the window, more shapes began to show themselves. A door with a long crooked crack down the centre, through which there was the same glow as from the window, appeared before them. And sounds, muffled and not easily identified, were coming from inside.

Sir Geoffrey casually raised his crutch and used it to bang on the door. There is something to be said for a man who can use a crutch so elegantly, but what that is, I haven't the foggiest.

There was some sort of debate taking place on the other side of the door. It started shortly after Sir Geoffrey knocked, and it involved some scuffling.

Eventually it was resolved when a small round man threw open the door and stood staring at their group for a very long moment. He wore a long simple black tunic with buttons down the front and held a staff in one hand.

He said something in Mandarin. The group turned around and stared at Jack, who smiled at them all, completely oblivious to their need for a translation.

The small round man spoke again, this time in Spanish. Timothy knew that it was Spanish because of his few holidays in Spain, but he had never bothered to learn the language.

Finally, the man tried English. "What do you want?"

And it seemed that it should have been pretty obvious from the beginning that that was what he had been trying to convey all along.

"We are here to see Duchess Rose," replied DeWit.

The round man took a sudden intake of air, but from somewhere behind him someone started to laugh rather hysterically. The round man looked back around the door and said a few sharp words in Mandarin, and the laughing stopped. He returned to stare at them.

"I'm sorry, but that is impossible. Goodbye." He slammed the door shut in their faces.

THE THIRTY-FIFTH CHAPTER

In which Timothy is introduced
to the game of fan-tan

Sir Geoffrey raised an eyebrow at DeWit. The pirate could barely contain his delight.

"Knock again," ordered DeWit.

Sir Geoffrey knocked again, and again there was a great deal of scuffling behind the door before it was thrown open.

"Do you not understand English?" the round man asked.

"Of course we do; we just spoke to you in English. But I am afraid your answer is not good enough. We have travelled a great distance and would like to speak with Duchess Rose, please," replied DeWit, taking a step in front of Sir Geoffrey in an attempt to assert his authority.

The laughing began again, and this time the door was opened wider to reveal the culprit. He was tall and very

Spanish-looking, with dark wavy hair and tanned skin. He, too, wore a simple long black tunic with buttons down the front. His face was as narrow as his companion's was round. He was the perfect exclamation to the round man's point.

"Sorry, sorry," he said with a thick Chinese accent that seemed entirely incongruous with his appearance. "But you see, no one just asks to see Duchess Rose. I take it as a great joke."

"Well, we are asking."

"And who is 'we'?" asked the small round man.

"Captain DeWit of. . ." DeWit paused briefly, knowing full well what the reaction was going to be to the second part of his sentence. "Of the *Ironic Gentleman*."

The tall man stopped smiling instantly and the round man took a step back into the building.

"The *Ironic Gentleman*. . ." The small round man took careful stock of the company in front of him and finally, for the first time, took stock of Sir Geoffrey. He let out a tiny squeak. "Indeed . . . ah . . . may I ask . . . what happened to Captain Steele?"

"Steele is dead," replied DeWit.

The round man gasped and stared wide-eyed at DeWit. "And you were the one who defeated the great captain?"

DeWit shook his head. "Actually, no." He placed a hand on Mr Underwood's shoulder. "He is."

The small round man stepped out from the safety of the door frame and approached Mr Underwood. He appraised the schoolteacher, examining his argyle sweater and round glasses in confusion. He stepped back and said, "Then the Duchess will be most interested in meeting him, of course. Of course."

"Excellent. Let us in," said DeWit.

"Oh, I cannot possibly allow all of you upstairs. The rest of you may stay down here. You may play if you wish." He gestured them into the small foyer.

"No!" said Alex, stepping forward. "Anywhere Mr Underwood goes, I go."

The small round man just stared at her.

"And there is no way that Alex gets to go and I don't," added Timothy.

"They should probably bring Jack with them. Duchess Rose is rather fond of him for some reason," added Sir Geoffrey, thoroughly enjoying himself.

The small round man sighed heavily. "Fine," he said. "The two small children and the strange man with red hair may join him. But no one else."

DeWit nodded at that. "O'Connell, Tanaka, keep watch. I'll stay here with Sir Geoffrey and we shall . . . play?" DeWit turned to the small round man, who nodded and, with a quick gesture, slid open the wall in front of them to reveal a much larger room.

The muffled, indistinguishable sounds from before suddenly flooded their senses as proper noise, as a large group of men and women were revealed to them sitting on the floor around two-thirds of the room. Trying to be heard above the noise, they were yelling and calling out to several small boys who were busy running around the space collecting coins. Sitting on his own with his back to them before the wall that had just opened was an old man, bald on top and shirtless, quietly and patiently minding his own business. He was carefully placing a number of the coins beneath a brass cover, and once he finished doing so he looked up at one of the boys. A silence then fell on the crowd as the boy came over with a long stick and used it to retrieve coins, carefully, from under the brass cover without revealing the contents beneath.

"What's he doing?" asked Timothy.

"Shh," replied Alex.

Shh yourself, retorted Timothy in his mind.

The young boy continued to retrieve coins and then stopped. There was a silence as the old man stared at the brass covering. Then the noise erupted again and the boys found themselves running around once more through the crowd.

"They are placing bets on how many coins are still hidden," explained the tall man.

Timothy nodded. *Three*, he thought to himself.

When all bets had been collected, the boys placed the cash on a series of square metal plates in front of the old man.

"Each plate represents a number," continued the tall man, "so you bet how many coins are left by placing your cash on the plate that corresponds with the number. That's one," the tall man pointed to right next to where the old man was sitting, "that's two, that's three, and that . . ." he pointed to the one closest to them, "is four."

Three, repeated Timothy to himself.

"You can bet many ways. You can bet on more than one number; you can make other numbers neutral. It is not complicated; it just sounds like it is."

Once the money had found the metal plates of choice, the crowd quietened down to a charged silence and watched as the old man slowly lifted up the brass cover and revealed to them the winning number. . .

"Three," said Timothy and smiled slightly.

"Three," said the tall man.

And the crowd went crazy again, collecting their winnings or cursing their losses.

"Come, come, enough watching. Do you want to meet with the Duchess or not?" said the round man.

Mr Underwood, Alex, Timothy and Jack (who was delighting in saying the number three over and over again) were escorted through the room and the packed crowd to a staircase leading upwards.

"Wow, look at that!" said Alex, looking up.

Timothy followed her gaze and had to admit he, too, was impressed.

For some reason, as humans, looking up is not often our first choice in looking places. We tend to look in front of ourselves, to see where we are going, and we look down a lot as well, at our feet when we walk so we don't trip. But looking up seems not to be as natural an instinct for many people, though up can be just as interesting as down. So it was in this case that none of them had even considered looking upwards until just that moment.

The fan-tan house rose three storeys above them and opened to a starlit sky, revealing that the room was actually a courtyard. On both the second and third levels, yet more men and women could be seen leaning over thick railings and placing bets into baskets that were then lowered to the ground floor. These players were better dressed and fewer in number, and Timothy reasoned they must be some of the more affluent citizens of Kaomai.

Their small party began to climb up the stairs, a silk embroidery weaving its way along the wall with them, depicting some sort of procession. And when they reached the second level, Timothy had only a brief moment, before he was rushed onwards, to glimpse a few players chatting quietly at a low table and a gentleman lying on a couch in a dark corner, a haze of smoke around his head and an old birdcage swinging behind him.

The third level was slightly brighter, lit not only by the light from the courtyard, but by a few lanterns set deeper into the space as well. Here, the wall hangings were hung so thickly that they each vied for attention, covering one another up. Swathes of silk hung from the ceiling to delineate different rooms, and that same hazy smoke hung like mist in the air.

Timothy walked slightly behind the others, feeling as if he'd walked on to some movie set. Everything seemed rather unreal, and, he thought, as he disentangled his body from a pink silk drape that had managed to wrap itself around his head, very impractical.

He caught up with the rest of the group just as they were passing through a set of curtains into much a darker area with a single stick of incense burning on a table in the middle of the floor.

"Wait here now," said the round man, and he continued through another set of drapes in front of them.

"Wait here now!" repeated Jack, and he sat down on the spot.

Alex, Mr Underwood, and Timothy stayed standing, though as the minutes ticked by they began to wonder if Jack had been wise to sit.

The small round man returned nearly twenty minutes later and held open the drapes for them.

"You may see the Duchess now."

Jack jumped to his feet and the four of them walked slowly towards the opening. They stopped just before the entrance and looked at each other. Then at the entrance. Then at each other again.

"Come in or don't," said a raspy voice from within. "None of this was my idea."

THE THIRTY-SIXTH CHAPTER

In which we meet Duchess Rose

It is said that Duchess Rose was once one of the most infamous pirates in all of China. Some say this is a gross exaggeration. Others point out that if you actually do the maths, it can be proven to be entirely accurate. Then those first people say that what they meant was that they couldn't believe it was possible to be that infamous, but that they knew it was true and it was just something they said because it was just so implausible that it could be seen to be a gross exaggeration even though it wasn't. And then those second people roll their eyes and say, "Of course you did."

Anyway, it is said that Duchess Rose was once one of the most infamous pirates in all of China because she had been. She was the tenth commander of the Fleet of the Nine Dragons (having inherited the position from her father) and in her heyday had had more than a thousand ships at her command. She was so successful, and so powerful, and just so darn impossible to deal with, that after a decade of her ruling the south China seas, the Chinese government had decided to offer her a rather unusual deal. They would give her land and a title, a great deal of money and an annual income, as well as leave her alone in any projects she might choose to undertake in the future, if she would just, for the love of all things reasonable, give up the pirate game.

Duchess Rose was not stupid. And being not stupid meant that she did not trust any offer made to her, even if it was by a group like the government, which was known for its honesty. But in being not stupid, she also understood that one could stay afloat in the pirating business, as it were, only for so long. So she hired a lawyer. And she got a contract drafted. And when she was secure in the knowledge that she was going to get quite a good deal, she took the government up on its offer.

Upon her leaving, the Fleet of the Nine Dragons disbanded. And each ship attempted to eke out its own living. Some went honest. Others sank in bizarre accidents. The rest kept at the pirating, but it just wasn't the same.

And then the Man in the Beige Linen Suit came along.

And the Fleet of the Nine Dragons was reborn, albeit with much smaller numbers of participating pirates.

Duchess Rose, in the meantime, had built up her empire on land rather well. She owned a hotel chain, several casinos, and had her own line of perfume: "Smell as Sweet". But she spent most of her time in the fan-tan house her grandfather had built. She enjoyed it. It was cosy. And it always reminded her of where she came from. And, more importantly, how far she'd gone.

Possibly, because of the size of her reputation, it will come as a bit of shock to learn that, in person, Duchess Rose was rather small. Short and squat, her figure was hidden behind a pale blue robe embroidered with a series of different flowers. Her black hair was streaked with grey and tied at the nape of her neck with a simple knot. She had painted her face white, her lips a bright red, and defined her eyebrows as well as her eyes with a thick black liner. Combined with the relaxed way in which she reclined, Roman style, on a series of silk pillows, she made Timothy feel uncomfortable. The more at ease she appeared, the less at ease he felt.

Duchess Rose examined each of them – Timothy, Alex, Mr Underwood and Jack – with raised-eyebrowed bemusement, then took a puff on her long, intricately carved pipe.

Exhaling, she said, "Ah yes, the old standing-like-lost-puppies-in-the-rain-routine; seems to be a popular one with my visitors." Her voice was low, with very little trace of any accent. She took another puff on her pipe.

Timothy was getting frustrated and couldn't understand why he was waiting for her to ask him to sit down. It was a formality he had never paid much attention to in the past. And so with an audible sigh, he took a seat in the middle of the room, slightly to Duchess Rose's left.

Duchess Rose stared at Timothy, her painted eyebrows meeting in the middle of her forehead. Timothy stared right back at her.

The small round man suddenly burst into the room. His speech was rushed together and unintelligible, though, of course, that was because it was in a language Timothy did not understand, but it would have been just as unintelligible to someone who spoke Mandarin as well. He fell down next to Timothy, giving him a look of intense loathing, and laid himself prostrate in front of the Duchess. It was obvious he was trying to apologize for Timothy's cavalier flouting of etiquette rules. Duchess Rose shook her head and began to laugh. As she responded to the man, he rose slowly and made a bow. He turned to leave, giving Timothy one last glare as he did so.

"Oh, he's mad you did that!" said Jack, clapping his hands together.

Obviously, thought Timothy, who was still not sure why on earth they had brought this supposed interpreter along with them, seeing as most people they had encountered so far spoke English.

However, just as he thought that, Duchess Rose looked up at Jack and smiled brightly.

"Jack!" she said and extended her hand to him. He took it and said something to her in Mandarin and she laughed again. He sat next to her and the two spoke for a good five minutes, though Timothy had a sneaking suspicion that Jack's conversation was just as limited in Mandarin as it was in English. And then Duchess Rose looked up at Alex and Mr Underwood and said, "Sit, sit. You can see your friend has the sense to do so. What frightens you?" She paused for a moment and then added, "Oh, that's right, I do!" And she laughed again. And so did Jack. And Mr Underwood chuckled nervously, while Alex just sat down quietly next to Timothy.

Duchess Rose calmed herself. She looked at Mr Underwood and shook her head. "I am sorry, but I simply cannot believe you were the one to vanquish the great Pirate Captain Steele the Inevitable. Convince me."

Mr Underwood glanced at Alex, who smiled at him encouragingly. "Well," he started quietly, "I doubt there could be anything I could say that would prove it to you. Jack, though, can attest to it."

"I attest, I attest!" said Jack.

Duchess Rose looked at Jack and then back at Mr Underwood.

Mr Underwood continued. "I'm quite good with the blade. I escaped from my cell, so I had the element of surprise working for me. And, of course, I had Alex's help."

Timothy looked at the girl, who grinned back at him.

"I know you will not believe it. I don't look like a fighter. But appearances can be deceiving. I'm sure," he added carefully, "that you yourself have had to deal with just that . . . issue."

Duchess Rose nodded slowly. "Appearances can be deceiving. So true." She raised her chin and squinted down her nose at Mr Underwood. She stayed in this position for a little bit too long. Then she lowered her chin and said, "Sir, I would be honoured if you would have a drink with me." And without any sort of signal, the small round man entered the room with a tray, on which he had carefully balanced three small ceramic cups and a small ceramic pitcher.

"*Shaojiu*," he said quietly, placing the tray between Duchess Rose and Mr Underwood, and left just as quickly as he had come.

Duchess Rose did not seem to notice that the wine had arrived by way of a small round man, but rather seemed to acknowledge its appearance as if she herself had caused it to materialize out of thin air. She raised her glass with both hands, and Jack followed suit immediately. The two waited until Mr Underwood realized he should do the same, and Duchess Rose made eye contact with him.

"*Kanpei*," she said and downed the beverage in one gulp. Jack did so at the same time and Mr Underwood a short moment after. He began to gasp and sputter.

Duchess Rose started to laugh again. Anyone else might have considered Mr Underwood's response to the wine a sign of weakness, but it seemed that so long as something amused the Duchess, she was willing to overlook many flaws.

"How much alcohol was in that?" asked Mr

Underwood, placing the cup less than delicately back on the tray.

"Oh, the usual; about forty per cent, I should say," replied the Duchess, her tears of laughter creating flesh-coloured streaks through her white make-up. To calm herself, she took another long drag on her pipe, which she had skilfully managed to continue to hold in her left hand throughout the entire interaction.

"Enough!" announced Timothy, standing. "Who cares about any of this? Can she help us or not?"

Duchess Rose looked up at him and reclined further into her cushions, making Timothy feel all the more anxious.

"Help you? What is this about helping you?" she asked.

"Well, we came here for your help," said Timothy, feeling all sets of eyes on him.

"You did? No one told me this? Small Round Man!" she called out.

The small round man ran back into the room. "Yes?" he asked, bowing low.

"Did you know these persons were interested in my assistance?" she asked the back of his head.

"No, ma'am," he replied.

"Because it would have been very wrong of you to not have informed me of this had you known," she added.

"I did not know."

"You may leave now, Small Round Man."

And the small round man left.

There was an awkward silence as everyone continued to stare at Timothy. *Come on, Alex*, he thought to himself. The one time he actually wanted her to talk, she was perfectly content not to.

"Why is everyone staring at me!" he finally shouted. "It's true, we need your help. That's why we came here. Not to drink wine or talk about Steele. Help. We came for help!"

Duchess Rose let him stand there in silence for moment. Finally, as she casually tipped the bowl of her pipe over a small ivory ashtray, she said, "What sort of help did you have in mind?"

"Well, we're looking for the Fleet of the Nine Dragons," said Alex, finally chiming in.

Duchess Rose turned to Alex and gave her that same scrutinizing stare she had given Timothy when he had sat down earlier. Timothy was impressed as he watched Alex stare impassively back at her.

"Oh, you are, are you?" said Duchess Rose quietly, adding an extra bit of rasp to her voice for effect.

"And we were hoping you would be able to tell us where it is," finished Alex.

Duchess Rose took a moment to think about this statement. Then she stood up, brushed her robe free of wrinkles, walked past Alex and Mr Underwood sitting on the floor, past Timothy still standing with his arms crossed, and out through the curtain behind him.

THE THIRTY-SEVENTH CHAPTER

In which Timothy takes a serious risk

Timothy turned and pushed through the curtains with Alex following close at his heels.

"Duchess!" he called out as he rushed through the space in what he hoped was the direction she had gone. "Duch—" Another silk hanging wrapped itself around his head, and he frantically pulled at the beast until he finally wrenched the whole thing from its support in the ceiling, pulling down not only it but several lanterns and a beaded curtain hiding a foursome of card players, who looked up in confusion. "What?!" asked Timothy, turning and bearing down on them.

"Timothy!" called Alex, grabbing him from the front and pushing him back. "What is wrong with you?" she whispered into his ear as he staggered back against a painted mural of several fish swimming upstream.

"What's wrong with me? What's wrong with you?! You can't tell me you like these stupid games!"

"No. I don't. I hate them. That's why I asked her the question instead of just standing there like, I don't know, you!"

Timothy opened his mouth and closed it again.

"We'll figure this out, OK? We will. But you can't just destroy a person's place of business, especially not if you want that person's help."

"I didn't do it on purpose!"

Alex laughed slightly. "Yeah, I know." She looked at the mess Timothy had made. "Man, you did a good job of it, though."

Timothy shrugged.

"Alex, Timothy," called Mr Underwood from somewhere ahead of them.

The two of them followed the sound, pushing their way through a few other draperies until they came out on to the balcony that opened out on to the courtyard. Mr Underwood was leaning against the railing, between a thickset man wearing a purple wig and two very pretty young women, both dressed in violet. He was looking down towards the pit where fan-tan was being played.

Alex and Timothy joined him. They followed his gaze down a level to the first floor and across from them on a bit of an angle. Duchess Rose was taking a seat in an elegantly carved chair, and all attention from down in the pit was focused upon her. Beside her stood the small round man, who banged his cane on the floor loudly. He announced something in Mandarin, and there was a faint muttering from the audience.

"Jack!" whispered Jack.

Timothy glanced up at the sound and then looked back down again. He took a moment to think, and then he turned to Jack once more.

"What's going on?" he asked.

Jack nodded emphatically and then stopped and smiled at Timothy, slightly open-mouthed. There was a pause.

"What's going on?!" Timothy wanted to grab the little pirate and shake him.

"Duchess is going to play now."

"Oh," said Timothy, looking back at the Duchess. He then glanced down at the bald shirtless man who was running the game downstairs. He seemed a little awestruck as he watched his young assistant retrieve coins from beneath the brass cover. When the boy had finished, and it was time to place bets, the bald shirtless man looked back up at the Duchess.

The small round man banged his cane once more, causing Timothy to look up again. The small round man was saying something else, and he looked rather upset.

"Now what?" asked Timothy to Jack.

"No one's betting," replied Jack. "Sad."

"Why not?"

"Why do you think?" replied Alex from his other side.

Timothy turned to her. "No one wants to play Duchess Rose. They're scared."

"Of what? They've been playing all night. Surely they don't care that much about losing."

"They're not scared of losing," replied Alex. "They're scared of winning."

"Games, always stupid games." Timothy shook his head.

Then a loud voice came from directly next to them. The thickset man in the purple wig raised his hand.

The muttering got much louder now, and Duchess Rose bowed her head slightly at her competition. There was a sudden flutter of activity as the two players placed their bets into small baskets in front of them. The baskets were lowered to ground level, and the boys quickly gathered them and put them on the appropriate plates.

"Why is he doing that?" asked Timothy to himself.

But Alex heard and replied, "What?"

"Why is the man in the purple wig betting that way? There clearly can't be any more than two coins under the cover."

"I don't know," replied Alex, but it was clear she didn't really have a good grasp of the game herself.

The cane banged on the floor for a third time and dead silence fell upon the crowd. The bald shirtless man took a deep breath and with a slightly shaking hand lifted the brass cover.

"One!" someone from the crowd called out. There was

a great cheer as the coins from both bets were placed into the Duchess's basket and raised up to her. The man in the purple wig shrugged and bowed to her. Duchess Rose stared at him for an instant, and then made a signal with her hand.

Out of the shadows behind the man in the purple wig appeared two tall, muscular men, dressed in the same black tunic as the small round man. They grabbed the man in the purple wig and dragged him away, screaming, back into the shadows.

Duchess Rose stood and yelled something out to the crowd, pointing her finger at them as she did so.

This time Timothy didn't have to ask.

"He let her win," said Jack. "She's mad."

That explained the betting.

"I guess some people want to try to impress her," said Alex. "I think she's a bit smarter than that. What do you think will happen to that man?"

"Nothing good," replied Timothy, distracted. He was thinking hard. If losing didn't impress her much, then maybe. . .

Duchess Rose sat down in her chair again with a scowl, and the small round man banged his cane once more.

"Like anyone's going to play her now," said Alex.

"Oi!" called out Timothy. Every head in the house turned to face him. Thousands of eyes were on him now, including those of Duchess Rose, who seemed surprised to see he was still around.

"Timothy, what are you doing?" whispered Alex, but Timothy brushed her off and moved along the rail until he was facing directly opposite the Duchess.

"I'll play," he announced. He glanced briefly at DeWit and Sir Geoffrey, who were staring up at him in complete amazement. He looked back at Duchess Rose, who, after a moment's pause, gave him a slight bow with her head, which Timothy returned in kind.

There was a flutter of activity as coins were collected and placed under the brass cover. In no time, Alex was by his side again, which was both really annoying and also kind of comforting.

"You can't really do this," she said. "If you lose, she'll think you did it on purpose and have you taken away like that other guy, and if you win. . ."

"If I win, maybe she'll understand that we're serious. Now are you going to keep talking or what?"

Alex shook her head. "It's a game of chance, Timothy!"

"There's strategy to everything," he replied, his voice lowered. "Watch the kid."

Alex turned and saw the boy with the long stick stand and watch the brass cover being placed over the coins.

"What am I watching for?"

"He holds his hands lower down on the stick when he's pulling out fewer coins."

"You mean he knows how many coins he's pulling out?"

"I don't think he does it on purpose," replied Timothy.

"But every time there is a higher number under that cover, he's got his hands like that."

"So we see where he places his hands, then?"

"Yeah."

Silence fell as the boy walked over to the bald man and extended the stick. He placed one hand low down, near the end of the stick, and the other close to the top, almost as if he were holding a pool cue.

"What does that mean?" asked Alex.

"I ... don't ... know," replied Timothy, leaning forward on the rail.

"What do you mean you don't know?" replied Alex, her voice getting louder.

"Shh, Alex, I'm trying to concentrate!" *On not throwing up*, he added inside his head. He had no idea what this new hand position meant. He had no clue how many coins were being extracted, nor, more importantly, how many were left under the cover. He was going to have to guess – gamble, in the real sense of the word. This was not good. Not good at all.

The boy stopped extracting coins and took a step back. The bald man looked up at the Duchess and then at Timothy. When they made eye contact, Timothy could read pure terror in the man's expression. *Yeah, that's helpful*, sighed Timothy to himself.

It was then that he noticed the basket for taking bets swinging just next to his head.

"Um, Timothy?" asked Alex.

"What?"

"Do you have any money?"

Timothy turned sharply and stared at Alex. It took less than a second to process the question and answer it, but in his head it happened a little more like this: the question was asked, and immediately Timothy's heart was in his throat. Of course he didn't have any money. Why would he have money? When had he had the opportunity to visit a bank on the way to China?

Money. Stupid stupid money. Always ruining things, like not-all-that-well-thought-out plans.

Wait a minute. . .

Wait a minute. . .

. . .

. . .

Unless of course it had sunk to the bottom of the . . . . . . after he fell. . .

Timothy suddenly became aware of a very familiar weight on his right side. A weight that had become so much a part of his jacket that he had stopped noticing it in the first place. A weight that matched perfectly with the weight of several bills of large denominations carefully vacuum-sealed in thick plastic that might have been appropriated when flying in a billionaire's helicopter.

Yes, this was the thinking that happened all in a flash of a moment when Alex asked him that question. But of course thinking time has little to do with actual time and so the actual moment happened thus:

"Um, Timothy?" asked Alex.

"What?"

"Do you have any money?"

Timothy turned sharply and stared at Alex. "Yes, yes, I do," he replied casually presenting the stack of bills from his pocket and dropping it into the basket.

There was a gasp from the crowd when they noticed the large sum lowered down to the pit, and Timothy almost forgot he was supposed to pick a number until the boy working the pulley of his basket called up to him.

Timothy looked at the boy and then at Alex, who was wide-eyed.

I don't know I don't know I don't know. . .

. . .

. . .

"One!" he called down, and held up one finger to make sure the boy understood completely.

The boy looked around and then back up at him, expecting him to place a smaller bet on one of the other numbers.

"Just one," said Timothy again, his voice cracking. "Put it all on one." He clenched the rail of the balcony tightly with his hands.

The plastic-wrapped wad of cash was placed on the plate representing the number one, and all attention turned to Duchess Rose.

Duchess Rose was sitting forward in her chair, her elbows resting on the rail in front of her with her hands pressed together, the fingers laced with one another

269

except for the two index ones placed just above her upper lip. She then leaned back and tilted her head over towards the small round man and spoke to him softly. The small round man placed an equally large sum of money into her basket and, as it lowered, announced the bet loudly.

Duchess Rose and Timothy made eye contact, and she held up three fingers with a smile. Timothy smiled tightly in return and they both shifted their gaze to the bald shirtless man.

The silence was overwhelming. As he stared at the shiny, sweaty bald head far below, he could feel the world start to swim around him. He tried to tell himself it was just vertigo, but he knew deep down it was pure unadulterated terror.

The bald shirtless man placed a hand on the top of the cover. He looked up at Duchess Rose and then up at Timothy and then down again. Then, bowing his head so low he couldn't see the result himself, he raised his hand, bringing the brass cover with it.

THE THIRTY-EIGHTH CHAPTER

In which Timothy has a serious conversation with Duchess Rose

"You wait here now," said the small round man.

Timothy nodded and shoved his hands into his pockets to stop them from shaking. Not that that did much, as his whole body was shaking, and his head was light, and his breathing a tiny bit shallow. Alex, Mr Underwood and Jack, along with DeWit and Sir Geoffrey, were all seated in the darkened waiting area before Duchess Rose's room, staring at him silently. Timothy couldn't decide if he would rather be here at the present moment being stared at quietly by everyone or in private conversation with Duchess Rose, as he was about to be. He decided neither was particularly pleasant and chose his room, in front of the telly, as the preferred option.

The small round man returned and held the curtain to the side once more for Timothy to enter. And Timothy did enter, sensing the curtain fall closed behind him. Before him, Duchess Rose reclined on her pillows as before, puffing on her pipe and looking at him casually.

Timothy sat without being invited to and waited for her to say something, anything.

Duchess Rose exhaled a smoke cloud in his direction and he resisted the urge to cough. Then she sat herself upright and crossed her legs. Finally she leaned forward and quietly said, "One?"

Timothy nodded slightly. "Yes."

"Very risky bet," she added.

"Yes."

"Some would call it a stupid bet."

"Yes."

Duchess Rose scrutinized him closely. What she was trying to read from his face even Timothy wasn't sure of, so he didn't bother trying to alter his expression.

"Well," said Duchess Rose, leaning back, "I personally would call it a lucky bet." Again without any signal, the small round man entered the room carrying the basket with the winnings and placed it in front of Timothy, then exited just as suddenly.

"Yes," said Timothy, or at least tried to say, his voice catching somewhere in the back of his throat. He stared at the pile of cash in front of him.

"Take it," said Duchess Rose. "Take it. You won it, fair and square."

Timothy removed his hands from his pockets, reached forward and took the basket and held it in his lap.

"I am impressed," said Duchess Rose.

"Thank you," replied Timothy, still staring into the basket.

"I am impressed you won, yes, but I am also impressed you played in the first place. If this were another time, I would have been interested in having you on my ship."

Timothy nodded.

Duchess Rose smoothed out the front of her robe with her hand.

"Why are you looking for the Fleet of the Nine Dragons?" she asked.

Timothy looked up from the basket. He felt his heart rate quicken. "Because I believe they have a friend of mine." It came out as little more than a whisper.

"The Fleet of the Nine Dragons does not typically kidnap anyone. There's not much money to be had in ransom. Plus it is a very dishonourable practice."

"With all due respect, Duchess, you are no longer in command of the Fleet. They have indeed captured a friend of mine. Worthwhile or not, dishonourable or not, it has happened." Timothy had found his voice again and it was surprisingly loud.

Duchess Rose remained calm, but looked uneasy at his response. "What makes your friend worth kidnapping in the first place?" she asked.

Timothy was tired. Despite the adrenaline pumping through his veins, he was tired. He was tired from all the adventuring, and he was also simply exhausted from all the stress he had been under in playing fan-tan earlier. He didn't care if he was being reckless by saying it. *No more games*, he thought to himself.

"My friend is a dragon."

Duchess Rose sat up straight.

"Explain."

Timothy explained. He was getting quite good at telling the story and had managed to shave a good several minutes off the act of telling it. And when he had finished, Duchess Rose stood up and began to pace about the room.

"With the power of this dragon, the Fleet of the Nine Dragons could return to its former glory."

Timothy watched the old woman think. He could not tell if she considered this a good or a bad thing.

"This must not happen." She turned and looked down at Timothy. "I have worked too long and too hard to establish my power in Kaomai. I will not have some foreigner usurp my position."

"Foreigner?" asked Timothy, standing because his neck was starting to hurt from looking up at her.

"The one they call the Man in the Beige Linen Suit. He captains my old ship. He commands my old fleet. It never mattered much to me because it had dwindled to so few ships. But if he has this dragon . . . I will not let him take away the glory of my achievements, my place in the history books!"

"Well, then, could you tell us how to find him?"

Duchess Rose nodded, and the small round man appeared at her side with a map. He unrolled it on the floor before them, and Duchess Rose indicated a little bay hidden just beyond the coastline of Kaomai. Timothy thought back to the map he had seen on the *Ironic Gentleman*. He was pretty sure there had been no such bay marked on that version.

"You cannot see the entrance to the bay from the sea. You need to go up the coastline and find this rock face." She indicated a jutting piece of land. On the map it was obvious a bay was behind it, but from the water it would have probably looked like a solid piece of cliff.

"May I take this map, Duchess?" asked Timothy, suddenly getting very excited.

"Of course." The small round man immediately returned to roll up the map for Timothy.

"How does he do that?" asked Timothy of Duchess Rose.

"Do what?"

"Know when to come and go like that, and what you want?"

"I have no idea."

The small round man handed the map to Timothy.

Timothy placed it in the inner pocket of his jacket, picked up his winnings, and stood for a moment staring at the Duchess.

"Well, then. . ." he said, feeling just a bit awkward.

"Well, then. . ." she replied with a slight grin. She was not going to make this goodbye easy for him.

"Uh, thanks." Timothy extended his hand. Duchess Rose extended hers, the palm facing the floor. Timothy stared at it for an instant, and then recalled times he'd seen his mother perform a similar action.

As quickly as he could, he kissed her hand and then turned and rushed out of the room, with the sound of Duchess Rose laughing merrily behind him.

THE THIRTY-NINTH CHAPTER

In which Timothy is taken by surprise

"I've got a map that will show us how to get to the fleet," announced Timothy to his waiting audience.

They all jumped to their feet, with Alex exclaiming, "Awesome!"

Timothy handed the basket of winnings over to Alex and took the map from his jacket. But before he could unfold it, DeWit said, "I think at this stage we should get it back to the ship as soon as possible."

"Oh, you are just so wonderfully trusting, aren't you, Captain," Sir Geoffrey said with a laugh.

DeWit ignored him and instead began to lead the others back through the maze of drapes towards the stairs.

"You were amazing," said Alex, moving up to walk in step with Timothy and handing him back his basket.

Timothy took it and shook his head. "It was just luck," he replied.

"Who cares? You took a risk and it totally paid off. It was a pretty good idea." She lowered her voice a bit. "I bet Duchess Rose considers you a friend now."

"Yeah, well." Timothy shrugged and started down the stairs.

"No, I'm sure she does! Come on, Timothy, you can't sulk through success too, that's just silly!"

Timothy was about to respond with his usual cynicism when he was interrupted by someone calling, "Captain!"

Timothy turned to look down the stairs ahead of him, where O'Connell was running up to meet them with a look of utter distress on his face. *Oh, this can't be good.* He glanced over into the pit.

"O'Connell, is everything all right?" asked DeWit.

"No, everything is not all right!" But it wasn't O'Connell who said it, but rather Timothy. He was staring at a figure, dressed all in black, making its way casually through the thick crowd, who were cowering slightly on the fringes of the playing area watching its progress.

Behind the figure in black were two men dressed in orange, their heads shaved. They walked in perfect step with each other, their faces expressionless. All three were heading towards the stairs.

"Who are they?" asked Alex.

"Well, I'm pretty sure the ninja is the same woman I met on the plane. Emily. The same one who pushed me out of the plane, actually."

"And she's taken out Tanaka. He's barely breathing, I

don't know how much time he has. We need to get him help, and fast," added O'Connell.

"What?!" DeWit took a step forward, or possibly just fell down one step in his shock. "What do you mean?"

"We were standing guard. There wasn't that much activity, and then we saw the two monks in orange approaching. We weren't sure exactly what they wanted, but Tanaka recognized them as being Shaolin, fighters like. So we prepared ourselves, and then, completely out of the blue, we were attacked from above by that ninja girl. It happened so quickly. In a flash she was on Tanaka, and the three of them fought good and long. I couldn't get a foot in there."

"Lovely story. I especially like the bit about me. Hello, Timothy."

O'Connell whipped around to find himself face to face with Emily. Instinctively, he charged her, but she merely stepped to the side and with a quick move of her hand helped him tumble down the stairs. She took a step up. DeWit and Mr Underwood moved instantly between her and Timothy.

"How did you find me?" asked Timothy, not sure if he should appreciate being protected or feel insulted that they didn't think he could take care of himself.

"There are ways," she replied and looked at the two men in front of her with bemusement. "Of course, when word reached us that the *Ironic Gentleman* was in town, with descriptions of the visitors – that was rather helpful as well."

Now, Timothy was an avid watcher of film and television. And he knew that for some reason in movies there comes a time when the villain of the piece has a nice long dialogue with the hero. Usually this is in order to get important information across to the audience, like letting them know a bomb is hidden somewhere in the building or something.

In real life, though, if we are faced with a villain of some kind, our bodies typically respond in one of two ways: fight or flight. Either you stay and engage in combat, or you run away. You don't stand and have a nice five-minute chat about personal motivations or anything.

Unless, of course, you have seen one too many movies, like Timothy. Fortunately, Alex, on the other hand, was a deeply practical person.

"Run!" she whispered loudly in Timothy's ear.

He looked at her, hearing the word, but not quite understanding it.

"Run!" She said it a bit louder.

"Really?" asked Timothy.

"Run!" This time she yelled it loudly, and Emily turned and noticed her for the first time.

And not because he usually considered Alex's suggestions to have much merit, nor because he couldn't clearly assess the situation for himself, but rather because he thought that maybe running actually was a decent idea, Timothy dropped everything and ran.

THE FORTIETH CHAPTER

In which Timothy runs for it

Timothy turned on the spot and charged back up the stairs to the third level, back through the maze of material that hung oh-so-impractically from the ceiling, until he reached the balcony of the courtyard once more.

He took quick stock of his situation. He could not very well jump down or anything. For one thing, it was a really far drop, and for another, the two Shaolin monks that had arrived with Emily were looking up at him from the centre of the pit. He also considered running back into the depths of the third level and hoping he'd find a door somewhere. Or possibly a window.

This is ridiculous, he thought, panic rising up from his stomach.

And then Timothy remembered to look up.

Standing on the third level put Timothy very close to

the opening of the roof. If he could just climb out of it, he would probably be able to move along the rooftops for quite a distance.

It seemed like the only rational decision.

Timothy moved along the rail of the balcony until he reached the corner where there was a thick wooden column acting as support for the roof. He gripped it with his right hand, his left raised above his head ready to grab the part of the roof that sloped down towards the pit. He swung one foot up on to the rail, and then, with a deep breath, the other one. The other foot, though not in as much pain any more, was still rather weak. He teetered slightly, and he grabbed the roof with his left hand to steady himself.

Now what?

Timothy turned his body so that his back was towards the courtyard and he was facing the corner with the wooden column. He contemplated the roof in front of him. Directly above the column was a decorative piece of wood that also connected the two perpendicular sides of the roof together. It jutted up and down, a bit like a very angular wave. If Timothy could hold on to that, he might be able to pull himself up on to the roof.

He took a tiny step back so that his legs were now quite far apart (any further and he'd be doing some rather painful splits). Then Timothy, in a quick motion, released the column and placed both his hands, palms down, on to the roof above his head. He only needed to get a bit of height before he would be able to get hold of the decorative piece of wood. With an inward roll of the eyes, Timothy pushed. He could feel a sharp pain jab up his right wrist to his elbow, and he squeezed his face tight with pain and the effort. Then, with all his might, he launched his left hand forward and grabbed for the piece of wood. He almost missed. But not quite. He took a moment to secure his grasp, and then the right hand joined the left.

Timothy started pulling himself up and found that his feet could use the wooden column to help give him momentum. It was when he was pretty close to getting his full body on top of the roof that he heard, "After him."

Unable to resist, Timothy glanced over his shoulder. The two Shaolin monks had each taken a side of the courtyard and begun to climb up towards him. No, not so much climb as casually walk and jump and occasionally flip their way up to him.

Great, just great. Timothy turned his focus back to the task at hand, and with one final pull and a push from the left leg, he hoisted himself up on to the roof. Sure, he was pretty proud of himself, but he didn't have much of a chance to bask in the glory of his accomplishment, seeing as the two monks were already at the second level.

Nor could he fully appreciate the view from up on the roof, which was something to behold. Ahead of him was a vista of rooftops, all of different shapes and sizes, with a forest of chimneys. Below, the lanterns were swaying in the strong breeze, along with some laundry that had been left out by accident overnight, and in the distance, the interior of the city's skyline was an impressive sight of flashing lights and tall buildings competing with each other in height. He took a brief glance at the building that dominated the others, sleek and with a giant rose at its very top, and felt encouraged by it.

Suddenly he sensed he was no longer alone, and he turned to see one of the monks standing on the other side of the giant hole in the roof that made up the courtyard. He said something in Mandarin, which Timothy took to possibly mean, "Enjoying the view?" The monk then started to run around the hole to his side.

Timothy turned and began to run, or rather stumble, as quickly as he could along the roof to where it met up with a neighbouring building, and jumped over the small space between them. Cleverly, he didn't look down. The next building had a much flatter roof, and Timothy was able to turn his stumble into a full-out run. He glanced briefly behind him and noticed the monk had made it to directly behind him now and was almost at the edge of the fan-tan house.

The monk called out something, and there was a response from Timothy's right. Looking across the narrow street to the other side, he noticed for the first time the second monk (or was it the first?) running practically parallel to him. *Man, these guys were quick!*

There was no way that Timothy was going to be able to outrun them. He had to come up with something else – a plan, possibly, maybe a miracle.

The answer did arrive slightly miraculously, but with an apologetic smile. Staring across the street at the other Shaolin monk had momentarily distracted Timothy from the difficult task of negotiating the obstacles that could be found on rooftops. However, his bad ankle called him back to attention by catching on a ledge and throwing him down to the ground. That is to say, the actual ground many metres below, as the ledge had served to delineate the end of its roof, and Timothy found himself falling between two buildings. He flailed his arms about, and his left hand managed to catch hold of a lintel above a window.

Timothy swung there, monkey-like, for a brief moment before noticing that the window was open. It seemed almost welcoming, and he quickly threw himself into the building. He scrambled to his feet and found he was in some sort of darkened storage room. He fumbled his way through the dark and found a door. He opened it carefully, discovered there was no one on the other side, and made a break towards the stairs and down to the exit.

He stepped as quietly as he could into the narrow alley, pulled himself back inside when he spotted a glimpse of orange that flew overhead, stopped, and dropped down just as Timothy had done between the buildings, only this time on purpose. Then it vanished through the same window. It was followed shortly by another orange figure, and Timothy decided he would stop witnessing this impressive athletic display and run for it instead.

He ran wildly down the alley and through the streets, twisting and turning, trying to put as much distance as he thought reasonable between him and the monks, who he hoped were spending at least a bit of time looking for him in the building. He turned a corner and found himself facing a dead end.

Right.

He whipped back around, only to find himself face to face with Emily, her arms crossed, standing in front of him.

THE FORTY-FIRST CHAPTER

In which Timothy makes a difficult decision

Timothy stood, paralysed.

"Impressive," said Emily. "Ultimately futile, but impressive. Now if you don't want this to be the last breath you take, I'd suggest handing over that key."

Timothy's mind was racing. Except that it wasn't getting anywhere. He could not think of a single thing to do. His thoughts were going in circles. Oh, great. His mind was racing, yes, but on one of those hamster-wheely-thingies.

"Or, I could just kill you." Reaching behind her back, she unsheathed a sword. Shorter than the ones he'd seen Alex and Mr Underwood use, and with a straight blade, it looked as if the top point had been filed off at an angle.

Though the moment was not wholly unexpected, it still surprised Timothy that it was happening pretty much as he had anticipated it would. Would Emily actually kill him? Well, she had practically killed Tanaka and pushed Timothy out of a plane. It seemed more than likely that she would. And unless someone right that moment came to his rescue. . .

No one came to his rescue.

Well, that option was out then.

Fold.

He heard the word almost as if it had been spoken aloud to him. When you don't hold the cards, it's time to fold, Timothy. *But I can't! I can do this, I can still win.*

Fold.

. . .

"Here." He took the chain from around his neck and held it out. It seemed for just that moment, the one where Emily extended her hand and he dropped it into her palm, that he was standing outside his body watching the interaction. He felt oddly disconnected from the whole thing, as if he were watching some other boy in a brown corduroy jacket and some other ninja.

Then he was back in his own body again, watching Emily scale a wall at top speed and vanish into the night.

"You could have said thank you!" he called out to the darkness. It was a really stupid thing to say, but he was feeling rather stupid. After all, he was alone in some alley, completely winded, and had just given up a very loyal friend to some pretty nasty people. No, wait a minute, he wasn't feeling stupid, he was feeling sick.

Suddenly Timothy found himself doubled over and

throwing up any last vestiges of dinner he hadn't quite digested yet. When he finished he righted himself and, feeling even more pathetic, began to drag himself back towards the fan-tan house.

It took him twice as long to make it back as it had taken him to run away from it, since he was moving at a snail's pace. And when he arrived he felt himself get queasy again. There was blood on the ground, a great deal of it. He could only imagine it had belonged to Tanaka.

"Timothy!"

Timothy forced himself not to throw up again as he turned to the voice, the very familiar voice that was, in this case, amazingly welcome. "Alex?" He called it out to the darkness because he had no idea where she was.

Alex materialized from the very narrow space between the two buildings he had jumped over a few minutes before. Giggles was at her heels.

She was covered in dirt, and there was a smear of blood on her forehead.

"What happened to you?"

"Oh, Timothy, I'm so glad you're all right!" And then she did a really strange thing. She lunged at him, and then . . . she hugged him.

"Yeah, I'm OK." He was too tired to struggle and so patted her back a couple of times. "But seriously, what about you?"

They pulled apart.

"Well, once you made a run for it, once you actually

climbed up on to the roof, which was, I mean, I don't know, either really stupid or really brave of you, there was a fight."

"A fight."

"I mean, you'd think that five against one would be pretty good odds, but man, that ninja girl, she's good."

"What happened?"

"She has these poisoned dart things. She totally got O'Connell and then DeWit. Mr Underwood was amazing and held her off until those monks came back without you and she suddenly left. Sir Geoffrey and Jack, of course, were no help at all. I bet they were hoping she'd win."

"Then what?"

"Then what? Then Duchess Rose appeared and just sort of took over everything. I don't know if it was kung fu or what, but it was those two monks against her, and she was holding her own. The small round man and that tall Spanish one took DeWit and O'Connell somewhere safe, I think, to look after them, and then it was me and Mr Underwood and the two pirates."

"But how did you end up here?"

"Well, Duchess Rose was handling herself just fine, and she also has all these guards people who just sort of showed up, like the two who took away that man with the purple wig? Anyway, Mr Underwood and I decided that it would be best if we made it back to the ship. So we rushed out of there, but then I realized that you might come back, and as much as I know he hated it, it made sense for one of us to wait for you. It seemed like both tasks were likely to be pretty dangerous, so I offered to stay because I knew I could fit in that space between the buildings. Besides it would take someone bigger than me to get Tanaka back to the ship."

"How is he?"

"I dunno, pretty bad. I dunno." Alex bit her lower lip.

Timothy really didn't want to have to deal with her crying, so he asked instead, "And what about Jack and Sir Geoffrey?"

"Well, Sir Geoffrey's gone off, totally ran away, or rather limped away, in the chaos. And Jack stuck around to help the Duchess. I think she's decided to keep him as some sort of pet, really. Not that he minds."

Timothy looked towards the fan-tan house, then back at Alex.

"What about you?" she asked. "How did you escape?"

Timothy found he couldn't look at her in the eyes, and so focused on her shoes instead. "I . . . I didn't."

Alex gave a small laugh. "What do you mean, you didn't? You're here, aren't you?"

"It's not funny!" It was after the words came out that he realized how loudly he had shouted them. "You're perfect! You do everything just as it's supposed to be done. Well, we can't all be like you, OK?"

He finally met her eyes, expecting to see them welling with tears, but she was just looking at him in bewilderment. "O . . . K. . ." she said slowly.

"You asked me if I escaped, and I said I didn't. Emily,

290

she didn't lose out on any great battle. She isn't nursing all the wounds I gave her or anything. For crying out loud, Alex, she is a trained ninja! She stalks and kills and stuff. I watch telly!" He took a few short angry breaths. "I didn't escape, because she let me go. . ."

"She let you go. . ."

"I'm not finished! She let me go because I gave her the stupid key, OK?! I gave her the key. I did. And don't go telling me how stupid that was, how you've all risked your lives and stuff, and how Tanaka might die and everything because of that key, because I know, OK? I know! I wanted to save my own skin. And so I gave up the key 'cause I didn't want her to kill me. Now Mr Shen is in major trouble. Probably this whole city is in major trouble. If those pirates get their strength back. You've all risked everything for me, and in the end, this what I do. I always do it. I am not a good person. I am not like you. I am a Grade A loser. No, that would mean I was good at something. I am a Grade C loser."

Timothy finished his rant and stared at Alex, willing her to challenge him. Deep down he kind of wanted her to yell at him. Throw things at him.

But she didn't. She stood quietly for a moment, registering all he had just shared. And then calmly, she said, "Well, then, we'll just have to get it back."

THE FORTY-SECOND CHAPTER

In which Timothy and Alex take matters into their own hands

"Don't you think it's time we took the matter into our own hands?" asked Alex. She and Timothy had found their way quite accidentally but rather luckily to a small park a few streets away from the fan-tan house.

"What do you mean?" Timothy was still feeling numb from Alex's response to his rather emotional display a few moments earlier.

"Well, I like to get things done, and it seems to me, for all their positive qualities, adults do like to talk about things a lot."

"Yeah, that's true."

"Right now, we're in a pretty good situation. Mr Underwood thinks I am waiting for you. For all he knows, I could have to wait for you all night. It seems to me we have quite a few hours at our disposal."

Timothy looked at Alex, utterly confused.

"Whatever you may think of me, Timothy, I believe I've done a few things that were clearly against the rules, especially in the last couple of weeks," she said with a smile. "Sometimes you have to go against the rules because the people who make them are not thinking clearly. I say we go and rescue Mr Shen ourselves. In fact, all we really need is the key. Once we get the key, we can get Mr Shen to help us out, and even though his powers are limited, they still exist. I really think this is doable."

"You're forgetting one thing, Alex," said Timothy, shaking his head.

"Yeah?"

"Someone has to give us the key. We can't just take it. I don't know how we will be able to convince them to hand it over."

"We'll think of something," replied Alex confidently, and she stood up, stretching her arms above her head.

"Alex, come on, we can't really do this." Timothy refused to budge. In fact, he sprawled himself out further on the freshly manicured lawn.

"You know what, Timothy, I'm getting really sick of all this. Every time something goes slightly wrong, you think it's a sign or something for you to give up. Like you've failed. Well, the only reason you fail is because you stop. If you knew that you would save Mr Shen in the end, despite everything that has happened, wouldn't you keep trying?"

"Yeah, but there's no guarantee."

"There's never any guarantee. It's called taking a risk. Kind of like what you did in the fan-tan house. You're just scared now, and that's fine, but you can't let it hold you back."

"But I mean, just us? Do you really think that makes any sense?"

"Timothy, when is the Lantern Festival?" Timothy didn't feel like answering that question, so Alex did for him. "Tomorrow. We don't exactly have time on our side. You honestly want to waste it by making our way back to the ship?"

Timothy really wasn't sure what to make of the current situation. He was rarely lectured on how to be rebellious, and he would have thought the chance to take care of the situation himself would be rather tempting. At the same time, what was rebellious about agreeing with someone else?

"OK, fine, let's do it, but we'd better get going," he finally said, and he removed the rolled-up map from inside his coat. It was a bit damp from his sweat, but fortunately it was printed on some kind of waterproof material, so everything was still intact.

Alex smiled triumphantly, which Timothy chose to ignore, and came to sit beside him. Together they examined the location of the Fleet of the Nine Dragons.

"Looks like a bit of a walk, doesn't it?" she said, running her finger along the markings that indicated the coastline.

"Yeah," agreed Timothy, "although. . ."

"Although?"

"What if we went right overland?"

Alex looked where he was pointing.

"You mean like up that big hill?" she said, looking up and nodding out to the landscape in front of them.

Timothy looked and considered the hill in the distance. There was the Spanish fort right at the very top, so it quite likely meant that there was some sort of path to get up there. What was on the other side would be another matter altogether.

"Yeah, I mean like over that big hill." He stood up. "It will probably take around two hours to get through the city and up to the top. Couple more to get down. We should still make it before dawn."

He heard Alex sigh. "Doesn't leave us much time."

"We can do it. I mean, you just said we could." He heard Alex laugh, and he turned and extended his hand to help her up. When she was on her feet, he paused for a moment to wonder why on earth he had just done that.

Alex, on the other hand, didn't seem especially fazed by the action, and instead simply said, "Well, we better get going. Come on, Giggles."

Timothy had totally forgotten about the cat, who had found himself a spot slightly off from them to mope quietly.

"Why does the cat have to come along?"

"Because he just does, OK? Besides he's pretty helpful in a pinch," she added.

"Fine, whatever."

And they set off, each a tiny bit concerned that their plan was really not much of anything at this stage in the game, but trying to convince the other it would work out all right in the end.

THE FORTY-THIRD CHAPTER

In which Timothy, Alex and Giggles find the Fleet of the Nine Dragons

There are certain bits of stories that, because of their nature, are rather dull. This is because very little happens in them. And for some reason they also always happen to take place over a rather tediously long period of time. So, yes, I could tell you of the five-hour trek Timothy and Alex took to reach the hidden bay. I could tell you that when they reached the fort, the view was rather impressive. I could also mention that Timothy lost his footing at one point as they made their way through the thick forest on the other side and, had Alex not grabbed the back of his jacket, his tale would have ended there rather abruptly.

But honestly. . .

Let's just get to pirate stuff already.

*

"There!" said Alex pointing. She, Timothy and Giggles were standing on the fringes of the forest, taking care to hide themselves in amongst the trees. They had spent most of their journey unconcerned about being noticed since it had been so dark when they left the city. But now the sun was just starting to come up.

Timothy had already seen the ships and didn't really need them to be pointed out to him. Indeed, you would be hard-pressed not to spot nine large pirate junks floating in a rather small bay surrounded by a dozen or so smaller vessels. He didn't say anything to Alex, though. He was tired. And also, what was the point in ruining her obvious excitement?

"Where do you think they have Mr Shen?" he asked instead.

"There's no guarantee, but I bet he's in the big one."

"Yeah, that kind of makes sense," agreed Timothy. The "big one" was a junk like the others, but, unlike the others, nearly twice their size, with seven masts. Its sails were bright yellow, which seemed more cheerful than menacing, but, Timothy supposed, the ship's savage reputation probably more than made up for the sunny cheer of the sails.

"So do we have a plan yet?"

Alex shook her head. "Though I bet they are all asleep right now, or most of the crew. That could be advantageous."

"I guess." Timothy didn't much feel like reminding her that at some point they were going to have to convince someone to give him the key. That would probably require waking at least a few ruthless pirates.

"Let's go get a closer look." Alex started to move quietly along the treeline, darting between open spaces. Timothy and Giggles followed closely at her heels.

It took twenty minutes of creeping before they arrived opposite the large junk. It was floating nearly in the middle of the bay, which wasn't a great distance from them, but at the same time not easily accessible either.

From their new vantage point, Timothy noticed that there actually was some activity going on on the ship. In fact, on closer inspection, it appeared that the two Shaolin monks that had been pursuing him earlier were performing guard duty. Didn't these guys deserve some kind of rest? "Unless, of course, they're robots or something."

"What was that?" asked Alex.

"Nothing, never mind."

"Did you see the monks?"

"Yes, I saw the monks."

"I wonder what monks are doing in such a violent business as pirating."

"Good question. You think about that, and I'll go save Mr Shen." He took a few steps out from the protective cover of the trees.

"Oh please, you know I'm coming with you!" She, too, took off her shoes and sweater. Timothy shook his head, but didn't protest as she joined him by his side. He watched as she contemplated the sword at her hip.

"Leave it," he said. "There's no point. If they catch us, you with one sword against a whole ship of pirates. . ."

"You don't think I could take them?"

"No, I don't."

"Eh, you're probably right." And she unfastened the belt, letting the sword fall to the ground.

When they were both ready, Alex gave Giggles instructions to watch over their things for them. The cat didn't seem to mind being asked to stay behind. Going for an early-morning swim was clearly not on his list of top priorities, and so he sat obediently.

The prospect of an early-morning swim was not exactly that inviting to Timothy or Alex either, but they could see no better way of getting to the large pirate junk. So they ran quietly down the beach to the water's edge, trying to keep as low to the ground as possible. And then they just kept walking into the water until they had to start swimming. The water was cold, but not unbearable, and it did serve to give them a bit of an energy jolt, which was much required considering they had been up all night.

The second jolt came a moment later when they were both unexpectedly grabbed from behind and pulled rather unceremoniously out of the water by two Shaolin monks and a ninja.

THE FORTY-FOURTH CHAPTER

In which Timothy and Alex are prisoners

I t is incredibly difficult to try to save a dragon when he is being guarded by two Shaolin monks and a ninja, not to mention a fleet of pirate junks floating innocently but ominously in the distance. Ninjas, you see, are rather stealthy and clever. And Shaolin monks are highly disciplined and perform acrobatic feats that any reasonable person would know to be impossible. Fleets of pirate junks . . . are simply daunting.

For a kid like Timothy, who had just recently outwitted the monks and contended with the ninja and overcome his fear of fleets of pirate junks, being thrown by exactly these same individuals into a small wooden room in the heart of the biggest junk of them all . . . was just plain insulting.

He wasn't exactly sure why he had chosen to bang on the door and yell things like, "Let us out!" and "You can't do this!" It wasn't particularly useful. I mean, it wasn't like he was going to break down the door or anything. And it was even less likely he was going to convince any of their captors to change their minds with the good sense of what he was saying – "You're right, we can't do this! Quick, let's let them out." No. Very unlikely.

"Timothy, what are you doing?" Alex had resigned herself to sitting quietly against the wall.

"I . . . don't . . . know. . ." Timothy stopped banging and turned to face her, sliding down the door so he was sitting. "This is just so infuriating!"

"You're telling me," replied Alex, but her mild manner seemed to suggest otherwise.

"Yeah, you seem real upset."

"What's the point in getting all worked up? Right now we have to think of a plan. And anyway, I've been in worse jail cells. At least this one is clean and bright."

Timothy shook his head and looked at Alex in disbelief. "So, then, what do we do now?"

Alex furrowed her brow and hugged her knees. "I think," she said, "we really do just have to wait and see what happens next."

"Great."

"Well, I think it's going to be kind of interesting. I mean, they obviously haven't killed us yet. So they are keeping us here for some reason."

"Yes, very interesting. Fascinating, really."

"You don't think so?"

"Alex, look, right now, I'm just tired and really angry, and we are majorly in trouble about Mr Shen. I mean,

301

we've got just over twelve hours here to help him. I've got other stuff to think about than why these pirates haven't killed us yet."

"Well, I think it is very important. Maybe we could short-circuit their plans if we figure out what they're thinking."

Timothy sighed and leaned his head back against the door.

Alex continued to talk. As she was wont to do.

"I mean, the last time this happened to me" – she said it as if she were talking about the last time she'd been to the dentist – "they wanted me to become a pirate with them. That could be a possibility. I think when pirates see kids, they see potential. They want a crew without any preconceived ideas on pirating. They want to teach them everything they know so the kids'll be more obedient than adult pirates."

"Yeah."

"Or maybe they want to ransom us. You know, offer up a deal to the *Ironic Gentleman* in exchange."

"Or maybe they want to use you as hostages. In case anyone tries to stop us getting Mr Shen to the Dragon's Gate," said a third voice.

In an instant Timothy and Alex were on their feet and staring at a previously unnoticed door on the far wall. Emily the ninja was standing smiling at them, still in her black, but with the mask removed. "Come on, Timothy. Our commander would like to meet you now."

"What about me?" Alex sounded offended.

Emily looked at Alex for a brief moment, then returned to Timothy. "Coming?"

It was a question, framed as such with an upward inflection and everything. But Timothy knew that he had no choice in the matter.

"No," he said, out of habit. But he crossed the room anyway and passed through the door.

THE FORTY-FIFTH CHAPTER

In which Timothy meets the Man
in the Beige Linen Suit

The Man in the Beige Linen Suit was known as the Man in the Beige Linen Suit for obvious reasons. He could have been known by his first name, really. His name was Edmund, which is a perfectly nice name and not worth covering up. But he himself had promoted the idea of being addressed by such a vague description because he thought it made him sound more mysterious. It also helped disassociate him from his rather famous father, and from a last name he had, over time, come to consider shameful.

His appearance was at once exactly as you would expect it to be and yet not at all. He was, as you would have guessed, dressed in a beige linen suit. Now, he had many of these suits, so it wasn't as if he just wore the same one over and over. He did have some concept of hygiene, after all. He also wore a white fedora. Because it went with the suit. And also because it was dashing.

But what was not always expected in his appearance was that he was a European. Well, it wasn't an entire surprise to Timothy, who had noticed Duchess Rose's description of him as a "foreigner". But had he not had this information, he might have been a little shocked when he came face to face with the man. As he was right now.

The Man in the Beige Linen Suit was also relatively young, maybe in his thirties, with dark hair and dark eyes, and a nice tan on his face and hands. He was sitting at a small desk and framed by a large window that looked out on to the bay. Emily seated Timothy in a chair opposite and quickly left the room. Not that they were entirely alone. A sour-looking man with a high forehead and long ponytail was standing guard at the door. Timothy felt a bit like he was in the headmaster's office about to get detention.

"What the devil are you doing here?" asked the Man in the Beige Linen Suit. He spoke English as if he had been speaking it his whole life. Which made sense, because he had.

Timothy didn't really know what to say. Though it was a pretty straightforward question, it was a surprising way to phrase it. "What?" he said as his usual last resort.

"What the devil are you doing here?" asked the Man in the Beige Linen Suit again.

"I'm sorry, I'm not quite sure I understand the question."

The Man in the Beige Linen Suit crossed one leg over the other and shook his head at Timothy. "Then we are at an impasse."

"I guess."

The two sat silently watching each other closely.

Timothy could sense the man in the ponytail start to fidget slightly. He didn't blame him. It was a fidgety situation.

The Man in the Beige Linen Suit gave in first. "I suppose what I meant was, what the devil are you doing here, considering you've given us the key and no longer bear any responsibility for the dragon?"

"Oh!" said Timothy, knowing full well that that was what he had meant all along. "Now I see." He stopped and pretended to think about it for a moment. "None of your business."

The Man in the Beige Linen Suit stood abruptly, turned to face the window and slammed his hand against it.

"Yup, I would find me frustrating too. Can I go back to the cabin now?"

He watched the Man in the Beige Linen Suit bow his head slightly. Timothy thought maybe he was sighing in frustration, but then he noticed the man's shoulders start to shake and realized he was laughing instead.

"Oh, Timothy, you're exactly as they described you." He turned around with a smile. "How pathetic."

"See, that I resent."

"I don't really care." The Man in the Beige Linen Suit

walked over to Timothy and, placing one hand on either armrest of his chair, leaned down close to his face. "You pathetic, petulant child. You want to pretend you're tough? You want to point out all the bad things you've done in your life? Well, go on then. What have you got? A few pranks at school? Well, bravo. Good for you. Running away from home? Gosh, how unique. So what is it, Timothy? What makes you so tough?"

Timothy was so close to the man's face that it had started to distort somewhat in his vision. It also looked oddly familiar.

"I'm here now, aren't I?"

"That makes you tough?" The Man in the Beige Linen Suit let out a humourless laugh. "That only shows how stupid you are. Try again."

"My parents hate me." Timothy expected the Man in the Beige Linen Suit to have a field day with that one. He knew it sounded stupid, but it was all he could manage.

Instead, though, the man stood upright and nodded slowly. "That's not easy, actually. Getting your parents to hate you. Parents are notoriously stubborn with the whole loving thing."

"Yeah." Timothy felt a tight knot in his stomach. It was pretty easy to notice, seeing as it was the only thing in there, the contents of his stomach having been left in an alley back in Kaomai.

"What are you going to do about it?"

"About what?" For a moment Timothy thought the man was referring to the knot.

"The fact that your parents hate you."

"The usual. Move out when I'm sixteen." It suddenly occurred to Timothy he was being rather forthcoming with answers. Why was he feeling so determined to prove himself to this man?

"I did that. Didn't solve anything. Try again."

Timothy finally felt his familiar indignant rage. It was like an old friend, and he indulged it warmly. Standing up he said, "No, I won't try again! Lock me up or whatever, but I'm getting really tired of this bonding exercise."

The Man in the Beige Linen Suit continued unperturbed. "Moving out solves some problems, but you'll learn, you'll see. They never really leave you alone. Even when they claim they'll leave you alone, like it's a threat, they do everything in their power to remind you that they are ignoring you. It becomes incredibly bothersome."

Timothy crossed his arms in front of his chest and shook his head.

"And then they become a problem."

At this the Man in the Beige Linen Suit sat back down. He was deep into his own thoughts, and Timothy wondered if he even remembered he was still in the room. Then he made eye contact with Timothy.

"This has all been a bit of an accident for you, hasn't it?"

Timothy refused to acknowledge the question.

"I feel for you, Timothy. A pawn in some old man's

scheme, suddenly given a lot of responsibility for something you never wanted. I dare say you became even a little emotionally involved. Still, I was impressed you gave Emily the key in the end. Shows you have some sense."

"Do you have it now?"

The Man in the Beige Linen Suit casually removed the key from around his neck and looked at it. "It's taken far too much effort to secure it. That dragon was impossible to deal with up until last night. Now we're down to the wire, the Lantern Festival is upon us. I just hate it when things get to the last minute."

The knot in Timothy's stomach moved up into his throat.

"Yeah, too bad I didn't just give the key to Sir Bazalgette. All this could have been avoided," said Timothy. He wanted the phrase to sound sarcastic, but because he kind of believed it, it didn't.

"I just love how that man's death has had relatively little impact on you. Shows you come from good stock."

"Death?"

"You didn't know?"

"I just ran away. I didn't stay to see what would happen. I'm not stupid. What, you mean Emily killed him to get the key?"

"Of course she did."

Timothy uncrossed his arms and shoved his hands in his pockets, clenching his fists tightly as he did so. Slowly, with much effort to avoid throwing up again, he said, "So you just killed some innocent old man for no reason."

The Man in the Beige Linen Suit started to laugh again. He laughed so loud, long and hard, it started to sound slightly manic. "'Innocent'? Oh Timothy, you didn't know Sir Bazalgette at all, did you?"

"I knew he was trying to save Mr Shen, I knew that! You must have hated that!"

"Oh yes, that was his plan, to save Mr Shen. You are so naïve, Timothy." The man stopped laughing and looked at Timothy with a shake of his head. "Sir Bazalgette never had any intention of freeing the dragon. All he's ever wanted is to pillage the world for the great hidden treasures of the ages. He was very resentful when the government made him return all those artefacts he had so carefully accumulated over the decades. He wanted to reclaim them, as a matter of pride, and then . . . well, then to sell them off to the highest bidder. Why do you think that Evans Bore character took the key in the first place? Even he, a fool and a coward, could see what Sir Bazalgette was like right from the beginning!"

It was Timothy's turn to laugh this time. "And you know all this how, exactly? Give me a break. You are just trying to manipulate me. How on earth could you have possibly managed to collect that information?"

"You are very wise to question me. In fact, the question itself is a great one. But, trust me, if there is one person I understand, it's Sir Bazalgette."

The answer didn't make any sense. And then suddenly

it did. Timothy actually found himself taking a spontaneous step backwards.

"Clever boy," said the Man in the Beige Linen Suit, noticing the move.

It was odd. Considering he had been pursued by deadly black cabs, pushed out of a plane, and threatened at sword point, Timothy hadn't really taken actual stock of how much danger he was in until that very moment. But now, now he was just simply terrified. He couldn't even phrase the conclusion he had drawn into any sort of articulate speech.

Fortunately the Man in the Beige Linen Suit was more than happy to do it for him. "Yes. Sir Bazalgette was my father."

THE FORTY-SIXTH CHAPTER

In which Timothy learns the truth about Edmund's father

"You killed your father."

"Had him killed; there is a difference." Edmund Bazalgette appeared to be quite enjoying the exchange. "Oh, don't worry about it. He wasn't a very nice man, you must have seen it. Why else did you refuse to give him the key?"

Timothy could not answer. He could hardly speak. Thoughts simply refused to form themselves into speech.

"My father disowned me the second I showed myself capable of independent thought. He didn't like my friends, and he certainly didn't like that I showed far more talent for treasure hunting than he did. Some of my most prized finds he still has hidden somewhere in his basement. I'm sure he even claims them as his. At first, of course, he was thrilled I was interested in archaeology, seeing as he introduced me to the subject. As a child I would spend hours in the museum with him, and family holidays would be for collecting new artefacts. Oh, how Mother resented those trips! But once I started getting good at unearthing treasures and began earning real money at the thing, even more than he . . . well. . .

"Of course, Mr Shen had always been a part of my life. My father had known of his existence since before I was born and had forged that false friendship immediately. I had been in on the plan literally from Day One. I cannot think of a time I didn't know of the dragon's history and how, when the time came, he and I would become the richest and most famous treasure hunters in the world. We even considered going after the elusive Wigpowder treasure."

If Timothy could have spoken, he would have relished sharing the news that the treasure had already been unearthed and that Edmund Bazalgette was too late. But he was still speechless.

"But as I grew older, as my talents increased, so too did his resentment, and yet, it would have been tolerable had Mother not died. She was the only person who could set us right, end the fights. My father blamed me for her death, saying that I caused her so much stress that she died of a broken heart. He became utterly unreasonable, and one evening when I was seventeen, I returned home to find the locks changed and my suitcase on the porch. It was a remarkable act of civility, really, his packing up my few things, but it was his last act of compassion. I left. And I never came back.

"I travelled the world, and I felt myself rather at home in the city of Kaomai. The pirate thing was something I fell into almost by accident. It was something at which I proved adept, and I enjoyed the freedom. But it wasn't until I decided to follow through with my father's plan for Mr Shen that I grew to any sort of position in the fleet. Of course, the trickiest thing was getting that key. Sure, I could have had Bore killed, but he is so prominent in the business world that there would have been some sort of investigation, and I just didn't want to bother with that. Then, of course, there was my father, who I knew would be trying to get the key himself. My father, the recluse. The one the world had all but forgotten even existed. They would notice he was dead. But not for a long time.

"I had to be patient. And as the time passed, I finally sent Emily to track his progress. And then, of course, you got involved. And made things much more complicated."

"I'm glad." It came out as a hoarse whisper, but Timothy was happy he had found his voice at last.

"What was that?"

"I'm glad." He spoke it with more confidence this time.

Edmund smiled. "Yes, I imagine you are."

"And it isn't over yet, you know."

"What was that?"

"It isn't over yet. Mr Shen isn't a dragon and the Lantern Festival hasn't ended. I could still make things complicated for you."

"Oh?"

"I managed to convince Bore to give the key to me. I could do the same with you."

Edmund started to laugh again. "If you think I am as easy to con as that fool, well, I am rather disappointed in your intelligence, Timothy." He leaned across his desk and gave him a hard stare. "Because there is nothing, nothing that will convince me to part with it. There is nothing I hold so dear, nothing that I prize above it, no one I wouldn't sacrifice. I've already killed my own father for it. In fact," he laughed even harder at his thought, "in fact, the day I give you the key is the day I meet my father again. The day I am dead and buried. Because the only way you are getting it is if you kill me for it. You will have to prise it from my cold, dead fingers." Edmund smiled broadly. "So what do you say? You going to try to kill me, then?"

Timothy just stood there. He knew, Edmund knew, that there wasn't even the remotest of possibilities that Timothy would try to kill him, kill anyone. There was no point faking it.

Timothy wasn't sure exactly what he was doing any more, in front of the Man in the Beige Linen Suit – heck, on this ship – in the first place. Rescuing Mr Shen was not even a thought. He could not actively imagine it, and when he tried, he had a funny feeling his brain was laughing at him. It was oddly at this moment that he thought back to the memory of being a little kid in a hospital bed, his mother and father at his side. Taking care of him. No. He shook the thought out of his head. Even if they could have been here now to help him, they wouldn't have done anything. They hated him. He was on his own.

He stared up at Edmund Bazalgette, who was still grinning at him.

"What the heck am I doing here?"

THE FORTY-SEVENTH CHAPTER

In which we set sail for Kaomai. Again.
This time with the pirates

T imothy was not sitting with Alex. For whatever reason, Emily had brought him back to a different cabin. If he had thought about it, he might have reasoned that Emily probably didn't want them to come up with any plans, however futile they might be. But he didn't much care at the moment.

Big boat, was all he thought instead.

And it was indeed. Once used to transport ambassadors to the far side of the world, the *Zhulong* was a rather impressive ship. Of course, it hadn't been known as the *Zhulong* at that time. At that time it had been called the *Silver Seahorse*, but of course Duchess Rose's father had changed the name to suit the dragon theme he had chosen for his pirate fleet. Zhulong was the dragon that blessed the lakes. It made sense.

Time passed slowly and was hard to gauge in the

windowless cabin. But it was several hours into Timothy's solitary confinement that he sensed the ship begin to move. The simple sensation of speed sent a jolt into Timothy's gut, and he sat upright. Moving meant only one thing. The Fleet of the Nine Dragons was on its way to bring Mr Shen to the Dragon's Gate. Timothy reminded himself there was nothing he could do about it, but the thought didn't seem to help. He felt anxious, out of control, and he stood up and began to pace the small cabin. As he did, he wondered where they were keeping Mr Shen, if he was OK. He got angry at the idea that they might have mistreated him and even angrier that they wanted to keep him as a slave for ever. Didn't they realize that "for ever" meant for ever to a dragon? That Mr Shen would be a slave long after all the pirates had passed on?

They probably didn't care.

Timothy turned to the door of his cabin. He was feeling a rush of adrenaline, which probably explained why he threw himself at it shoulder first. He fell back on to the floor, his shoulder and arm in a lot of pain. Then a cannonball flew past his head.

Timothy sat perfectly still, just in case another cannonball was to follow the first. When it seemed as if it wouldn't, he turned to the wreckage and the hole in the wall of his cabin and peered through it. His first thought was relief at smelling the fresh air, and his second thought was concern. Half a dozen ships of the fleet had made their way out to sea and were fast approaching the Kaomai harbour. He could see three of the smaller ships ahead. They apparently had no cannons and were returning fire with guns. The guns had a limited range and were not coming anywhere close to their target.

Which was the *Ironic Gentleman*.

On the one hand, it was thrilling to see the *Ironic Gentleman* in the distance and to watch it come to the rescue. On the other, it was firing cannonballs at Timothy's head. Timothy wasn't sure that was such a good tactic.

Obviously neither did the crew of the *Zhulong*, because just as he thought that, one of the Shaolin monks burst into his cabin, picked up Timothy, threw him over his shoulder, and carried him out on to the deck. It happened so ridiculously quickly, as most things with the Shaolin monks seemed to happen, that Timothy didn't even get a chance to explain that he would have been more than willing to follow the monk, had he simply told him where they were going, when he was dropped down next to Alex right at the bow of the ship.

Edmund Bazalgette was standing at the prow, staring out at the *Ironic Gentleman* through a long telescope, and when Timothy arrived, he ordered both Timothy and Alex to be brought up next to him. Meanwhile, just off to the side, Emily was waving a giant flag. It wasn't an act of surrender. The flag was red.

"I think they're trying to get the *Ironic Gentleman*'s attention," whispered Alex.

"To let them know we're on board so they stop shooting at us?"

"Exactly." Alex leaned closer to him. "You OK?"

"Fine."

"I . . . uh . . . I could hear the whole meeting through the wall . . . I thought you handled yourself very well."

"Whatever."

"I think they've stopped, sir!" announced Emily, putting the flag down and joining Edmund. Edmund nodded and pointed, collapsing the scope and placing it on the deck.

Passing to their port side was another of the larger junks, one that did have cannons. She was making great speed and heading right for the *Ironic Gentleman*.

"The *Yinglong* will have no problem with her."

The three smaller ships had gathered around the *Ironic Gentleman*'s stern, and the larger ship, the *Yinglong*, made to broadside.

There was a loud explosion as the *Yinglong* fired. And then another loud explosion from the opposite direction as a cannonball flew over the *Zhulong* and struck the mizzenmast of the *Yinglong*. The mast shattered and scattered large splinters across the deck as it collapsed into the rigging.

"Where on earth did that come from?" Edmund spun around and looked towards land. They were still a good few leagues from Kaomai.

"The fort!" Alex pointed up the hill that she and Timothy had just recently climbed. There were figures moving around the old fort and several bodies manning the long cannons that ran along the outer wall facing the sea. Timothy could not believe that the old guns were still in working order.

"Your orders, sir!" Emily stood rigid in front of Edmund in expectation.

"Orders are. . ." Another cannonball whistled over their heads, this time landing in the water, mere centimetres from its target. "Orders are – proceed to Kaomai," said Edmund.

Emily didn't move.

"Well?"

"Well, sir," she said slowly, "it's just that, well, we could probably shield the *Yinglong*. After all, no one is willing to attack us with the children on board."

Edmund took a step towards Emily. She kept her position, but took a quick inhalation of breath at his approach. "Time check," he said softly.

"Nine hours and forty-seven minutes," she replied instantly.

Edmund raised his eyebrows at her. "We proceed to Kaomai." He spoke each word as if it were its own sentence. Emily bowed her head, turned, and made towards the stern of the ship.

Edmund snapped his fingers. The man with the ponytail stepped forward. "Send word back to the bay, to the rest of the fleet, that we are going to need their assistance, and tell them we need the *Panlong* here, and pronto. Apprise them of the . . . situation."

It was the man with the ponytail's turn to nod and he disappeared belowdecks.

Edmund turned to Timothy and Alex. "Your friends won't stand much of a chance once the rest of the fleet gets here."

It was probably true, but Timothy had to wonder what would happen to the few ships that were presently under attack. Not that he was terribly concerned for their well-being. He was, of course, rooting for the *Ironic Gentleman*. But deserting one of his own ships still seemed like something that the commander of a pirate fleet might, at the very least, wish to reconsider. Couldn't really be good for morale.

When neither Timothy nor Alex responded to the comment, the Man in the Beige Linen Suit adjusted his hat roughly on his head and left them in an angry huff. Alex and Timothy suddenly found themselves alone, and with what appeared to be at least some freedom, at least compared to their earlier confinement.

Timothy looked over at Alex and could see she was doing her thinking thing again. Then he watched as she reached for Edmund's discarded telescope and peered through it.

"The *Ironic Gentleman* looks OK still. A bit banged up. . . Timothy!" She turned and looked at him with a smile.

"What?"

"It's Mr Underwood! He's captaining the *Ironic Gentleman*."

"Good for him."

Alex shook her head at Timothy and turned to look through the scope one last time.

Timothy sighed. He hadn't meant to be mean like that. "Yeah, OK, it's cool that he's come to help us," he said, trying to explain himself. "But we can't do much about that from here now, can we? Look, can we go look for Mr Shen now maybe instead?"

Alex collapsed the scope and put it on the deck. "Do you think that's a good idea?"

Timothy shrugged. "What can they do to us? Like you said, they need us."

Alex nodded. "You're right. Let's go look!"

There was only one entrance down into the bowels of the ship, and the two of them made their way over to it and down the stairs. It was a maze belowdecks, narrow halls and cabins that led on to other cabins. They were given strange looks as they passed. Timothy imagined they must be an odd sight, two kids wandering about as if they owned the place. He felt an enjoyably reckless feeling. Timothy could tell Alex was experiencing it too, especially after she waved happily at an extremely large man who seemed entirely made up of folds of flesh. The look he gave her as she passed made Timothy grab her by the arm and quickly speed up their progress.

They checked out half a dozen cabins before they came upon Mr Shen. When they did, Timothy almost couldn't believe it. He hadn't thought that Mr Shen would be so easily accessible in an open room. *Then again*, reasoned Timothy, *why not?* There was nothing Mr Shen could possibly do to escape. He was now Edmund Bazalgette's servant.

It had been weeks since Timothy had seen Mr Shen. And when they made eye contact, for a brief instant, Timothy couldn't help but feel happy, despite their current circumstances. The dragon, though, looked at him sadly, and Timothy's appearance seemed to upset him even more.

"Mr Shen!" Timothy ran over to the dragon, who had lowered his gaze. Mr Shen said nothing.

"Mr Shen," tried Timothy again, "I'm so sorry for everything. It didn't have anything to do with you. I should never have given up that key. I was just so scared, and everything seemed so hopeless . . . I'm so sorry. It was awful of me!" Timothy was starting to feel desperate, as the dragon was still not acknowledging his presence.

"Timothy, don't get all mad at yourself," said Alex. "You're here now, aren't you? That has to count for something."

Timothy appreciated the sentiment, but it didn't make him feel any less guilty.

"I'm a bad friend," he said instead.

He sat down in front of Mr Shen, trying to force the dragon to look at him once more. "Mr Shen, this is Alex." He pointed over at her and she gave a small smile. "And together we are going to help you. To save you. I . . . don't exactly know how yet. But Alex is pretty smart too, and I know we can do this."

He stopped talking because he didn't believe it himself. He was starting to feel that tired sense of hopelessness again. His whole body felt heavy as lead.

"I'm sorry," he said for a third time. Then he smiled weakly and added, "Hey, thanks for saving me when I was pushed out the plane. Finally the air-currents thing worked properly, huh?"

But there was still no response, and Timothy was too tired and despondent to keep trying. So he stopped talking and just sat there. Alex joined him, and the three of them sat quietly waiting for something, anything, and in this way the hours passed in silent hopelessness.

THE FORTY-EIGHTH CHAPTER

In which we seek out the Dragon's Gate and Alex does something impressive

They arrived in Kaomai hours later. Timothy, Alex and Mr Shen had been found and brought up on deck by the two Shaolin monks. Timothy noticed that other boats were giving the *Zhulong* the same sort of wide berth as the *Ironic Gentleman* had been given upon its arrival. He also noticed around a dozen medium-sized junks with pink sails making their way out to sea in a regimented line.

Emily had seen them as well.

"Five hours and fourteen minutes," was how she greeted Edmund as she continued to watch the junks sail by.

"What does Duchess Rose have to do with any of this!" Edmund slammed his fist on the deck rail and glared out at the passing junks. "What's she up to?"

"I have no idea. But it is unlikely she's on our side," replied Emily.

"What's going on?" asked Alex.

Edmund turned to her and gave her a dirty look. Still, he explained the situation to her. "Those ships belong to Duchess Rose. She may have given up pirating, but she never gave up her love of the sea. I think she's heading out right now to help your friends. And I haven't the slightest idea why."

"It's probably because she likes Timothy," replied Alex simply.

Edmund turned and fixed his dirty look on Timothy. It really didn't impress, annoy or frighten him. It was just an expression on a man's face. Timothy gave a slight shrug, indicating that what Alex had said was probably true. *Odd, really*, he thought. *Not that many people like me. How fortunate, though, that one of the few people who do is also one of the most powerful people in Kaomai.*

The shrug seemed to call Edmund into action, and there was a flurry of activity. Suddenly Timothy found himself heading to shore with Alex, Mr Shen, the two Shaolin monks, Emily and, of course, Edmund. It reminded Timothy very much of the night before, as the sun had begun to set, and they landed their longboat very near the same spot as the crew from the *Ironic Gentleman* had.

When they had all climbed on to the dock, Edmund turned to Mr Shen and said, "Take us to the Dragon's Gate." He took hold of Timothy by the arm, and Timothy watched Emily do the same with Alex.

Mr Shen nodded and started to lead them away from the water.

Timothy had wondered when the issue of the location of the Dragon's Gate was going to come up. He thought that maybe they would have to locate another map or something. He hadn't really considered that Mr Shen might just quite simply know the location himself. He also hadn't realized the Gate could have been in Kaomai itself. While this made things easier for the pirates, it also made them more difficult for Timothy, who had hoped that maybe in the time it took to find the Dragon's Gate, he could come up with some plan. Making a beeline for it, though – that wasn't going to be that helpful to him.

They were going at quite a pace despite the fact that the streets were now packed with revellers singing and dancing and enjoying the end of the New Year's celebration. The restaurants and shops that they passed were full of people, with long queues out through the doors. And colourful lanterns lit their way as brightly as sunlight. Occasionally they would pass large lit displays, mostly of dragons. They only served to cause the knot in Timothy's stomach to tighten even more.

Their group continued to weave their way past all these sights, Edmund seeming to take no notice of them, until suddenly Emily and the two Shaolin froze. This caused the rest of them to walk on a pace before they noticed that the others had been left behind.

"What's going on?" asked Edmund.

Emily raised her hand and stood for another instant, listening.

"Now!" she called out just as seven attackers in black dived down upon the ninja and Shaolin monks, almost as if they had dropped from out of the sky. They were obviously very skilled as they began their assault, but Emily and her monks were better. It was very difficult to see what exactly was going on. Only the Shaolin monks made any sort of impression, as they were still dressed in their bright orange. And even they came across as bright orange blurs and nothing more. A moment later the action stopped. Three bodies lay on the ground in front of Emily and the monks as the rest of the attackers scattered.

"After them," she ordered. And the monks disappeared into the darkness.

Emily approached Edmund and grabbed Alex's arm once more. "Let's go. And quickly."

As they started walking again, Timothy noticed Alex was looking at Emily with an unreadable expression. He was pretty sure she had come up with some kind of plan. He only wished he knew what it was.

They were practically running through the streets now, Mr Shen having taken the order to speed up very literally. Timothy could feel himself start to panic. In no time at all they would arrive at the Dragon's Gate. He still didn't have any kind of strategy. He was starting to feel desperate.

Why could he never come up with plans?

Plan making, Timothy had learned, was second nature

to Alex, however, and he could sense she was about to put one of her own into action. It proved to be a slightly incomplete plan, but it was obvious she had definitely decided to take matters into her own hands.

Timothy saw everything perfectly. Alex and Emily were ahead of him, and Edmund and Timothy practically fell over Alex when she suddenly decided to stop still. Timothy managed to weave his way around her and as he turned to watch what she was doing, so too did Edmund.

By stopping in her tracks, Alex also surprised Emily, causing her to lose her footing slightly. That's when Alex did a kind of spin under Emily's arm, managing both to break Emily's grasp on her and to unsheathe the small sword Emily wore at her hip.

Both Timothy and Edmund were taken slightly aback by the action. Timothy was aware that Alex was indeed an impressive swordswoman ... -girl ... -person. Whatever. But the fact that she thought she could take on a ninja, well, it was remarkable, and also slightly foolish of her. At least, in Timothy's opinion.

At first Alex seemed confused by the sword in her hand. It was, after all, a completely different kind of blade than she was used to. She was also probably thinking something similar to what Timothy was thinking and seemed to be rather surprised with herself that she had decided to take on a ninja in one-on-one combat. After all, seven skilled attackers hadn't been able to fell the ninja, so what hope was there for her?

The two were standing some distance apart, staring at

each other. Alex adjusted her grip on the sword and moved it through the air a few times. Then Emily glanced at Edmund, who gave her a wave of permission, and out of nowhere, two sharp pieces of metal shaped like stars were sent soaring towards Alex.

Alex sent them flying off in separate directions with the blade of her sword.

"Cool," said Timothy.

Alex appeared impressed with what she had just done, but took no pause to give herself kudos. Instead she took the moment of Emily's confusion to make an attack at the ninja's right arm. She sliced through the air towards it, and Emily produced a black fan from somewhere on her person, parrying the sword easily. Alex found herself making a full circle and facing Emily once more.

"You have a lot of stuff," she said.

The fan vanished back to wherever it had come from, and Emily reached behind her back and grabbed her longer sword, the same weapon she had used to threaten Timothy the night before.

Timothy watched as Alex clenched her jaw and prepared herself for an attack. Emily was brutally quick in her movements, and it was difficult to follow the action. Alex appeared to be on the defensive, parrying attacks and ducking out of the way. She seemed to bring her blade to Emily's only just in time on each swipe, and Timothy was starting to get very nervous for her. He could hear her breathing hard, and the look in her eyes was focused but frightened.

He desperately wanted to run in and help her and had just made up his mind to do so, however foolish an action it might have been, when suddenly Emily was on her knees, her sword fallen at her side. In an instant, Alex picked it up and held it at the ninja's throat.

It took a moment for Timothy to register what had just happened. He had seen Emily attack Alex's head, and Alex defend it by holding her sword above her. He had seen Emily's sword glance off Alex's, sliding down it, but he hadn't seen what had caused Emily to fall to her knees.

He simply had to ask.

"There's a bundle of nerves on the upper leg," replied Alex. "Basically puts the whole leg to sleep if you hit it. Mr Underwood taught me that. He thought that because I was so little, it might be useful to know. I took the pommel of my sword, this bit," she tapped the bottom of the sword's handle, "and just hit that part of her leg really hard. And it worked!"

"Yeah, it worked."

It should have been a moment of celebration, and Timothy was really impressed with what Alex had just done. But he also suddenly felt concerned when he noticed that there was something cold pressed against his temple.

"Put the sword down, or he dies."

Ah, the end of a gun, reasoned Timothy, though he dared not turn his head.

Instantly Alex removed the sword from Emily's throat

and let it and the other sword fall to the ground, but the ninja was still out of commission and so didn't move.

"I'm not sure what you were hoping to accomplish with all that, but I have to say it was entirely pointless. The fact is, you are both entirely pointless to me now. We're almost at the Dragon's Gate. I don't need you any more."

Timothy felt the cold metal pull away from his head, and he saw Alex's eyes open wide. He turned and looked at Edmund and saw the gun now pointed right at Alex. She looked so small, standing in the middle of the street standing next to a fallen ninja and two swords that seemed too big for her.

Timothy wanted to reach up to Edmund's arm, to knock the gun out of his hand, but he was held fast in his grip. All he could do was struggle. But his range of movement was seriously limited. He could barely even kick at Edmund's shins. In desperation he bit Edmund's arm. He tried stamping on the man's feet.

But nothing worked, and he watched helplessly as the shot rang out into the air. He watched as Alex closed her eyes and turned her head away. He stopped breathing as he saw her fall down to the ground.

And he almost collapsed in relief when he saw the bullet strike the wooden front of a small novelty shop far to Alex's right.

THE FORTY-NINTH CHAPTER

In which we encounter a ghost from the past

Timothy was confused. He was also very relieved. But confusion was uppermost for a moment. How had Edmund missed his mark so completely? And why had Edmund suddenly released him?

Timothy realized that he didn't much care about the answers. He ran over to Alex, who was still on the ground, staring in the direction the bullet had taken.

"Are you OK?"

Alex nodded, but she was shaking all over. "Just sort of collapsed. I think I almost fainted." She seemed to find that more shocking than being shot at. Then she said very quietly, "Who's that?"

As he so often did, Timothy followed Alex's gaze. It was his turn to feel faint.

It wasn't the act of following the gaze that made him feel that way, but rather the person he saw, and it became very clear what had distracted Edmund from his mark. Timothy quickly turned to look at him and found Edmund leaning against a wall, the only thing keeping him upright.

"You!" Edmund pointed out ahead of him.

"That's. . ." Timothy stammered. "That's . . . Sir Bazalgette. Or at least . . . I mean . . . well. . ."

"His ghost." Alex finished the thought. And the way she said it made it sound even probable. Though that might have just been her tone of voice. Alex tended to make most things sound probable.

Sir Bazalgette was standing stopped in the middle of the street a few buildings down from them. He was wearing a long dark coat, and his face was gaunt and pale. He offered his son a blank expression with his one good eye. Horribly, his patch was missing from the other, revealing a dark hollow covered in scarred skin.

"But . . . but you're dead!" Edmund squeezed the words out through panicked breath.

Sir Bazalgette nodded slowly at him.

Edmund shook his head violently, as if trying to shake the image of his father from inside his mind. "It's too late!" he yelled when the shaking proved futile. "I have your dragon! I have the key! There's nothing you can do about it!"

Mr Shen waved sadly at the ghost of Sir Bazalgette.

The ghost of Sir Bazalgette chose to ignore the action.

"I win!" Edmund's voice was rising in pitch and starting to sound slightly hysterical. "Do you see that,

Father! I win! You're dead, I'm alive, I get the dragon . . . I . . ." He stopped speaking and fell to his knees. He held his face with his hands. After a few moments, he looked up again. "Why don't you leave me alone! You could never just leave me alone! All those messages. How did you always track me down? I had to go to the far side of the earth to escape you! Why would I have come home after you kicked me out! Why would I have done anything for you? You tried to say you are sorry but you aren't sorry. You needed me, but . . . you never cared about me."

"I did." Sir Bazalgette's voice was soft but clear.

Edmund pointed at Sir Bazalgette again. "You needed my help. You could never do it alone. And you didn't do it alone. You failed. But I did it, didn't I, Father? I did it!"

Sir Bazalgette just stared back at his son. He didn't say a word.

"And you're not remotely impressed, are you?" As Edmund spoke, Sir Bazalgette's form was obscured by two large men moving between father and son. When they had passed, the ghost was gone.

Timothy, Alex, Emily and Mr Shen stared at Edmund sobbing into his hands.

"I don't think I like ghosts much," said Alex.

"I don't think Edmund does either," replied Timothy. "And, I mean, meeting your dead father, the one you had murdered . . . well, that's got to be the worst kind of ghost." Timothy laughed slightly at the joke. And then stopped when he had a very surprising thought.

"Timothy?"

Timothy seemed to forget all about Alex. Instead he turned and made his way over to the prostrate Edmund, picking up the larger sword from the ground as he did so. He placed the tip of the blade at Edmund's throat.

"Timothy, what are you doing! Don't! You can't!" She covered her eyes.

He made one quick movement with the sword, and then marched back towards Alex, Edmund's head still firmly in place and still sobbing.

"You can open your eyes now," he said with a smile. He watched as Alex tentatively removed her hands from her face. She gave a gasp when she looked at him.

Timothy had extended the sword directly under her nose. And dangling at its tip was the key on its chain.

"You have the key?" She spoke the words in awe.

"I don't know, let's see." Timothy brought the sword to his side and reached for the golden key. Despite his earlier insight, Timothy couldn't help but expect his fingers to pass through it, as he had seen happen to others many times before. But they didn't. He grabbed it firmly in the palm of his hand, and his fingers encircled it nicely. He drew the chain along and off the end of the blade. Without hesitation, he put it around his neck. It felt familiar and comfortable.

"What happened? How did you do that?" asked Alex. She was wide-eyed.

"I dunno, I just had this thought. He'd said he would give me the key when he met his father again. Obviously he meant that I would have to kill him to get it – or that he would have to be dead. I don't think he ever expected that he'd actually meet his father again, in this life, or . . . whatever. But he did. And I just thought that since he had actually promised me the key, you know, said the words, that now that he'd met his father again, I could take it from him."

"And you could!"

"And I could."

"Timothy, you're a genius!"

"I know." He smiled at Alex, who was grinning at him like crazy. Then he turned to Mr Shen.

"OK, Mr Shen. Let's get this over with!"

For the first time since they had been reunited, Timothy saw the dragon smile. Mr Shen came bounding up to him like a puppy and gave Timothy a big hug. After having been so ignored, Timothy was quite overwhelmed by the action.

"I knew you could do it, Timothy. I just knew it. And I know you would never have given me up on purpose. You came all the way to China for me! That is amazing! And I am sorry about earlier. I had been ordered not to talk to you, even look at you. It made me very sad to obey." The words came pouring out of the dragon, one on top of the other.

"Yes, well, good." Timothy smiled slightly, though inside he was filled with joy. "Anyway, look, we should probably get to the Dragon's Gate soon. . . Time?" he called out.

Emily's reply was automatic. "Three hours and fifty-seven minutes."

"See? So come on . . . I know it's nearby. Take us to it," commanded Timothy with a grin.

"Of course!"

Mr Shen led them away from Edmund and Emily, who were both sitting in their respective heaps, and both temporarily paralysed – one by a little girl's quick aim, the other from the horror of seeing his dead father's ghost.

They followed Mr Shen down the street. They made a few twists and turns through some narrow alleys until they found themselves in a large square lit by several hundred lanterns. There were people everywhere, and some musicians were setting up in the middle.

"We're here!" called out Mr Shen happily.

"Where is it?" Timothy had expected the gate to be fairly well hidden. It was ancient, after all, probably no more than a ruin. He was surprised that it would be found in a public square. "There!" Mr Shen pointed.

Or that their long-sought goal could just have a really big sign indicating its location.

Towering in front of them was a large black building built like a fortress. And flashing on and off in bright pink neon over the only entrance, and conveniently spelled out in both Mandarin and English, were the words: "The Dragon's Gate".

THE FIFTIETH CHAPTER

In which Timothy finds himself in
a very familiar situation

The Dragon's Gate was a very modern-looking building. It was also one of the most popular dance clubs in all of Kaomai, and thus its appearance was meant to impress upon the casual observer that there was absolutely no way anyone would be cool enough to even be in its presence, let alone enter it. It was a giant black box with a single door at its front, guarded by two very burly bouncers. Only in Kaomai could a club of such size have just one entrance/exit and no windows. No other city on earth would have allowed any organization to so callously flout fire safety regulations.

After taking a moment to stare at it, the trio made their way to the club. There was a long queue of revellers of all ages waiting to be let in, but Timothy didn't take much heed of them, and simply bypassed them all.

There was much vocal opposition to this action, but the three of them did not particularly care.

"Name." The large muscular bouncer said it in English.

"No, we're not on the list, but we really have to get inside," replied Alex.

"Can't come in unless you're on the list."

"Look, this is really important. We'll be quick, in and out," said Timothy.

The bouncer shook his head. "Do you know how many people have tried to get in tonight? Even if you are telling the truth, I just can't let you in. The Dragon's Gate is hosting a very exclusive party in honour of the Lantern Festival tonight."

"So what?"

"Well, the only way to make something exclusive is to make sure that the only people let in are on the list!" The bouncer paused for a second. Then he said quietly, "I'll tell you what, you come back at one a.m., when the party is going strong, and no one will notice a few extra people, I'll let you in."

"One a.m. is too late!"

"That's all I can do." The bouncer went back to examining his clipboard.

Timothy felt a sudden rush of wind as Alex rushed past him, grabbed the bouncer's clipboard, and threw it on the ground. "Don't just ignore us like this! Do you have any idea what we've been through? Do you?!"

The bouncer bent down to pick up the clipboard.

"Alex." Timothy grabbed her arm.

"This is too much!" She turned to him, shaking him off. "You can't tell me that after all we've been through, you're going to let this guy ruin everything!"

"Uh." Timothy turned around. The queue behind them was watching the scene with intense interest. This was a tiny bit embarrassing. Then again, she did have a point. Timothy's eyes shifted focus down the dark street beyond the club.

"Exclusive party. Who cares? So a bunch of people want to dance for a bit and feel special," continued Alex, returning to berate a very confused-looking bouncer.

Two bright lights appeared in Timothy's line of vision.

"I cannot let you in. You are not on the list. And you are not rich or famous." The bouncer stopped for a second. "Are you?"

"Yes, yes I am!" replied Alex instantly.

The bouncer appraised her carefully.

"I am a . . . movie star . . . one of those child actors."

"Alex."

"And he is my costar. And," she pointed at Mr Shen, "he's the director."

"Alex."

"Timothy, I'm a bit busy here."

"We have to leave." He grabbed her by the arm once more and dragged her away from the club's entrance.

They made their way quickly around the corner, and Timothy let her go.

"What are you doing?" she asked. "I almost had him convinced."

Timothy shook his head. "It isn't that. . ." He looked around. "Where's Mr Shen?"

"I think we left him behind in the queue."

Timothy swore quietly to himself.

"Whoa, Timothy, we can just go back and get him. No need to get all worked up about it."

Timothy held up his hand and slowly made his way back to the corner of the club. He peeked around and then brought his head back, placing himself flat against the wall.

"We're in trouble."

"What are you talking about?"

"OK, so remember what I told you about everything I'd been through before I met up with you guys."

"Yeah."

"Remember the black cabs?"

"Yeah, that was weird."

Timothy looked at her hard.

Alex returned the look.

"Alex!"

"What?"

"Did you know the black cabs were back?" asked Mr Shen, joining them and leaning on the wall next to Timothy.

"Mr Shen!" Timothy pulled the dragon around behind him and stared out once more towards the club. A black cab had pulled up in front of it and was inching along to their location, Mr Shen having conveniently led it to them.

"OK, everyone, so here's the plan. I think it makes the most sense to split up. I'll go on my own. Mr Shen, you stick with Alex. We aren't losing you again. As far as I know, there are three of these guys. They can show up anywhere, so watch your backs." The other two nodded at him. "We'll meet back at the club."

Without pause, the three of them turned on their heels and ran off down the road away from the club. Timothy took a right, and watched as Alex and Mr Shen took a left. He had faith they'd be able to take care of themselves, but he couldn't help but worry.

He ran down his street and made it to the rear of the club. He peeked around the corner and found himself staring into the bright spots of a set of headlights. The cab charged and roared past the entrance to the street. Timothy heard it screech to a halt and knew it would have to take a moment to turn around. And Timothy was going to take advantage of that moment. Quickly he darted out into the crossroads and plunged down the continuing street on the other side. There were more people down this one as everyone was starting to make their way to the square.

"Out of the way, out of the way!" Timothy muttered, using his arms to bat them aside. He hoped that, because of the crowd, the cab would choose not to follow him.

He thought wrong.

There was a scream from behind him, and he glanced over his shoulder as a mother with her child dived out of the way just in time as the cab barrelled past them. This event was followed by a general panic as the other pedestrians tried to get out of the way. Only Timothy continued in his forward trajectory. And then he wondered why he was doing that. So he took the next right, which happened to be a street market. There were stands of lanterns, clothes and small toy dragons. Calendars were hung in profusion, and there were food stalls as well, selling steaming meats and refreshing drinks. There were people everywhere.

Of course, the cab had no shame.

The wreckage was pretty horrible, though thankfully, it appeared no one got hurt. A small fire had broken out from one of the fallen lamps, but the woman managing the stall put it out quickly. The cab had hit like a tornado, and Timothy vowed that he was not turning down any more pedestrian streets if he could avoid it.

The cab, covered with a few dresses and one plastic dragon, followed him out on to the square that bordered the club. It screeched as it turned to follow Timothy down one of the larger streets. This time Timothy had to dodge the traffic coming at him, but thankfully, so did the cab, and this slowed down its progress somewhat. Timothy had finally managed to gain some sort of lead, when he noticed the second cab coming towards him. Taking stock of the situation took less than a moment. So, too, did running inside the souvenir shop to his right. He hoped that the cabs wouldn't crash into it. He hoped they had enough sense not to.

He heard them pull to a stop outside the shop, their

motors purring. Or they could just wait till he left. Timothy looked around and made his way through the shop.

"T-shirts half price!" said the shopowner as Timothy charged past. There had to be a back door. He pushed his way into the back room, found the door, and opened it. Only to be faced with the third cab. He slammed the door shut.

Think. Think.

"T-shirts half price," said the shopowner as Timothy returned from the back room. Timothy shook his head "no" again as he passed. Then he stopped, turned around and looked at the man. "And by no, I mean yes," he said quickly.

THE FIFTY-FIRST CHAPTER

In which we witness an unexpected reunion

Timothy opened the front door to the shop slowly, trying to look as casual as possible. He kept his head low, hoping he was doing an effective job at hiding his face under the brim of his wide novelty hat. The T-shirt he had purchased was a little big for him and had a ridiculous cartoon of a dragon giving a thumbs up on it. His jacket, which he had turned inside out, was now tight on him.

He walked past the two cabs. It was stressful being so close to them and walking so slowly. But he had to pretend he was just another resident of Kaomai, all dressed up for the night's events.

He made it past the cabs and back into the square. He quickly turned down one of the narrow streets again and picked up his pace. He noticed a pair of familiar forms approaching him.

"Alex, Mr Shen!" he called out to them.

"Timothy, is that you?" Alex picked up her speed and approached him. "Why are you wearing all that?"

"Well, I thought I wasn't getting into the spirit of the evening like I should, so I picked up a few things . . . I'm in disguise, Alex!" Alex gave him a look. Timothy sighed. "You guys OK?"

"Yeah, the cabs weren't really after us. I mean, we ran for a bit, but then it just started to feel silly, so we turned around."

"Look, I don't know how much time we have before the cabs show up again, so. . ." Timothy stopped for a moment to think.

"So?"

"It's obvious the cabs are after me. And I think it isn't me they want, but the key. So. . ." He began to take the chain from around his neck. "If you take it and take care of Mr Shen, then I can lead them away from you as you try to get into that club."

"You really want to do that, Timothy?" Alex seemed stunned, and he couldn't understand why.

"Is there any other choice?"

"Wow."

"Wow? What are you going on about? Just take it."

"I'm really honoured that you trust me like that."

Timothy hadn't really thought of it that way. But he was suddenly really surprised that he trusted her like that too. He couldn't remember the last time he had relied on anyone but himself. *Oh, whatever.* "Just take the key."

"Wait! We don't have the time." Mr Shen pointed behind Timothy, and without having to turn around, Timothy knew. It also helped that appearing in his line of vision was another black cab. The third appeared from down to his right. He turned, and, sure enough, there was a cab inching its way towards him. They were surrounded, trapped, framed perfectly in the light of three sets of headlights. It was blinding, and the three of them huddled close together. He could feel Alex place a hand in his, and he reached for Mr Shen's. He felt awful, and frustrated, and yet, oddly, not scared. All he could think was that it wasn't fair. He had got so close, defeated so many obstacles, only for it all to end now. And as the hands in his gripped him more tightly, he couldn't help but feel really horrible for the two individuals he had got into this mess. He had a very empty feeling in his stomach.

"I'm sorry," he said quietly just as the cabs suddenly shot at them at full speed. It seemed a really silly idea, as they would most likely hit each other as well as the three of them, but the drivers obviously didn't mind.

This was it. After all they had been through. Death by crazy black cabs. What a way to go.

Suddenly a shadow darted out in front of them. It raised what must have been its arms and waved wildly. There was the horrible sound of screeching brakes as all three cabs jerked to a halt.

"Stop, stop, stop!" said a very familiar voice. "What are you doing?!"

As the cab in front turned off its lights, the shadow turned into a figure. Evans Bore appeared to them, his forehead beaded with sweat and a frantic expression on his face. He was panting hard.

Timothy stood there, still gripping tightly on to Alex and Mr Shen's hands. He stared at his former boss in total and complete shock.

Bore ran around to the driver-side window of the first cab. "What on earth are you doing?" he repeated.

"You said you wanted him dead or alive," replied the soft voice of the driver.

"That's just an expression! Don't you know that's just an expression?"

"How is that just an expression?" Timothy finally managed to utter, his voice cracking.

Bore turned back to him. "It's something people say, you know . . . like on the wanted posters back in the Wild West."

"But on the wanted posters back in the Wild West, they meant it."

Bore seemed taken aback. "They did?"

"Mr Bore, what's going on?"

By then Timothy had become aware he was holding hands with a girl and a dragon and suddenly felt embarrassed. He let go quickly and glanced at them briefly. Alex just seemed puzzled. But Mr Shen waved happily at his former master.

"I just wanted to make sure you were all right!" said Bore, returning the wave slightly less enthusiastically.

Timothy was still perplexed. "What?"

"After I gave you the key that night, I couldn't sleep. I was so worried you'd give it to Bazalgette. And I felt I just had to explain everything to you, so I had my driver take me to Bazalgette's place in the middle of the night. But when I got there, Bazalgette was unconscious, and he didn't seem to have the key on his person. You were nowhere to be found, and I just had no idea what was going on, so I sent my driver after you, asked him to contact some of his friends, while I dealt with Bazalgette."

Timothy interrupted. "Wait, what do you mean?"

"What do you mean, what do I mean?"

"Sir Bazalgette. He's not dead, then?"

Bore shook his head. "No, no, he isn't. I've sort of done this citizen's arrest thing. He's my prisoner for the time being. In fact, I brought him along with me; thought maybe he could have a word with his son."

"You did?"

"Yes. I sent him off with some of my staff to a hotel not far from here. Would you like to see him?"

Timothy shook his head and gave a small laugh. "So he isn't dead. He's not a ghost or anything."

"A ghost? No . . . what? No. I would never have . . . killed him . . . I mean . . . what a horrible thought . . . I could never kill anyone, no matter how much they had betrayed me."

"You know you almost killed us, like, several times, right, with those black cabs of yours?"

"I didn't know. And I'm sorry about that."

"You really are clueless, aren't you?"

"Yes, I'm afraid I am."

Timothy ran his fingers through his hair. Bore's apology seemed small comfort, but he really couldn't feel angry with the man. It would be a bit like being mad at a small child for flushing your wallet down the toilet. Justified, but ultimately pointless.

"Look, I wasn't the only one who was concerned about you, you know!" said Bore.

And, as if on cue, two figures emerged from around the corner.

"You've got to be kidding me," said Timothy. He could feel his shoulders tense, and he took a protective step backwards.

"You have some nerve, young man, coming to China without our permission!"

"Now, now, dear. You see he's all right. Let it go."

THE FIFTY-SECOND CHAPTER

In which everyone goes out for dinner

T imothy's parents looked extremely out of place in Kaomai. His father was dressed in khaki trousers and a light blue windcheater, the consummate tourist. And his mother was wearing a pair of skinny jeans that didn't exactly suit her frame, and a white wrap over her shoulders.

Emotions flooded his innards. He was paralysed with confusion. Here they were, his parents. They had actually come for him, just as he had secretly hoped they would, back when he was talking with Edmund on the *Zhulong*. Yet while on the one hand he was thrilled they had come to help him, on the other, he was thoroughly indignant that they didn't believe he could take care of himself. Why were his feelings towards them always so messy?

He got a bit of his own back when all the adults

insisted they go somewhere to discuss the situation. After having been the one to make all the decisions, it was pretty insulting to Timothy (and, he had a suspicion, to Alex as well) that suddenly they were back to being "kids" with no say in the matter. He protested loudly as they found their way to a restaurant, leaving the Dragon's Gate far behind them. Alex made some utterance to the effect of, "This is insane, we don't have time for this!" and tried again a few moments later with "There is this sea battle going on", but was ignored by the adults.

Eventually, his parents settled on what in any other country would have been labelled a Chinese restaurant but here was simply a restaurant, and were led to a large round table at the back. They were very lucky to get a seat, as the place was teeming with customers because of the celebrations, but for some reason the Freshwater party and friends had been allowed to bypass the rather long queue.

They placed their orders – well, Timothy's mother ordered for him – and when the server took the menu from her, he commented, in very stilted English, "Pretty sweet."

"I don't care, just bring it," replied his mother.

The server nodded and smiled and left.

There was silence as they waited for their meals. Timothy noticed that the table was shaking slightly. He looked over at Alex and saw she was tapping her foot anxiously on the floor. He couldn't blame her; he was feeling pretty anxious himself. It seemed insanely ridiculous that instead of rescuing a dragon he was sitting down to a dinner with his parents. He should just get up and leave. But for some reason he found himself rooted in his chair.

Fortunately they were served dinner relatively quickly. Timothy could sense all eyes were still on him and he kept his focus on the green tea in his hands.

"Well?" asked his mother loudly. The din in the restaurant made it very difficult to hear what anyone was saying.

Timothy refused to say anything.

His mother paused for dramatic effect, then tried again. "So you just refuse to say anything?"

Timothy felt a soft hand on his and looked up at Alex. She looked concerned, and all he felt was embarrassed about his parents, and of course Evans Bore. And a little about himself.

When he still refused to speak, Alex finally took matters into her own hands. "I know you are upset with Timothy. If I were a parent, I would be very worried about my child going to China without my knowledge. But that still doesn't change the fact that Timothy has done some very amazing things in the last few weeks, not the least of which was defeating the commander of one of the most powerful pirate fleets in the south China seas."

"Oh my!" said Timothy's father, placing his hands over his mouth.

"But the thing is, right now, this moment, we really have to help Mr Shen."

"Yes, we must!" insisted Bore with his mouth full of food.

Timothy finally looked up at that. "What are you going on about? You never made any kind of effort to help Mr Shen."

"Not true, not true! I booked a flight to China at the end of the summer. But then I started to get these threatening notes, from, well. . ."

"Sir Bazalgette."

"Yes."

"Coward."

"That I am. That I am." Bore shook his head sadly and took another large mouthful of food.

"Anyway, we really are running out of time," said Alex, insisting they keep on track. "We have to get Mr Shen into the Dragon's Gate, and we are having huge problems with that. There's this exclusive party going on, and they won't let us in until after midnight."

"That's a problem," said Timothy's father.

"Not to mention the fact that right now our friends are fighting a battle at sea just off the coast, and we really need to get back to help them."

"Of course."

"Of course? What do you mean 'of course'?" Kathryn Lapine turned to her husband.

"I just mean that maybe right now isn't the right time to punish Timothy. They have a very serious mission to accomplish. It was probably a bad idea coming here for dinner."

"Every time," said Timothy's mother, shaking her head, "every time. It's never the right time to punish Timothy. When is the right time, dear? Maybe when he's been expelled from every school in the city? Oh, wait a moment, he has."

"I do punish him."

"You never enforce it."

"Well, maybe if you were home once in a while to help with that. . ."

"Don't you dare; you knew what things would be like when you married me. You knew I wasn't giving up on my dream!"

"I thought by now maybe you would have had your fill of your dream. Or at least have had some success so that you wouldn't have to take every stupid, humiliating job that came your way!"

"Stop it! Both of you!" Timothy shouted. "Just stop it." Everyone at the table stared at him. "Mum isn't around, Dad has too much on his plate. Who cares? It's not your fault I was expelled from all those schools. It was mine. I'm the screw-up. Me. My fault."

The silence that followed this pronouncement was full of tension so thick it could be cut by a knife. And it was. At that moment their waiter happily placed the dessert in the centre of the table and cut into it with a long thin knife. He then turned to Timothy's mother and once more said, "Pretty sweet."

This time she just ignored him and served herself a slice of the cake with shaking hands.

"Enough of this." Timothy finally found that he could get up out of his chair and did so with probably a bit more force than necessary. He threw his napkin on to the table. "You guys enjoy your dessert. Alex and I have a dragon to save. Come on, Mr Shen." Both Alex and Mr Shen rose obediently.

"Don't you dare leave the table, young man. We still haven't discussed . . . things. . ." Timothy's mother rose and started to follow her son as he weaved his way back towards the entrance. The loud din in the restaurant turned into a distracted muttering as they walked past each table.

When they got to the door, Timothy's mother pushed past Alex and Mr Shen and grabbed her son by the shoulder, turning him around to face her. They stared, each not sure what the other would say. And then they were interrupted cheerfully by their waiter, accompanied by another man in a tuxedo who must have been the restaurant manager. They both smiled warmly.

"Pretty sweet," the waiter said again.

"Stop saying that!" Timothy's mother looked as if she were about to grab the waiter as well.

The waiter turned to the man in the tuxedo, and there was a short exchange until the man in the tuxedo started to laugh. The waiter looked slightly embarrassed.

"Please forgive him," explained the man in the tuxedo. His English was stronger, yet still heavily accented.

"Yes, well, being told everything is pretty sweet is not terribly helpful to a patron," replied Timothy's mother.

"He is just a little, how do you say it, struck by the star?"

"I beg your pardon."

"Stuck by the star. You are a performer, right?"

Timothy and his mother exchanged a look. She looked thoroughly confused.

"You are in *Pretty Sweet Tension*."

"I am?"

Timothy stared at the man. And then at the diners sitting at the tables around them. They were all looking at his mother in awe. Then he remembered how easily they had been given a table.

"Not *Pretty Sweet Tension*," he said. "*Sweet Pretensions*."

"Is that what it is called where you are from?" The man in the tuxedo seemed thrilled to learn this piece of information.

"But," protested Timothy's mother, "that show was cancelled years ago. It was" – it was obvious she was embarrassed to mention it – "a terrible failure."

"No! We love it! We have just finished watching the plot line about the missing keys. That was very exciting. Do you mean to say that you do not still make it?"

"I'm sorry." Timothy's mother seemed genuinely apologetic.

The man in the tuxedo looked sad. "Well, that is very too bad. I do not know how it is in the rest of the country, but here in Kaomai everyone watches it."

"Do they?"

"We have clubs. And at my last birthday party the theme was the show."

Timothy's mother looked faint. The waiter appeared to notice this and quickly grabbed a chair for her. She sat down slowly. "They've been saying 'pretty' to me since the airport. I just thought they thought I was . . . pretty." She looked up at Timothy. He wasn't sure what to say. He knew how much this meant to her. She had spent so much time and energy trying to become famous to very little success, and here, suddenly, without even trying, she was.

"Well, there you go," he said.

Her husband and Bore had made their way into the scene. Timothy's father bent down next to her and took her hand in his. "I'm very proud of you."

"I'm . . . I'm famous. . ." She looked at her husband with tears in her eyes.

He laughed and gave her a hug. "Yes, you are."

They held each other for a few moments, and when they parted, Timothy's father helped her up to her feet. There was some applause from the customers, thrilled to be watching a live-action version of *Pretty Sweet Tension*. Timothy's mother bowed, but not in her usual way. She seemed genuinely humbled by the experience.

When she turned back to her husband, he said, "Now that you're a success, don't you think maybe it's time to be a member of our family again?"

She looked at him, and then her son. "It's too late," she said quietly.

"Never."

"He can't stand me."

"I know something that will help make it up to him." Timothy's father stood up and faced him. He suddenly appeared a few inches taller. It was weird. "So this exclusive party. You think they'd let in a soap star?"

THE FIFTY-THIRD CHAPTER

In which we finally reach the Dragon's Gate

The party was in full swing as their group entered the club. The music was loud, the lights pulsating. They had got into the club with ridiculous ease. The bouncer had seen Timothy's mother coming from far away and, recognizing her instantly, yelled out instructions to give her a clear path. None of the people in the queue seemed to mind at all, but were awed that they got to stand so close to a celebrity as she passed by them. When the bouncer had made to prevent the rest of the group from entering, Kathryn Lapine had launched into a fantastic monologue about the importance of family, and how she refused to enter any club that would not allow her only child and his friends entrance. Though she was obviously in character, the conspiratorial wink she offered Timothy as they passed through the doors suggested she'd also meant it. Timothy hated that that had made him feel happy.

And now that they were inside, Bore immediately found his way to the dance floor, while Timothy's parents moved to the side to observe, their arms around each other.

It was left to Timothy and Alex to look frantically about for something that Mr Shen could scale. For a gate he could pass through.

"You see it?" he asked Alex. She shook her head no. But Mr Shen somehow knew exactly where he was going and made his way to the base of the spiral staircase leading up to the bar. He stood motionless, staring.

Timothy looked up. At the very top of the stairs was a tall grey stone archway serving as an entrance to the bar area. It was lit by lights that changed between pink and purple every few seconds, highlighting the club's namesake for all to see. The arch wasn't highly decorated, though Timothy could just make out some faint markings that had obviously worn down with age. The Dragon's Gate wasn't even all that impressive-looking. But the way that Mr Shen stared at it definitely convinced Timothy that they had found what they had been looking for.

Timothy and Alex stood with Mr Shen at the base of the staircase. Timothy looked at Alex, and she smiled brightly and moved to join Bore on the dance floor.

"Let's get going, Mr Shen!" Timothy yelled it right into the dragon's ear.

Mr Shen just stared back at Timothy.

"You can do this. You'll be fine."

Mr Shen's bottom lip started to quiver. Timothy grabbed the dragon by his shoulders.

"Look. If I can get a dragon to China, you can do this. Come on. I've had to deal with pirates and ninjas and Shaolin monks, and have had to run over rooftops. The least you can do is climb a set of stairs. Besides, you have no choice. I order you to."

"I am frightened." Timothy couldn't hear Mr Shen, but he read his lips.

"You should be. You haven't thought for yourself in centuries. You should be terrified! Doesn't mean you won't be able to take care of yourself. And anyway, you'll never be totally on your own. I mean . . . you know . . . you can always ask me for help and stuff." It was a nice sentimental moment. One that Timothy knew was sincere. And was slightly marred by the fact he had to shout it into the dragon's face to be heard over the music. Anyone watching would have assumed he was giving Mr Shen a telling-off.

Mr Shen nodded. He smiled one of those brave and utterly terrified smiles. Then he turned, took stock of the Dragon's Gate and of the stairs, and began to scale them. Timothy walked close at his heels. It was slow going as the crowd on the stairs was thick, but in no time they were both standing just before the arch.

They stared at it in awe.

There was an angry burst of Mandarin from behind them. Timothy turned around and a frustrated patron pushed past them under the arch and made for the bar, giving them a dirty look as she did so. Timothy laughed at this. To him and Mr Shen the arch meant everything, and passing beneath it would be life-changing. To the other patrons at the club, it was just an arch they had to walk under in order to get a drink. They barely even registered its existence.

"OK, Mr Shen, let's do this thing."

They gave each other one last look. Then with a collective intake of breath, they walked under the arch. They stopped on the other side. And then for good measure walked under it one more time back towards the stairs.

Timothy wasn't sure what he was expecting. Though he did know he was expecting something. So when nothing happened next, he was just a tiny bit frustrated. And when after they returned back downstairs and still nothing had changed, Timothy was downright perturbed.

Alex ran over to them and Timothy turned to meet her.

"So?" she asked, breathless – whether from excitement or trying to keep up with Bore, it was hard to tell.

"So what? So that." Timothy pointed at Mr Shen.

"Whoa."

"Yeah. Exactly. Nothing. Now what?"

"Um . . . Timothy?" It was Alex's turn to point at Mr Shen.

Timothy turned around and took a sharp jump

backwards. Mr Shen was glowing. He was glowing. A kind of blue kind of glowing.

"Maybe we should get him outside," said Timothy.

"Good idea."

Timothy made a signal to Bore, who in turn signalled Timothy's parents. Then they all rushed out of the club, Timothy practically dragging Mr Shen behind them.

They made it out into the square and found themselves packed into a tight crowd that was observing something in the middle.

"Move!" ordered Timothy as he barrelled through the crowd, Mr Shen in tow. They pushed their way roughly through the people until the crowd opened up and they found themselves in the centre of the square. Right in the midst of a performance of the dragon dance.

"How ironic," said Alex.

There was booing as the dance was halted by their appearance, but none of their gang paid any attention to it. Instead, Timothy placed Mr Shen in the middle of the square, where there was the most room, and took several steps back. It felt a bit like when he'd played with fireworks – he'd light them, and then run away fast before they could explode in his face.

When the crowd noticed Mr Shen standing glowing in the middle of everything, the booing stopped and was replaced by an inquisitive silence. Even the dragon dancers removed the large dragon they were wearing and stood to stare at the little man.

Mr Shen gave a small wave and smiled a little

nervously and waited along with everyone else to see what would happen.

Time froze.

Except that it didn't.

It just felt like it did.

In reality time kept going for five minutes and everyone else froze.

. . .

. . .

Then everything went bright. The kind of bright that happens when you are asleep and someone turns on the lights when you aren't ready for them. The kind of bright that blinds everything around you so that even if you were able to keep your eyes open you wouldn't be able to see anything. The light began from Mr Shen and emanated outwards. It started blue, but, as it grew in strength, turned to a hot white. Timothy covered his eyes, and everyone in the crowd followed his example. When the backs of their eyelids turned from red back to black, and they felt safe opening them again, they did.

And, standing in front of them, was a real, honest-to-goodness dragon.

THE FIFTY-FOURTH CHAPTER

In which Timothy must free Mr Shen

M r Shen was huge. He filled the entire empty
space of the square, and his tail wrapped around
Timothy protectively. He was blue. Timothy had never
even thought to ask him what colour he would become,
but blue seemed to suit him perfectly. It wasn't clear if
the colour came from the scales or somewhere within
the dragon, his hide being almost translucent. He had no
wings, but his long worm-like body was incredibly
powerful. Timothy could feel the muscles contracting in
the tail. And as he stared at his friend, Timothy noticed
a large golden collar around the dragon's neck, at the
base of the large ruff that encircled it.

"It worked," said Mr Shen. His voice boomed across
the square and sounded nothing like what Timothy had
got used to over the last few months.

"Uh . . . yes." Even though logically, he knew it was Mr

Shen, he couldn't help but feel a bit frightened of the beast before him.

The crowd had backed off slightly, and people from the club had started to spill out on to the street to see what was going on. No one spoke.

Mr Shen obviously could sense the unease in Timothy's reply and asked a little more quietly, "Are you scared of me?"

Timothy didn't know what to say. He couldn't say yes. That would upset Mr Shen, and this was supposed to be a happy moment for the dragon. He took a deep breath and made eye contact with him for the first time.

Staring back at him, from a whiskered dragon's face, were Mr Shen's eyes. The same eyes that had laughed at Timothy, almost mocked him. The same eyes that had cried when they were separated. And the same eyes that always looked ever so slightly resigned about every situation. Right now, however, they looked deeply concerned.

"No," replied Timothy. "I'm not scared of you." A moment ago it would have been a lie, but now it was true. Mr Shen's expression turned to one of pure joy. "Now get over here so I can free you."

Mr Shen bent his long neck down low in front of Timothy. He turned slightly away from him, exposing the keyhole in the collar. Timothy drew the golden key from inside his shirt, took the chain from around his neck, and held the key in his fingers. They were shaking, though he didn't know why.

Slowly and deliberately he brought the key to the keyhole and then placed it inside. He turned the key. There was a clicking sound. The collar and the key within it disintegrated into golden dust, which didn't float down towards the ground, but rather flew up into the air.

Mr Shen turned to Timothy and said quietly, "So I am free?"

"I guess. Let's see. . ." He thought for a moment. "Go over to the club and sit on the roof."

Mr Shen thought about it for a second. "I would prefer to stay here," he said to Timothy. He thought about it some more. "Hey!" he said. "I would prefer to stay here!"

He started to laugh, which came out as a low rumble, and the audience watching wasn't exactly sure what was going on.

"I am free!" he called out happily. "I am free!" And he took off into the sky, bursting up into the air like one of Timothy's fireworks. And, like one of Timothy's fireworks, was watched with awe and with an occasional "Ooh!"

Suddenly the musicians from the dragon dance started to play again, and the crowd moved into the centre of the square. Some wanted to talk with Timothy, others started to dance. Others continued to stare into the sky, watching Mr Shen zoom around performing intricate flips and spirals and just having an awesome time.

"Timothy!" Alex ran up and gave him one of her hugs. "That was so cool!" She released him and grinned.

"Yeah, well, I didn't really do anything."

Alex started laughing. Laughing kind of like a crazy

person. She wiped the tears from her eyes and said, "Timothy, you are impossible! You didn't do anything? You did everything! Don't be stupid!" And she smacked him playfully on the head.

Timothy smiled sheepishly. He knew he looked like an idiot smiling like that, but he was feeling a little proud of himself. And he wasn't used to that feeling.

Bore came running over next, sweaty from having resumed his dancing. He left a disappointed crowd who had decided they just loved his dance moves and had become his groupies. "This is amazing!" he exclaimed. "Absolutely amazing! The dancing, the musicians, dragons. . ."

"I told you I'd get you your fancy party, Mr Bore." Timothy meant it as a joke, and, in a strange way, as an apology. But as usual, Bore saw it as completely sincere.

"You did brilliantly! It is by far the best fancy party I've ever been to!"

Timothy decided not to mention that it was the only fancy party Bore had ever been to.

"Thank you, Timothy!" It was his turn to give Timothy a hug, which was a bit more unpleasant than Alex's, considering he was covered in sweat. But Timothy just shook his head and hugged him back.

Just as they broke apart, his parents appeared. Timothy felt a bit like he was in a reception queue at a wedding, one person after the next waiting to congratulate him. They stood staring at him slightly awkwardly. Timothy stared awkwardly back.

"Uh. . ." he attempted. *Whatever.* "Thanks, Mum."

And in her standard over-the-top way, she let out a wail and flew over to him, grabbing and drawing him in. She placed a hand at the back of his head. "You do know I love you, right? Always have, always will?" Her voice sounded a bit as if she should be in some Shakespearean play. But he knew that she was acting over the top because she was feeling pretty emotional.

"Yeah," he replied.

"Good work, son," said his father as they pulled apart.

"Yeah."

They shook hands.

This tender and very unnatural moment for all three Freshwaters was interrupted suddenly by a dragon landing in front of them. Mr Shen hadn't had a lot of practice landing, nor still any concept of his size, and so came down to the square with a loud thud, nearly squishing a dozen revellers who had managed to duck out of the way just in time.

"I had forgotten how enjoyable that was!" said Mr Shen with a great smile.

"Looks like it," agreed Timothy.

"Would you care for a ride?"

Timothy smiled and looked at the dragon's back. He then turned and looked at him in the eyes again. There was still one thing that had to be addressed.

"Actually, I was wondering if you would do me a favour."

THE FIFTY-FIFTH CHAPTER

In which we witness a sea battle, and Mr Shen is very helpful

Timothy and Alex held on for dear life. It wasn't as if they thought that Mr Shen would intentionally let them plummet down to the earth or anything, but that it just felt as if he might accidentally. Of course Timothy pretended that he wasn't the least bit concerned, and he glanced back at Alex and she waved happily. Then she grabbed out in front of her with a look of panic as they hit an air pocket.

"I can see them now!" called out Mr Shen over the wind that was rushing around them and making it difficult to hear anything.

Timothy leaned over the side and looked down at the dark water below them. He saw a few lights in the distance. It was hard for either Timothy or Alex to tell which ship was which. There were so many vessels on the water, some belonging to the Fleet of the Nine

Dragons, others under the command of Duchess Rose.

"There!" called out Alex. She was pointing down to their right. Timothy switched sides to follow her gaze.

The *Ironic Gentleman* came into view. She was still afloat and seemed relatively unharmed, though it was rather difficult to tell in the dark and from their height. She was, however, in a rather precarious position.

"It looks as if Duchess Rose has surrounded the ship, but the pirates are breaking through her protective circle." Mr Shen relayed the action back to them, his keen eyesight allowing him to share with them this play-by-play narration. "She must have been holding them off for a while. Why are they so determined to attack your ship, Timothy?"

"It's not my ship," replied Timothy. Realizing that wasn't what he'd been asked, he added, "I don't know."

"I think it's 'cause the *Ironic Gentleman* used to be one of the most powerful pirate ships in the world. They're probably trying to make some sort of statement." Alex shouted it loudly from behind.

"Yeah, well, I'm not sure what kind of statement they're making. I mean, doesn't mean much, defeating a ship now owned by a schoolteacher!"

"It's a symbol!"

"It's a what?!"

"Symbol," tried Alex louder, "it's a. . ."

There was a sudden lurch as Mr Shen began his descent.

"What's the plan?" asked the dragon as they went into free fall.

"I don't know, do something to help the *Ironic Gentleman*!" replied Timothy, pretty sure they should have discussed this a little earlier.

"But what?"

Timothy turned to Alex, but she was focused on holding on to the dragon, and couldn't hear their conversation anyway.

"Mr Shen, I can't make all the decisions for you, you know that," said Timothy into the dragon's ear. "You know your powers better than I do. I trust your judgement."

Timothy stopped talking and stared as the *Ironic Gentleman* seemed to fly towards him, even though he knew very well it was he who was flying towards it. Mr Shen levelled himself off and they soared over the ships, just missing the tops of their masts. They were so close that he could see Mr Underwood at the helm, totally taken aback by having a dragon fly just over his head.

Mr Shen then turned up, and started towards the sky on a steady incline. Timothy felt a pair of hands on his shoulders.

"I'm sorry," said Alex. "But you've got his hair and stuff to hold on to, and all I have are scales. And right now I'm pretty sure if I don't hold on to you I'm going to fall."

"That's OK," replied Timothy. She tightened her grip. It kind of hurt, but was also reassuring.

"All right," announced Mr Shen. "I have a plan!"

He continued his climb a few more metres, and then he levelled off.

And then, suddenly, he stopped. Stopped still. In mid-air. He had no wings, so the fact that they were flying at all had already weirded Timothy out. But the fact that they were now stopped in the air, with seemingly nothing holding them up, that was totally freaky.

The rushing wind stopped instantly, and Timothy could now hear the sounds of battle below. The ships continued to fire at one another, but with far less accuracy. Timothy assumed this was because they were distracted by the dragon hovering above them.

"Let's see if this works," said Mr Shen nervously.

It wasn't obvious that Mr Shen was doing anything. Nothing had changed in him physically. Timothy had learned not to expect much in that way, but Alex appeared a bit confused.

"Is he doing anything?"

Timothy couldn't answer because he honestly didn't know. And then. . .

The Fleet of the Nine Dragons began to move away. They just started sailing . . . backwards, it looked like. Timothy noticed that their sails were full of wind, but that the wind was blowing unlike any wind he'd ever known of. That is to say, it was blowing the ships in several different directions at once, and all away from the *Ironic Gentleman*. The Fleet's tight circle around the *Ironic Gentleman* was expanding wider and wider. Odder still was the fact that the inner circle of ships belonging to Duchess Rose was still standing stationary.

"That's cool," said Alex.

The wind got faster and faster, and water began to rise with it, causing a fine mist in the air. The ships were moving further and further away at a great speed now. Those that were directed towards the shoreline soon met their mark and crashed against the large rocks. But the others that were sent further out to sea seemed to have an infinite distance to travel.

"Let's just let the current take them, shall we. . ." said Mr Shen.

Timothy noticed the water below the ships start to flow away from shore. The current rushed and boiled around them and pulled the ships along with it further and further out to sea until they disappeared into the darkness.

Suddenly there was a loud crash of thunder that caused Alex to tighten her grip, practically choking Timothy in surprise. An impressive lightning storm began. It danced and flashed across the sky for several moments, puncuated by the rolling of the thunder. Then with one final explosion of sound, the thunder stopped, the lightning ended, and everything fell silent.

"Was that last bit really necessary?" asked Timothy after it was all over.

Mr Shen laughed. "I suppose not. But I enjoyed it tremendously."

THE PENULTIMATE CHAPTER

In which Timothy, Alex and Mr Shen experience a final showdown

There was a faint sound of cheering from the ships below. Timothy and Alex smiled at each other, a great sense of relief filling them both. Suddenly there was a loud roar of propellers and Mr Shen lurched violently, bucking up his middle and almost throwing both Timothy and Alex into the air.

Timothy twisted around to see a small open-cockpit biplane fly out before them, make a wide circle and come back in their direction.

"Mr Shen, you're bleeding!" called out Alex.

Timothy followed her gaze and noticed the gaping wound at the base of the dragon's tail.

"I think I've been shot," replied Mr Shen. He was still hoveing on the spot and so made a perfect target as the plane flew past again. This time Timothy could hear the sounds of a machine gun chugging out bullets in their direction, though the plane was a little too far away for the bullets to reach them. It wasn't too far away, however, for Timothy to see who was sitting behind the gun, the cockpit having no roof.

"Is that Edmund Bazalgette?!" Alex was stunned.

"It sure is!" replied Timothy. "And I think that's Emily flying the plane. She's good at that." Timothy leaned down to talk to Mr Shen. "Mr Shen, let's go and see what they want."

The dragon came out of his shock and narrowed his eyes. He shot towards the plane like an arrow.

The plane started a nosedive and Mr Shen changed direction in an instant. They levelled off in sync and soon the two were flying next to each other.

"What are you doing?!" called out Timothy. He watched as Edmund started to reload his gun.

"What am I doing?" Edmund looked up at him with a manic expression in his eyes. "I'm getting my dragon back! You think I'm going to let my father win?"

"What are you talking about?" The shouting was starting to wear down Timothy's voice.

"It's all his fault that you got the key. He distracted me! All he's ever wanted is to see me fail! Even now that he is dead, he still wants to see me fail!" He aimed the gun at them and began to fire. This time Mr Shen dodged the bullets easily, though Timothy and Alex couldn't help but instinctively duck.

"He's not dead! That wasn't a ghost," replied Timothy as Mr Shen returned to fly next to the plane once more. A light rain had begun to fall, and it only served to add more noise that he had to yell over.

"You must think I am an idiot!"

"No, listen to me." Timothy wasn't sure why he was attempting to reason with a madman who so obviously wanted him dead. "Evans Bore is here. He found your father alive that night at his house and he brought him to Kaomai. That wasn't his ghost!"

Edmund Bazalgette looked over at Emily. "You told me he was dead!"

Emily looked at her boss, looked over at Timothy and Alex, then at Mr Shen. She turned back to Edmund. "Why would I kill the man when he didn't have the key on him?"

"I gave you explicit instructions I wanted him dead!"

"I don't care! I'm not your slave, I'm not your dragon. I am a person, and I didn't think it was right to kill someone who didn't have the key."

"You are pathetic and weak!"

"I am not! I tried to kill the boy several times. I have done almost everything you've ever asked of me. What sort of credit do I get for it? Nothing. Why does no one ever appreciate my skills? Without me, you would be nothing. I am getting tired of all this. You know something. . ." She stood up. "I quit."

Emily jumped. Out of the plane. Into the sky. The others watched as she fell towards the water. Alex clutched on to Timothy's back even harder. A moment later a large black parachute opened, and the ninja floated gently to the shoreline.

"Who needs you anyway!" called out Edmund to the sea.

He crawled into the front seat. The plane was unsteady in the air, flying wildly now, but Edmund seemed convinced he could control it and fire his machine gun at the same time. As proof, he sent out another round of bullets.

"Stop doing that!" yelled out Alex this time.

"I will when you give me back my dragon!" he screamed in response.

"Get it through your thick head!" yelled Timothy back. "You can't have him!"

"I don't need your permission, little boy!" Edmund seemed to have no end of bullets and was reloading the machine gun for a fourth time.

"No, you don't." The voice was booming and resonant and cut through all the noise and fury easily. Mr Shen was using his new dragon vocal cords to great effect, and it was his turn to speak. The dragon brought his head close to Edmund's, startling the man so that he gave a little yelp. In a voice that sounded less like words and more like a low rumble, he said, "But you do need my permission."

The rain was pouring down faster, and Timothy had to hold on to Mr Shen's ruff with all his might. He glanced down below and noticed that the sea was beginning to churn. He could feel the wind whip around his face. All the while, the *Ironic Gentleman* was floating in perfect stillness, as were the ships belonging to Duchess Rose. Timothy suddenly realized that the weather was not doing its thing because of any natural influence. It was reflecting Mr Shen's mood. And judging from the state of the weather, Mr Shen was really, really angry.

Edmund Bazalgette had never really had much of a chance against the dragon. But, even now, he persisted and reached behind him again to fire off another round in their general direction. The plane was completely out of his control and was obviously only being kept in the air by Mr Shen and his not-so-limited powers concerning air currents.

"One last chance," said Mr Shen. "Stop it now or I let the wind take you to some small deserted island somewhere."

Edmund stood up and yelled out loudly, "Never!" This time it was his turn to jump, but instead of jumping down he jumped out towards them. He grabbed at the dragon as he did so, but his hands slipped on the scales. Instinctively, Timothy reached for Edmund's hand and clutched it just in time. Edmund flailed about for an instant and then reached about his person, pulling out his gun. He fired a shot, grazing Timothy's shoulder. The pain was searing, and in reaction Timothy let go of Edmund's hand.

As he fell to his end, towards the rushing waves of the churning water far below him, Edmund fired again. This time the shot hit Mr Shen and the dragon flailed wildly. Timothy could barely hold on. Alex, who had only a moment ago been using Timothy to keep herself from falling, was now doing everything she could to hold him safe.

Timothy tried to stay conscious, he really did. But the wind and the rain, Mr Shen's acrobatics in the air, as well as the searing pain from the gunshot, all just got the better of him, and he found himself succumbing to the enclosing blackness.

THE LAST CHAPTER

In which all the loose ends are tied

"Ow!" Timothy sat upright and stared wildly around him.

"Yes, as ever, my hard work in saving your life goes unappreciated," came a sarcastic voice from beside him.

Timothy looked at Shakespeare, who was sitting patiently holding several bloody bandages.

"What?"

"Lie down, Timothy, I'm just changing your bandages. Though watch out, I think Alex is about to attack you."

Alex had a bit more sense than to simply jump on someone who had been recently shot, but she still charged the bed, stopping just short of leaping on him.

"You're awake!"

"I know how much my being awake thrills you," replied Timothy, lying back on the cot.

"Well, it's good to have you back. Things were getting a bit boring, really, without your unique personality," she replied with a big smile.

Timothy looked at her and sighed. She was holding Giggles tightly to her and the cat gave him a small hiss.

"I was hoping he'd been left behind," said Timothy.

"Oh, don't say that. Giggles totally saved us. You know he found his way back to Duchess Rose?"

"Did he tell her we were on the ship, then?"

"No, don't be silly. He can't talk. No, she just realized that if he were on his own, something must have happened to me. She put two and two together and notified Mr Underwood of our predicament. She's the one who was firing at the ships from the fort, as well. Did you realize that?"

"How could I have known that?"

Alex shrugged and grinned. She seemed giddy with excitement.

Timothy rolled his eyes. "OK, fine then, fill me in on everything. You know you want to. What happened to Edmund?"

"He fell into the sea. Hard to know, really, but from our height, it's unlikely he made it."

Timothy wasn't sure how that made him feel. It wasn't that he had any sympathy for Edmund, but it also didn't feel good to learn he was dead. "And how about everyone else?" he asked, to take his mind off the thought.

"Well, DeWit and O'Connell have recovered nicely

from the poison darts. Tanaka is still pretty critical, but it looks like he will pull through. DeWit has taken command of the ship again from Mr Underwood. Man, that was so cool, wasn't it? When Mr Underwood captained the ship to try to save us? I didn't know he had it in him!"

"Yeah, cool. And what about Mr Shen? Is he OK?"

There was a silence that greeted the question. Timothy sat upright again, causing Shakespeare to mutter, "I give up" and walk out of the surgery.

"Is he OK?" asked Timothy again. This time his voice was shaking.

Alex didn't say anything again, and Timothy jumped off the cot. "Where is he?" he asked her.

Alex still wouldn't speak, but she pointed towards the stairs that led up on deck.

Without pausing, Timothy took off and ran up the stairs and on to the deck. He could feel panic as he stepped out into the fresh air and found that the *Ironic Gentleman* had already taken sail and was moving through a thick fog.

"Mr Shen!" Timothy turned in a full circle, but couldn't see the dragon anywhere. "Mr Shen!" he called out again, startling a few passing sailors.

"Timothy?" A disembodied voice returned the call.

"Mr Shen, where are you?"

"What do you mean where am I? I'm right here!" was the reply.

"Where?"

"Right here, with you."

"What does that mean?"

Alex came up to Timothy's side. He turned and looked at her. "Is he dead? Is that his spirit? I don't understand, just tell me!"

"Yeah, that whole ghost thing really freaked you out, too, didn't it?" she replied.

"Alex."

"Timothy." She led him towards the bow of the ship. "It was meant to be a surprise, but I didn't think you'd get like this." She pointed out into the fog in front of them. "He's right there!"

The fog had started to lift, and Timothy could see a large dark outline ahead of the ship. "Mr Shen, is that you?"

"It is indeed!" replied the large dark outline, which was becoming less and less of an outline and more and more like a giant blue dragon. In another moment, they were free of the fog, and suddenly Timothy understood what was going on.

"We're flying!" He looked down over the deck rail and could see water sparkling far below them in the morning sun.

"You better believe it!" laughed Mr Shen.

Timothy approached the bowsprit and noticed the large thick ropes that were harnessed to the dragon, allowing him to pull the *Ironic Gentleman* through the sky.

"Why are you doing this?" asked Timothy.

"Because I wanted to. It's my small way of expressing my gratitude. You have done so much for me, it is the very least I could do."

Timothy was moved. "Are you sure you are well enough to be pulling a giant ship behind you, though?" he asked, examining the dragon carefully. "I mean, you were shot a few times!"

"Oh, it is nothing, dragons heal very quickly. I am only relieved to find you are all right!" And he smiled at Timothy before turning his focus back facing front.

"Timothy?" Timothy turned to see Mr Underwood approach him.

"Oh, hey." He wasn't really in the mood to talk with the teacher. He really wanted to hang out with Mr Shen instead.

"I'll be really quick. I just wanted to let you know that I am planning on starting a school on this ship."

"Yeah, I think Alex mentioned that back when she told me her story and stuff."

"Of course she did, I apologize. At any rate, I was wondering if you'd be interested in studying here with us?"

Timothy looked at Mr Underwood closely. Though he had faced down pirates, ninjas, crazy black cabs and a psychopath, he felt as though he were facing his real adversary at last. A teacher. His one true nemesis. And then he laughed to himself. After everything he had been through, it seemed so ridiculous to waste energy in combat with this man. Especially seeing as this man had saved his life many times, was willing to put up with his attitude, and was, Timothy concluded, pretty cool in general.

"Yeah, OK. Why not."

"Excellent!" Mr Underwood stuck out his hand and Timothy took it. They shook. "I think your dad wanted to talk to you about something?"

Timothy noticed his parents standing a little way off. His mother sent him a smile and he returned it. He then made eye contact with his father, who approached him.

"You guys still here?" Timothy said it out of habit, not because he minded.

"Well, we needed to get home. Captain DeWit was kind enough to allow us to come along."

"No, yeah, of course, that's cool," said Timothy quickly, trying to make up for the attitude.

"How are you feeling?"

"Fine."

"Good." His father seemed a little nervous. "Um . . . so I see you and Mr Underwood talked."

"Yeah."

"You think you'll give it a go, then?"

"I think so."

His father knelt down and placed both his hands on Timothy's shoulders. "I really think, Timothy, this is an excellent opportunity for you, and I really hope . . . that is, it would be really great if this time . . . you didn't get expelled. What do you think? You think you could do that?"

Timothy looked down at his father looking up at him with those same frightened eyes. He wanted to laugh. It was so obvious that, despite it all, his father could not imagine Timothy ever wanting to be a student anywhere or to cooperate with anyone. Couldn't his father see that being a student on board a ship – with a crew Timothy already knew and sort of . . . liked, and the fact that he actually had a friend in Alex – couldn't he see that studying on the *Ironic Gentleman* was just about the most wonderful suggestion Mr Underwood could have made? He would have to explain it to him. Sometime. Later.

Right now he simply said, "Whatever."

There were so many small details that needed to be filled in because of his short absence from his own adventure. Alex, the consummate storyteller, was more than happy to oblige. So she and Timothy crawled out along Mr Shen's back and sat up close to his head, and the three of them talked and listened and laughed their way back towards home.

"I wish I could take a picture of this!" said Alex, looking back towards the ship. "Of us sitting up here, of Mr Shen pulling the ship, of how high we are in the sky. It would be awesome."

"It would," replied Timothy. He said it to indulge her. After all, it was a pretty cheesy thing she'd said, really. However, it was also true that such a picture would be awesome.

But Alex couldn't take a picture of it. So she couldn't

see how impressive the sight truly was. Nor how Mr Shen's bright blue hide contrasted nicely with the dark red of the *Ironic Gentleman*'s sails. She could not see the speed with which they flew through the air, or how the sunrise cast a beautiful light on the whole scene. Nope, neither she nor Timothy could see any of this. But we can. And we can enjoy the view for as long as we like.

It's really rather something, isn't it?

THE "THE END"

In which there is no more left to tell.